Laird of the Mist

PAULA QUINN

FOREVER

NEW YORK   BOSTON

Copyright © 2007 by Paula Quinn

Cover illustration by Jon Paul
Hand lettering by David Gatti

Forever is a division of Grand Central Publishing.

The Forever name and logo is a trademark of Hachette Book Group USA, Inc.

The poem from page xiii is from *Children of the Mist* by Frank McNie. Reprinted by permission of Frank McNie.

Forever
Hachette Book Group USA
237 Park Avenue
New York, NY 10017

Printed in the United States of America

ISBN-13: 978-0-7394-9125-6

For the MacGregors

*"While there's leaves in the forest and foam on the river
MacGregor despite them shall flourish forever."*

Acknowledgments

TO MY HUSBAND, who patiently listened and learned about this brave clan and understood why their story made me cry. And to my children, who lovingly roll their eyes when I try (and fail) to speak with a Scottish burr.

To my editor, Michele Bidelspach, for each and every word of encouragement. Thank you for your insight and for helping me make this book all it should be.

To my agent, Andrea Somberg, who always makes me feel like I can do anything. Thank you for your faith in me.

To Rika, Gabrielle, Terra, Christy, Rabbit, Willow, Melissa, January, and Dublin, you make every page I sweat over worth it. Thank you for your support and your friendship.

And to God, for His grace in my life.

Children of the Mist
by Frank McNie

We're the children of the mist with no land to call home,
descended from kings but destined to roam.
We were honoured in battle then hunted like game,
but the proof of our mettle is we're still proud of our name.

They outlawed our clan and the mode of our dress,
but we never measured allegiance by chance of success.
Some things we're not proud of were circumstance led,
but what prince not a rogue to see his children are fed?

Our friendship was valued by high born and low,
our steadfast belief earned respect from our foe.
No great castles had we and our numbers were few
but our clansmen before us kept our legacy true.

Chapter One

GLEN ORCHY, SCOTLAND
SEVENTEENTH CENTURY

KATE CAMPBELL LOOKED her enemy square in his lifeless face and then swung. Her blade severed an arm, but the torso remained intact. Mindless of her uncle's men honing their battle skills around her, she lifted the ax she gripped in her other hand and grunted as it sank deep into her opponent's straw chest.

Swiping her hair away from her eyes, she spied her uncle Duncan crossing the small bailey of her holding. He had arrived in Glen Orchy a few days ago to bring her to Kildun Castle, in Inverary. He'd promised to bring her and her brother to his home when they were children, but at the end of each visit he left without them.

Their mother died giving Kate life. Their father was killed at Kildun twelve years after that, just before Duncan was named Earl of Argyll, and Kate and Robert's guardian.

Kate watched him stalk toward her, his equine legs encased in fine woolen breeches and boots of polished obsidian. His frame was slight, his shoulders narrow beneath an olive doublet. He was built more for priesting than for fighting, though he often bragged of his victories in battle. These battles kept him away from Kildun for months at a time, he'd reminded them many times during his visits, planting a kiss on their foreheads before heading for the doors. Soon he would come to bring them home with him. But he never did. Not even when her father's vassals began leaving, save for a small handful who raised them.

Kate met the earl's gaze briefly, and his gray eyes grew dark with intent that made her skin crawl. He may not have wanted her as a child, but he wanted her now.

"You brandish your weapons well, Katherine." He came up behind her and ducked to his right when she hefted her ax over her shoulder for another crushing swipe, this time to her enemy's thigh.

Aye, she and Robert had been made to practice day after day. "Amish and John taught us well."

Behind her, she heard a tight snort. "They have remained loyal soldiers to my brother these many years. But their duty to him is over now. I will see that they are rewarded." He leaned over her so that his whispered breath clung to her cheek. "It pleases me to know you would fight back should any man try to ravish you."

Kate clutched the handle of her ax and thought about flinging it over her shoulder. "Truly, Uncle, your concern for mine and Robert's well-being has always warmed my heart. Especially when you used to remind us how fortunate we were that it was the McColls who raided Glen Orchy every other fortnight, and not the murderous Mac-Gregors." He hadn't cared that a Highlander might ravish her while she was growing up, or that there were but a handful of men left in the garrison to fight them if they did.

"When you were a child, the only thing the raiders wanted was sheep. I knew you were safe here. But now you are a woman and the Highlanders will take more than your livestock." His breath glided over her throat. Kate cringed and brought her ax down hard on her opponent, raining hay on their heads.

"I do not fear any man who thinks to come here to steal my virtue, Uncle."

"And if our enemy should fall upon you?"

Kate knew whom he meant. He'd spoken of them countless times over the years. "There are hardly any Mac-Gregors left in Scotland worth fretting over. I'm certain I shall never meet one."

"There are enough of them left to continue to back the royalists' cause." The earl curled his finger around a raven lock that fell over her shoulder. "We must not forget how they joined forces with their Catholic Marquis of Montrose against us. Or how many of our kinsmen have died during their murderous rampages. Remember I told you how they massacred the Covenanters without mercy at Kilsyth? I will not let you fall to them, as well. You will do as I say and come home with me." He gave her hair a tug, as if to remind her that he would not let her refuse.

"This is my home," she said, stabbing her opponent in the throat.

"Not anymore." When she stiffened at his sharp retort, he softened his tone. "Robert is eager to see you. It has been near three months since he has set eyes on his beloved sister."

Kate missed her brother terribly, but he had chosen his path. "My brother has waited years to give his service to the realm, but I am content here, Uncle."

His laughter raked across her ear. "With a few old men and a handful of servants? What could you hope to do against the Devil, should he find you?"

Kate was certain he already had and was standing behind her at this very moment. Her uncle was trying his best to frighten her into leaving with him, by reminding her of the horrid MacGregors the way children taunt each other with tales of beasties. The most terrifying of them all: The Devil, who had killed over fifty Campbells six years ago in a massacre that had made him legend—and made her and Robert orphans.

Duncan hauled her closer and gritted his teeth. "Have you forgotten already that he killed my father and yours?"

"Nae," Kate answered without turning. "I have not forgotten." Indeed, Kate hated him, but she did not concern herself with legends or the foolishness of fearing them.

"And you do not fear such a blood-lustful man?" he demanded while she swung again.

"Nae, I will kill him if ever I meet him," she vowed, decapitating her enemy with her sword.

"You never will." The earl slid his hand down her arm until his fingers covered hers. He jabbed her blade into her lifeless opponent, a groan tangling in his throat as he pressed her back to his chest. "Tomorrow you will return with me to Kildun. Only there will you be safe from our enemy."

Kate stopped fighting and ground her teeth when he kissed the back of her head. "You are my enemy, as well," she murmured as he swaggered back to his men. She brought her ax upward instead of down; it struck and wedged tightly between her opponent's legs.

Leaving the ax where it landed, Kate sheathed her sword and walked off toward the meadow where her sheep grazed oblivious and innocent to the lusty wiles of men. It sickened her when she thought of why her uncle wanted her. She'd known of his depravity for some time but had never told Robert. She hadn't truly thought Duncan would come for her, even after Robert went to live with him, so there was no need. But now he was here and so anxious to get her out of Glen Orchy, she was certain he would drag her there tied to his horse if he had to. Did he think Robert would let him touch her once they arrived at Kildun? Fool. Her brother would slice off Duncan's hands, uncle or not. Robert was noble and valiant, with a strong sense of duty to protect his clan. It was he who taught her Malory and Monmouth's tales of Arthur Pendragon and his knights of the Round Table. And it was the terrible tales of the savage MacGregors that drove him to leave their home three months ago and join the other knights of Inverary.

Robert had begged her to go with him, but Kate did not want to leave her home, and she certainly did not want to live with her uncle. She was safe here. The raiders were bothersome but not terribly dangerous.

Amish had made her and her brother vow to never lift a weapon to the mountain men. Their raiding, he had told them, was a way of life. They did not come to kill, so long as they were not attacked. Not so the MacGregors. For over two centuries they were considered the scourge of Scotland: uncivilized barbarians with no regard for honor or a man's family. So heinous were their crimes against the Campbells and their allies that their name had been proscribed over fifty years ago.

Amish and John never spoke ill of them, though, even after the Devil killed her father. Hatred, they told her as her father had, was poison to the soul.

Kate wiped her fist across her ear, where the stale smell of her uncle's breath still lingered. Hatred might be poison, but if he ever touched her again he would feel the power of it when her blade sliced open his heart.

A thunderous cry from the braes above pierced her thoughts. Her face paled. Raiders! She turned, looking back at her uncle's men already drawing their swords. Nae! She sped toward them, praying as she ran that she could reach her uncle's men before the Highlanders did.

⁓

Callum MacGregor, clan chieftain of the MacGregors, reined in his mount atop the crest of a hill and watched the small battle taking place in the vale below. His dark brows creased over his eyes as he scanned the men engaged in the melee around the Campbell holding and those lying dead in the grass. Duncan Campbell was not among them.

"Looks like we've stumbled upon a raid by the Mc-Colls," said one of the four men flanking him.

"Ye said the Earl of Argyll would be here, Graham." The chieftain cut his gaze to his first in command.

"He's here," his commander assured confidently while he rotated the cap tilted jauntily atop his mane of honeyed curls to a backward position. If any man had reason to be so certain of his words, 'twas Graham Grant. After pretending to be a Campbell from Breadalbane and living in Kildun Castle for the last pair of months, Graham knew all there was to know about the Inverary Campbells and the tenth Earl of Argyll. "This was his brother Colin's homestead. He's come here to retrieve his niece." Graham pointed into the vale at the soldiers. "Campbell's men are here. Mayhap he hides in the keep. We know he lacks courage."

"Save fer when he's brandin' MacGregor women," said another man, a bit broader of shoulder than the rest. He popped the cork off a leather pouch dangling from his belt and raised it to his mouth.

"Can ye no' go anywhere wi'oot yer poison, Angus?"

Angus took a swig, belched, and then swiped his beefy knuckles across his thick auburn beard. "Brodie, ye know I like killin' Campbells wi' a bit o' auld Gillis's brew in me." He grinned at his cousin stationed beside him. "It fires up me innards."

Callum refused when Angus slapped the pouch of brew against his arm, offering his laird to take part. Callum did not need whiskey to fire his innards. Hating the Campbells was enough. They had taken much from his clan. But they had taken everything from him.

"The McColls are puttin' a quick end to the Campbells. They'll be less fer us."

"Dinna fret over it, Brodie," Angus said, corking his pouch. "We killed us enough o' the bastards already at Kildun before we got here."

"It will never be enough," their laird growled low in his throat.

"If Argyll is there, the McColls might get to him before

we do," Jamie Grant, Graham's younger brother and the youngest of Callum's men, pointed out.

"There's a lass fightin' among the men!"

"That's no' a lass, Brodie." Angus guzzled another swig of whiskey. " 'Tis a Campbell wi' mighty long hair."

Brodie flashed his larger cousin an incredulous scowl beneath his dark whiskers. " 'Tis a lass, ye dull-witted bastard."

Callum heard the side of Angus's sword smack against Brodie's head, and Brodie's subsequent oaths before he pounded his fist into Angus's chest. The chieftain ignored his kinsmen and observed the object of their disagreement. The mounted warrior certainly looked like a lass. He'd never seen a lass fight before, though many times he wished he had. His mother's screams still haunted his dreams. He'd been a lad when Duncan Campbell's father raided his village and his men raped and branded the women, though no hand had been lifted against the earl's men.

But here was a woman who had the spirit to actually fight to save her life.

" 'Tis a lass," he said, more to himself than to his men. "Mayhap Argyll's niece."

"Aye." Graham nodded, watching her lush raven mane swing around her shoulders while she whirled her horse around and deflected another mighty blow. "She tires against the McColls. I know she's a Campbell," he said with only a hint of regret, "but it looks like a good enough fight. Shall we aid her, Callum?"

Graham smiled at his friend's slight nod, and then he flicked his reins and took off a moment after Callum kicked his stallion's flanks and raced toward the melee.

The MacGregor chief cut a straight path to the lass, swiping his claymore through anyone in his way. His men fanned out around him, killing the rest. The closer he came to her, the harder he rode, his dark hair snapping behind him like a pennant. Her arms were growing weary. She was having difficulty lifting her blade to parry the flurry of strikes hammering down on her. He told himself, while he hacked at a McColl riding up behind her, that he was rushing to her defense to keep her alive so that she could tell him Duncan Campbell's whereabouts.

She whirled on him just as he reached her, and Callum felt something in his gut jolt. Her skin was pale alabaster against a spray of soft obsidian waves, dampened by exhaustion. Her eyes were beautiful as black satin, and when she looked up at him, they told Callum she had just lost hope in surviving this day.

He did not expect her to swing at him, looking as defeated as she did. For an instant, he merely gaped in stunned disbelief at the blood soaking his thigh. Then he lifted his claymore over his head and brought it down hard on another McColl. The lass turned away from the force of his deathblow, but a moment later she returned her gaze to his. Callum responded to the great relief in her expression by wheeling his mount around and calling out to his men to guard her on every side. There, they shielded her until the only men left in the yard, besides them, were dead or wounded.

When Callum turned his mount around to face her again, her sword slipped from her fingers. He glanced at it, then lifted his eyes to hers. "Are ye injured?"

She blinked as if emerging from a daze. Her breath still came heavy enough to part her lips.

"Are ye hurt?" he demanded again.

She shook her head nae. "Are you?" Her gaze slipped to his thigh. "My deepest apologies for wounding you. I did not know who you were, or—"

"Are ye Duncan Campbell's niece?" he interrupted.

She either didn't hear him or chose to ignore his query. "I must find Amish and John. They are old and—"

"Woman," he cut her off again, this time his voice hard enough to make her blink. "Are ye Argyll's niece?" When she nodded, his expression went hard. "Where is he?"

She looked around at the fallen, presenting him with the delicacy of her profile. "I had hoped he was here. But he must have run off with one of my sheep."

A hint of amusement crossed Callum's expression before he angled his head and barked out another order to the four men around her. "Brodie, check the keep with Angus and Jamie. If ye find Argyll, bring him oot to me."

"Who are you, that I may properly thank you for aiding me?"

Callum's gaze swung back to her. For an unsettling instant he lost all ability to reason, save that he knew he would be content to look at her for however many days he had left on the Earth. 'Twas not fear that made her bonny eyes appear so big, but reverence. Admiration from a Campbell! Since he had never saved the life of one before, he was not prepared for her awe. He shifted again, feeling damned uncomfortable and blaming her for it.

"I am Callum MacGregor." Best to get it over with sooner rather than later, though a part of him regretted having to watch that veneration turn to hatred when he spoke his name aloud. He was not disappointed. Her face paled to such a milky white he thought she might faint dead away and tumble from her horse.

His eyes were usually very quick, and on any other day Callum MacGregor would never have missed an enemy reaching for a weapon. But for a moment her beauty made him forget about fighting and hatred and blood. A moment was all it took for her to slip her hand beneath her belt and retrieve the small dagger she had hidden there.

The glimmer of surprise that sparked Callum's eyes belied his cold, impassive voice. "Ye have courage to point yer dagger at me." She swung, and he moved in a blur of speed, yanking her from her horse to his. Pressing her chest to his, he closed his arms around her, pinning her dagger securely behind her back. "Ye insult the laird of the clan MacGregor with such a meager weapon, lass."

"Let me go, vermin!" she hurled at him and spent the remainder of her energy kicking and wriggling, trying to free herself. "Let me go if you be a man, and let me fight you with my sword."

Callum glanced at Graham, mirroring the commander's expression of admiration at her furious promise. She was a fiery, braw lass, something all Highlanders valued.

But she was a Campbell.

"Is Argyll in the keep?" Callum asked her, barely straining a muscle against her attempts to be free of him.

"I told you I don't know where he is, but when you find him, take him to hell with you!"

Aye, now this was more like the reaction he expected from a Campbell. She was no more innocent than the rest. "Graham, get me some rope. The wench tires me."

Her fight came to an abrupt halt. She glared up at him with the promise of retribution frosting her eyes. "Will you prove yourself naught but a savage by raping me?"

Briefly, his gaze fell to her lips, then drifted over the rest of her body in a leisurely inspection of her feminine aspects, as if he were considering it. "Woman, I am much more than a savage."

Her nostrils flared. "I would cut off your—"

Over her shoulder, Callum saw one of her uncle's men exit from behind the house, cocked bow in hand. He had no time to shield her as the arrow whistled toward them and penetrated her right shoulder, just above her breast. Though it happened within the space of a breath, he watched it pierce her perfect form, watched the breathtaking spark of life grow dull in her eyes. As Graham raced toward the guardsman, Callum's eyes met hers again when she realized she'd been hit.

"Och, hell." Her breath was a ragged whisper, sweet against his chin. "That was likely meant for you."

Chapter Two

FIRE LANCED UP KATE'S ARM and seared her chest. Every inhalation of breath became more excruciating than the one before it. It wasn't helping that her captor still held her firmly pressed against his body.

On second thought, mayhap it was. For she couldn't move or flail about as agony gripped her. Her thoughts began to fade, but she fought to cling to consciousness. She had never fainted before, and she was not about to do so now whilst in the arms of a MacGregor!

"Be still with ye, lass."

"Dear God, it pains me," she groaned, covering her face in his shoulder.

"Let the pain settle." His pitch lowered to a comforting murmur. His arms loosened around her while she tried to slow her breathing. He turned to his men, who were exiting her home.

"Argyll isna inside," one of them called out. "We found only a few servants, nae old men among them."

"They must be there." Kate fought the MacGregor's

hold on her and then swooned as red-hot agony tore through her arm.

"Yer brew," the chieftain commanded to another one of his men, and then caught something in his hand. "Drink this." He held the nozzle of a small hide skin sack to her lips. "It'll dull the pain."

She glared at him with tears misting her eyes. "Did you kill Amish and John?"

He stared at her, unaffected by her sorrow. "I dinna kill old men. They are no' here. Now drink the brew." The intensity of his piercing gaze compelled her to obey.

She covered his hand with hers and took a long guzzle. Then she began to choke. Mother Mary! She had never tasted anything so foul! It was like drinking liquid fire. Her skin tinged green, and she shivered so violently her teeth rattled. She brought her hand to her mouth to stop herself from crying out . . . or from throwing up.

"It'll pass." Her captor moved slightly away and commanded her to look at him. When she did, his eyes fastened onto hers, and something in their ardent depths told her he did not expect to see weakness in her. She inhaled deeply. He would not find it.

"It's poison," she finally coughed.

"'Tis only whiskey." A smile lurked at the edges of his mouth, but that was the only evidence of softness in his striking features. An instant later, even that was gone. "Where is yer uncle?"

"For the last time, I don't know." Kate closed her eyes to stop herself from weeping all over her enemy. Amish and John had been like foster fathers to her and Robert. Dear God, where were they? Where was her uncle? "He was here earlier. We were to leave for Inverary tomorrow. He must have fled when he saw the McColls."

"True to his cowardly Campbell nature."

Kate looked up at him. Cowardly was killing old men, or slicing open her father's spine as one of this vermin's kin had done. "Take your filthy hands off me, MacGregor."

For a terrifying moment, Kate thought she might be looking at the Devil MacGregor himself. For his eyes were the color of fire: blue-gold embers that singed her flesh as they regarded her beneath the sable fringe of his lashes. Then his mouth crooked into a ruthless smirk as he opened his arms and released her.

Kate grasped his forearm to keep herself from slipping from his lap and crashing to the ground. She gritted her teeth as a fresh assault of withering pain ripped through her. "Damnation," she swore, narrowing her eyes on him through a haze of tears. "You bastard."

Her insult earned her a look of cool indifference. "Though ye look like ye could use some coddlin', I dinna have the heart fer it."

"I expected no less from a MacGregor," she countered, then stiffened and grimaced when his arm snapped around her again.

The pain was beginning to dull, along with her senses. Dear God, she'd never been wounded so. Damn the Mc-Colls. Raiding her cattle was one thing. Trying to kill her was another. They had never done the like before. But today, because her uncle's guardsmen had joined in the melee, the McColls had fought to kill. When two of the Highlanders swung at her, she'd had no choice but to unsheathe her blade and fight back. After over a quarter of an hour, her strength had been drained and she knew she could not hold them off much longer. She'd thought she was going to die. Though she had spent many years learning to wield a sword, no straw opponent could have prepared her for true fighting. She had been frightened many times in her life—three years ago, when the crop had failed and she'd thought her small family was going to starve. When her nursemaid Helen grew ill with the fever and did not recover. And after that, when Robert left and the wind howled and battered against her door at night, like a demon trying to enter. But she had never been as frightened as today, too weary to save her life, waiting for the strike of someone's cold blade to cut through her flesh. Then *he* came.

She was not afraid of the MacGregor laird, though when she had first laid eyes on him sitting atop his great warhorse, the hilt of a bloody claymore clutched in his hand and a dozen dead McColls around him, she had been certain her death was imminent. But instead of killing her, he saved her life. Even after she had wounded him, he fought to protect her. Why would a MacGregor do the like?

Her head suddenly felt too heavy to hold up. Just before her eyes closed, she gazed up at the warrior cradling her in his arms. He smelled of heather and mist. The scent covered her, going straight to her head. The sun hovered just behind him, splashing light over his shoulders like a golden mantle, reminding her of Robert's tales of Camelot. She smiled and then went limp in his arms.

~

Callum watched her head loll back, spilling her hair over his arm. His gaze fell across her throat, over the beguiling mound of her bosom pushed slightly upward by the brown bodice cinching her waist. God's fury, he must be going daft, but he found her completely mesmerizing. She fit so perfectly in his arms. Indeed, he had the feeling that they had been crafted this way and he hadn't known she was missing until this very day. Nae, he reminded himself, she was a Campbell, someone he was born to hate.

He had come here to kill the Earl of Argyll, not to save the bastard's niece. He looked away from her, and his eyes burned with frustration. "Gather the men and let us be away from here."

"And the lass?" Graham asked before turning to the others.

"Well, *I* dinna want her if she canna hold her whiskey." Coming up behind them, Angus laughed when his laird tossed him back his pouch.

She had held it better than most, Callum decided, unable to help himself from looking at her again. Others usually retched after just one sip of Gillis's potent brew. The way this woman had fought the whiskey's worst effect revealed the kind of strength he valued and had never expected to find in a Campbell.

"I'm takin' her," Callum said, raising his gaze back to his men. "If Argyll wants to see his niece alive again, he will have to find me and finally face me in battle."

"And if he finds our holding in Skye?" Graham asked.

"Let him." Callum's snarl was razor sharp. "He fears me and will nae doubt garner another army to bring with him. We will see them coming from ten leagues away and strike them doun as we did in Kildun. Argyll will die slowly, though."

"What if the lass dies before we reach Skye?" Jamie asked, dropping a small pink bud he'd been inspecting in exchange for the girl. Her skin was deathly pale and her breathing shallow.

"Ye dinna die from an arrow in yer shoulder," Brodie scoffed.

Angus swiped him in the chest with his fist. "How's he supposed to know that? We've never seen an arrow in a lass before."

"Women are more delicate than men," Graham agreed, tossing a lingering glance on the lass in Callum's arms. "She's a bonny one too."

"What in damnation does that have to do wi' anything?" Angus asked after another deep pull of his brew.

Callum glanced down at her again. "She will live. He shifted his arm to cradle her at a more comfortable angle when his thigh began to ache, and then scowled when she groaned—it sounded to his ears like a purring kitten after a healthy supper. She cuddled deeper against his chest, and his arms came up closer around her, mindful of the arrow jutting out of her shoulder. Here was something that certainly would have torn away his fierce reputation had anyone but his most loyal men witnessed it. A Campbell clutched in the crook of his arm!

"Should we no' take the arrow oot, Laird?" Jamie asked, keeping a close pace beside Callum as they rode out of the vale.

Callum had considered it, but the thought of causing her any more pain did not appeal to him. Still, he did not want his men thinking he was going soft, and over a Campbell, no less. "We'll take her to the Stewarts. They're no' far from here. Ennis's wife is a healer. Once the arrow is oot, the lass'll need herbs to fight infection. I'll need her alive if I'm to use her as leverage against her uncle."

"Ennis Stewart is a traitor," Graham reminded him. "He might not welcome MacGregors into his home."

"He will if he wants to live," Callum growled back at him.

Graham studied his best friend with a spark of amusement gleaming in his green eyes. "Here, let me take her. Ye seem more sour than usual since ye put her in yer arms."

"I've got her," Callum warned succinctly. "Stop gapin' at her."

"Aye, stop gapin' at her," Jamie intoned with a forced scowl aimed at his brother. "Callum fancies her and willna have his woman fallin' fer ye like them at Camlochlin."

"I dinna fancy her, Jamie," Callum corrected with an extra dose of disgust thrown in for the convincing. "She's a Campbell."

While Jamie often proved himself worthy to be ranked among the MacGregors' most fearsome men, his downy flaxen hair and large blue eyes rivaled those of the most innocent child. "So ye hate her, then?" Those huge eyes looked up to Callum.

Aye, Callum thought, he despised the blood that flowed in her veins. Her clan was responsible for killing almost every MacGregor laird for the past four generations without pause. They'd tortured the only person in his life he ever dared to love, until naught remained in him but anger, and darkness, and revenge. Aye, he hated her. But he could not find the stomach to utter it. He clenched his jaw tight instead and kicked his mount into a full gallop.

"Aye." Jamie nodded, and then took off after him. "He hates her aright."

Chapter Three

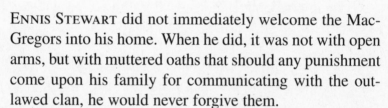

ENNIS STEWART did not immediately welcome the Mac-Gregors into his home. When he did, it was not with open arms, but with muttered oaths that should any punishment come upon his family for communicating with the out-lawed clan, he would never forgive them.

"Ye're a MacGregor lest ye ferget, Ennis," Graham reminded the old warrior. "Yer name may have been changed, but yer blood is, and always will be, MacGregor blood."

Standing aside to allow them entry into his small bothy, Ennis mumbled a few more blasphemies, then poked his head outside after everyone entered. He looked left and right, then slammed the door shut and bolted it.

"M' faither was a MacGregor," Ennis acknowledged, turning to Graham. "M' brother and his family were killed because of it. Lest *ye* ferget, the name MacGregor is *proscribed*. I can be hanged fer aidin' ye." He went to his wife, who stood by a small table in the center of the room, wringing her hands together. Ennis put his arm around her and pulled her close as if the door were about to burst open and they be found guilty of harboring the rebels. "Yer defiance will get ye all killed." He turned to Callum and shook his head with the pity of it. "How long will ye continue yer war? Ye're strong and young. Life is no' so bad now. It willna be long before the monarchy is restored under Charles II. MacGregors have fought fer him. Surely he will remember it. Change yer name, fer the mercy of God, and live a peaceful life."

Angus stepped forward and towered over Ennis with a scowl as cold as a Highland winter night. "Mind yer tongue. 'Tis yer laird ye address."

Squaring his shoulders, Ennis tilted his head up to look the huge warrior straight in the eye. "M' laird is Connor Stewart now."

Angus regarded the old man with a look of disgust. "Ye're a coward, Ennis MacGregor."

"Nae! I protect m' family!"

"So do they!" Graham shouted at him. He stormed forward and slammed his fist on the table, ignoring Mae Stewart's startled leap back. "They protect their clan and their family name. I'm proud to say the Grants stand at their side."

"How are they protected?" Ennis demanded. He pushed his wife behind him and faced the group of warriors boldly. "D'ye protect them by arrogantly announcing yer names to yer enemies? How does that protect yer families?"

Now Callum moved forward. When he reached the table, he swept his arm across it, clearing it of bowls and a vase full of flowers. He bent forward, laying the woman in his arms across the surface. Straightening, he closed his fingers around the hilt of his sword.

"I protect them with this. Anyone who thinks to do harm to my clan will die by my sword, and the offense will never be forgotten. If I have sons, I'll train them to be warriors, as my faither taught me, so that when I die they'll protect the clan in my stead. And my clan is Mac-Gregor." His voice grew low with firm conviction. "I will no' hide my kin in the darkness of fear in order to protect them. If we die, then so be it. We die as MacGregors. Now, I've no' come here to d'ye harm, nor to shame ye fer what ye feel is right, Ennis. This lass is in need of yer wife's healin'. We'll be gone before the sun sets." He turned to Mae. "Will ye help her?"

"Aye." She nodded up at him. "Ye look in need of some of m' special salve yerself." She motioned to his leg, where blood had dripped and dried in thick rivulets down to his knee.

"I'd be most grateful," he said and watched while she began her examination of the woman on the table.

"Who did this to her?" Mae looked up from pulling the edge of the woman's bodice and shift off her shoulder.

"One of her uncle's guardsman," Callum told her, unable to look away from the smooth complexion of the lass's shoulder. She moaned, and he blinked his gaze away.

"Her uncle?" Ennis asked, his interest in her piqued. "Who is she, then?"

When Callum told him, Ennis tossed him a doubtful look. "Ye're aidin' a Campbell?"

"Aye, but he hates her." Jamie hastened to stand at his laird's defense.

"He doesna hate her, whelp." Brodie shoved his elbow into Jamie's gut.

"Ye're all going to have to wait ootside," Ennis's wife

declared, exasperated by the sudden bickering. Besides, she was going to have to undress the lass to get to the wound, and it was not proper for any man to see her. "Oot with ye now," she ordered, shooing them away.

"Ye see what ye did, Brodie?" Jamie hissed at him. "She thinks us barbarians because of ye."

"That's no' it." Brodie pushed him along. "She doesna want us to see the lass's breasts."

They were already heading in the direction of the door when Callum gave both men a harsh shove that catapulted them the rest of the way. "Mind yer mouths now and move yer arses."

Once the men left the bothy, Ennis looked over his shoulder every five breaths. Within ten, he had worked himself into a frenzy. Any moment now, someone was going to wander by to bid him a fine day, take one look at the five giant warriors, and go screaming throughout the holding that MacGregors were afoot. Then, Ennis thought, rubbing his forehead, he and his poor Mae would be cast out and left to starve to death on the moors.

Callum's hand on his shoulder startled him. "Dinna fret so, Ennis. Should anyone happen by, I'll put my sword to yer throat and ye can explain to yer laird that we forced ye to aid us."

Ennis knew the MacGregor was not berating him for his fears. The chieftain was indeed willing to lay his head on the block for anyone in his clan, even one who had chosen a different name to stay alive.

"I've thought aboot retreating to yer holding on the isle, laird." Ennis admitted, unable to help but respect the courage it took to stand firm against their subjugation. "But this is m' home now."

Callum nodded and patted his back. "Camlochlin will welcome ye if ye ever change yer mind."

Ennis finally managed a smile, but a moment later he resumed his pacing, scowling now and then at Brodie and the others while they hurled insults at each other.

"How did ye come to possess a Campbell?" Ennis asked the chieftain, to keep his mind off the panic rising in him.

Callum explained what had taken place in Glen Orchy.

"What d'ye intend to do with her?"

"I will hold her until Argyll comes fer her, then release her to her brother in Inverary." Callum ground his jaw, his penetrating gaze fixed on the heather-lined meadows before him. "The sooner I am away from the wench, the better."

"And the earl?"

Callum's eyes cooled to embers as he turned to his reluctant host. "He dies."

Ennis arched a bushy gray brow at him. "Will ye punish him fer what Liam Campbell did to ye, then?

"Aye," Callum nodded. "He will pay fer his faither's crimes, just as I paid fer mine. And he will suffer fer the MacGregors he has killed and the women's faces he has branded."

Ennis grew quiet. He'd heard about the women put to the iron by the Earl of Argyll. Damn pity 'twas, but 'twas naught out of the ordinary. The Campbells had been trying to tame the MacGregors since the time of Robert the Bruce, but to no avail.

Aye, Ennis knew that his clan was not entirely innocent. They were a bloodthirsty lot, killing Campbells for more years than Ennis could ever count. There were dozens of acts of Parliament's Privy Council against them, granting barons and other noblemen the right to pursue the outlaws with fire and sword. But when the MacGregors had massacred the Colquhouns at the battle of Glen Fruin fifty years ago, King James VI decreed them into extinction. Most Highlanders knew the Mac-Gregors did not deserve the punishment they'd received, for treachery amongst the Campbells and their allies abounded. But Callum and Margaret MacGregor had been innocent. That they had escaped Liam Campbell's dungeon at Kildun Castle was a miracle, everyone agreed. *How* they had done it, and what had become of Callum after that, was another matter entirely, depending on who was asked. Some called the laird of the mist braw, while to others he was a madman. One thing was certain, though. The MacGregor was a proud man, choosing, by his own words, never to hide in darkness. But as Ennis looked down at the leather cuffs encircling Callum's wrists, he wondered how long the young chieftain could hide behind those terrible years of his youth.

Ennis's thoughts were interrupted when his wife opened the front door and peeped her head out at the men standing around her doorway. She smiled when she met the MacGregor's gaze. "'Twas a clean injury. I've re-moved the arrow and dressed and bandaged her wound. She's awake, though a bit groggy from m' herbs. Proba-bly why she asked fer the arrogant bas—" Mae caught herself from repeating what the Campbell lass had called him. She blushed and gave her chest a pat. "—man who raided her holding. I presume she's meanin' ye, laird."

Angus immediately puffed up his chest and stepped forward. "I believe she most likely meant me."

Brodie snorted a laugh. "If she meant ye, she woulda asked fer the fat sot with a sack o' brew hangin' oot o' his mouth."

"Well, she didna mean ye, that's fer damned certain, Brodie MacGregor," Angus shouted. Ennis Stewart looked up and beseeched the heavens to open and take him where he stood.

"I think she meant Graham," Jamie offered honestly. "He's always smilin' at all the lasses with them devilish dimples of his."

"Stay here," Callum ordered his bickering kin and ducked his head under the doorframe, stepping into the bothy. When he saw her lying on the table, a strange tightness settled in his chest, causing his steps to pause. Her hair dripped over the side in long, rich locks he wanted to touch. God's fury, she had not even cried out when Ennis's wife removed the arrow from her flesh. When she turned her head to look at him, her eyes blazed with anger and tears.

Unprepared for the effect the sight of her had on him, he cursed himself for wanting to take her in his arms and comfort her.

Chapter Four

KATE WAS RIPPED from her dreams of being cradled in the arms of her rescuer and came awake with a choking gasp. With painful clarity, she remembered being shot. She looked around the unfamiliar bothy, with understanding dawning on her that she'd been taken from her home, as well. And not by some knight of the realm, but by a Mac-Gregor! There was little she could do now, fighting the dizzying effect of herbs, no doubt fed to her by the woman standing over her and wiping Kate's blood from her own hands with a small cloth. Or by that horrendous whiskey, as deadly as her rescuer . . . er . . . abductor. Good God, she'd been abducted! Where was her captor? She asked the woman, who gave her no answers, save for a reassuring pat before she hurried for the door. MacGregors! Kate's head reeled. Was it only this morn that her uncle was warning her about them? Pity she had wounded the laird in the leg. She ought to have sliced open his spine like they had done to her father.

She turned her face toward the door when she heard

someone enter. She hated this man's clan for terrorizing her kin for so many years, but she had to have been daft to lift a meager dagger against him. Why, he was even taller than Robert, and solidly built beneath a shirt of dyed saffron and belted plaid. He moved with the confidence of a conqueror. Two wide bands of brown hide encircled his wrists. Dried blood caked his bare knee and disappeared beneath the rim of his kidskin boot. But even the slight limp from his wound did naught to thwart his dominating presence. He paused for a moment, his eyes settling on her like a tempest, turbulent and dangerous.

Kate leaped from the table and stumbled back against the wall. Let all of Scotland fear the MacGregors. She would not! Her eyes darted around the room for something with which to hit him. She picked up a stool with her uninjured arm and raised it to ward him off. She fought a moment of sheer panic when he picked up his steps again. Pain resonated though her body, but she was not about to stand here and allow him to kill her without a fight. Gritting her teeth, she squeezed her eyes shut and swung.

When her stool came to a dead halt, she opened her eyes to find the chieftain's broad fingers closed around one wooden leg. He towered over her, so relentlessly compelling, his gaze on her so unforgiving.

"Ye will cease tryin' to do me bodily harm," he warned, taking a step even closer. "Or I'll be forced to confine ye."

"I mean to kill you." Kate stared up at him and gave the stool another tug.

Her would-be weapon flew across the room and crashed into the trivet with a mighty clang. Kate barely had time to startle before he swooped down and caught her in his arms. He lifted her to his chest, cradling her in a stone embrace. She struggled to free herself, but to no avail.

"Where are you taking me? Unhand me!" she demanded more forcefully when he did not answer right away.

"I'm bringin' ye to the bed."

Kate froze. Did he mean to ravish her? Aye, he had threatened to do the like earlier, had he not? She turned to look at the small mattress in the corner and fought to quell the drum of her heart. "If you dare touch me, I will rip out your heart."

"How might ye do that?" he asked, sounding somewhat amused. "With yer teeth?"

Kate wished she had the fortitude to do just that. She stiffened. It was true she could never overtake him with one arm. She reasoned she could not even fight him with two. She tried appealing to his sense of honor, hoping he possessed some. "I'm betrothed," she lied.

He peered down at her and then scowled for all he was worth, his eyes darkening to a smoky blue. "To whom?"

Kate drew the corner of her lower lip between her teeth, trying to come up with a name. She remembered one Amish had mentioned a time or two when he used to speak of his youthful days fighting the English. "To Lord Mortimer of Newbury. My uncle is very close to our lord protector, Cromwell, and I have been promised to Lord Newbury as an—"

"Newbury?" His scowl deepened into a glare that would have caused the most battle hardened warrior to blanch. "Ye're goin' to wed an Englishman?"

Kate glared right back at him as he crossed the room. "Aye, and I'm told he has an army two hundred strong."

The MacGregor snorted and shrugged his shoulders as if he didn't care if Lord Newbury's army numbered over a thousand. "I have nae intention of dishonorin' ye, woman."

He laid her in the small bed, then sat at the edge, beside her. "'Tis bad enough ye're a Campbell. If ye considered weddin' an Englishman, ye're a fool, as well."

Kate lay there glowering at his profile. She had the mind to slap him, preferably with an ax! Still, he made no move to ravish her, which meant her lie had worked. Either that, or he hated her as much as she hated him. The latter seemed more likely, since every time he set his eyes on her, he frowned.

"Being a Campbell and a fool is better than being a MacGregor. *My* kinsmen never cut off a man's head and sent it to his sister, causing her to lose her mind."

He angled his head to look at her fully, his expression hard and unyielding. "Ye're correct. Yer kinsmen have done far worse."

Kate drew in a deep breath and forbade herself to tremble, though that trembling had less to do with fear and more with the rugged beauty of his visage. His dark hair swept past his shoulders. A strand on either side was braided at his temples and tied with thin leather strips. His jaw was shadowed with a few days' worth of whiskers, but not enough to conceal the alluring hint of a dimple in his chin. His nose was straight and noble, his lips full and sensual.

"Worse than carrying the head to a church and swearing on it to uphold the wicked deed in defiance of the king?" she demanded, pushing herself up into a sitting position. She tugged on his plaid when he began to turn away again.

He took a moment to let his gaze drift over her features, then riled her temper with a slow, slanted grin that made her feel like the biggest dimwit in Scotland. "Ye speak of the forester John Drummond, woman. The Mac-Gregors killed him almost seventy years ago after he hung a number of them fer huntin' deer on their own land. Have ye nothin' more recent to remind me what ruthless bastards my kinsmen are?"

Kate blinked, and then her eyes flashed. "Aye, the worst among you killed my father and my grandfather."

His grin faded, but his voice still mocked her. "Are ye certain?"

The door burst open, stopping her from asking him what he meant. Angling her head around his arm, she surveyed the four men filing inside the small bothy, one in front of the other. They pushed and shoved their way toward her. Then the smallest of the bunch, a pleasant-looking young man with enormous blue eyes and pale yellow hair, stopped and grinned at her.

"Jamie Grant makes yer—"

The man behind him bumped into Jamie's back then swatted him across the back of the head. Another warrior, standing slightly to their left, took the opportunity to gracefully step around his comrades and bow to her.

"Graham Grant, of the clan Grant," he said, sweeping his midnight blue cap off his head.

Kate watched his mop of deep golden curls catch the light of the hearthfire as he straightened. He looked like an angel compared to the rest of them. An angel, she concluded an instant later, with a wickedly seductive smile.

"How do ye fare, Katherine?"

She arched a brow at him. "How do you know my name?"

"I spent the last pair of months with yer brother, Robert, in Inverary. He told me much about ye."

The mention of her brother drew a curious slant to her lips. He knew Robert? She had trouble believing her brother would consort with any friend of the clan responsible for killing their father. "Why would my brother tell you anything about me?"

"We were friends."

Kate offered him a suspicious smirk, certain he was lying.

"Ye see? She fancies him," Jamie pointed out, seeing her smile. "I told ye she meant Graham."

Graham reached for her hand and was about to lift it to his lips for a kiss, when the MacGregor snatched her wrist back and returned her hand to her lap. His fingers remained, covering hers possessively. He used his chin to gesture toward the rest of his men, ending any further charming introductions. "Brodie, Jamie, and Angus. There, now get the horses ready. Ennis and his wife have put themselves in harm's way long enough."

"Can she travel so soon?" the one named Angus asked. He was eyeing a barrel of what Kate imagined was whiskey. She suspected he was not really concerned for her well-being as much as he was about getting into that barrel. He was an enormous man with wavy red hair and a scar that laced his face from his left temple to his neck. When he looked at Kate, his expression softened and he reminded her of a fearsome dog she once had who used to lick her face clean after he'd chased raiders around her land, eager to take a bite out of one.

"I will not be traveling with you," Kate assured them. The chieftain rose to his feet. "She can travel, Angus," he said as if she had not spoken at all. "She's a fit lass."

Kate glared up at him and pronounced each word clearly so that he understood her this time. "I'm staying right here until my brother comes for me, you callous swine."

His expression did not change as he bent to her and scooped her off the bed and into his arms once again, ignoring her protests. He stopped when he reached the elderly couple waiting at the door and offered them his thanks, muffling Kate's venomous insults with his hand over her mouth.

Mae Stewart looked ready to swoon when the Campbell lass took a bite out of one of his fingers. Callum MacGregor was a large man with a taste for blood that rivaled the kings of England. Mae shoved a small package into his hand, hoping to stay his temper before he struck the poor lass and killed her. "Her salve," she offered him nervously. "She can apply it to her chest, but she'll need help applyin' it on her back. Try no' to strangle her, laird, if ye be the one applyin' it." She rushed to a small shelf and picked up another package, this one larger than the one she offered Callum, and handed it to Graham. "Just some dried meat and black bread fer yer journey."

The men thanked her, though Angus continued eyeing the barrels like a man being torn from the presence of his only love. Graham shoved him out the door, and Ennis followed them outside.

"Remember," Callum told him, placing Kate on her feet hard enough to make her teeth knock together. He leaped into his saddle. "If ye're questioned, ye were forced to aid us."

He leaned down, fit his hands around Kate's waist, and lifted her sideways to his lap.

"Does yer arm pain ye much?" he asked her, a little too softly and close to her ear for her liking. She pushed herself away from him and nearly tumbled to the ground. He caught her, snaking one arm around her belly.

"Laird," Ennis entreated one last time. "Scotland is changin'. Leave the past where it belongs."

"I have tried," Callum answered solemnly. "But the past willna free me."

Ennis nodded and bid him farewell with a smack on the horse's rump. He stood in the grass, watching them leave, and offered up a silent prayer that the unruly bunch make it to Camlochlin alive.

Chapter Five

KATE CURSED HER SKILL for failing her and herself for not killing this MacGregor when she had the chance. She swore by the saints if he ever muzzled her again, she would bite his fingers completely off! Her arm throbbed in perfect rhythm with her heart. Where were they taking her? She fought the panic rising in her chest. Screaming would do no good. The miscreants would likely take great pleasure in her hysteria. She consoled herself with the knowledge that at least she had not been abducted by the Devil MacGregor. This chieftain might be the most arrogant man she had ever met, but he did not behave like a madman bent on killing Campbells. In fact, he had risked his life saving one. She relaxed a bit and shifted across his hard thighs, trying to gain a little more comfort if she was going to have to remain perched upon them all the way to . . .

"Where are you taking me?"

Before he answered her, he grunted something in

Gaelic, then pushed her dangling legs off his wounded thigh. "To Skye."

She swung around, hitting his chin with the top of her head. "Skye?" She hoped she hadn't heard him right. She wasn't exactly certain where Skye was, save that it was far from Glen Orchy, but its name conjured visions of some very far away, heaven-bound place. Mayhap where he sought absolution for whatever sins he had committed. And being a MacGregor, he surely had many.

Tilting her head back, she peered at his face. He kept his gaze fixed on the trees straight ahead. "Why are you taking me there? What do you intend to do with me?" Her eyes narrowed on his features, the indomitable set of his jaw. There was an air of cool detachment in his bearing that made Kate doubt he even cared about his transgressions. Well, she did not care about them, either. She wanted to go home.

He glanced down at her, weighing her with a dark, brief look of impatience. "I'll answer one of yer queries."

"Only one?" Kate quirked her mouth at his attempt to intimidate her. Why, this brute was even more arrogant than her uncle!

"Aye."

"Are you always so uncompromising?"

He inclined his head, giving her his full attention. Kate defied the urge to pull back at the virility in his bold gaze, the vivid beauty of flames fired with the power of some fervent purpose within. She met his strength of will head on—until his eyes swept over her face, lingering on her mouth and heating her cheeks.

"Verra well." He returned his gaze to hers. "To show

ye that I'm agreeable, I'll allow ye to choose which query ye want me to answer."

Kate's brows flew up at his haughty self-importance. "Two queries," she parried, challenging his amiability.

He conceded with a slight nod.

"Why are you bringing me to Skye?"

"Because there are over fifty dead bodies loiterin' on yer doorstep in Glen Orchy."

"Och." She blinked. "I see." She twisted her body forward and leaned back against his chest with a heavy sigh of relief. She had forgotten about the bloody battle on her front lawn. She certainly did not want to return to *that* alone. She would have to bury the bodies, unless her uncle returned to retrieve his men, which she could not fathom him doing. And there were the McColls to consider. They would seek revenge once they discovered what had become of their kin. "I confess, you have a point. It would not be wise to return home just yet." She turned toward him again and gave him a measured look. "I thought you were abducting me." His lips curled into a smile she suspected he'd used a hundred times before to frighten a horde of enemies. Kate's mouth tightened; she refused to yield so easily. "You are a MacGregor, after all." She shrugged her shoulders and her expression relaxed. "But you did save me, and I don't want you to think that I—"

"I dinna trouble myself with thinkin' of ye at all."

His curt insult grated on her last nerve. "Of course." She shifted her position again and brought her legs down with resounding thumps on his injured thigh. His body went rigid, but he did not move her.

"What do you intend to do with me?"

"Slicin' off yer head would be a good beginnin'," he ground out through clenched teeth.

"Och, but then who would you practice your frightful scowls on?"

Her bravery to mock him right to his face fired his blood. "Yer kin."

Oh, what Kate wouldn't have done for her sword at that moment. "Alas, then, you would frighten no one." To prove her point, she didn't turn away when his eyes swept over her face. She should have, though, because the smile that graced his lips made her heart quicken.

"What are your plans for me?" she asked again, turning away.

"I have no' decided that yet."

Kate prayed she hadn't heard him right. He had not decided yet? What did that mean? Was he going to return her to her brother, safe and sound? Or was he going to kill her?

"Well, I'd rather go home than to Skye," she informed him, deciding that he was simply trying to frighten her again. "So I've made your decision for you."

Dear God, how could she find a MacGregor so dangerously appealing? Damn her, but the indulgent slant of his mouth made her knees go soft.

"Thank ye. That is exactly what I will do."

Her eyes widened. "What?"

"Return ye home to yer brother."

"To Inverary?"

"That is where he lives."

She lowered her gaze lest he see the trepidation in her eyes. She didn't want to live with her uncle. Oh, why had Robert left Glen Orchy?

The chieftain leaned forward, and his breath caressed her temple when he spoke. "Ye have made it clear that ye dinna care fer yer uncle. Why?"

She raised her eyes to his, unable to find the sudden concern in his voice any less noble than that of the most gallant knight. She shook her head at herself. Was she daft? This was no knight, but a savage outlaw. Kin to the beast who murdered her father. She could be thrown into the tower for finding him anything but vile. But he had rushed headlong into a melee of swinging swords and saved her from certain death. He had not abducted her. He had carried her all the way to the Stewarts' homestead to remove her arrow, when he could have easily left her to tend to herself. He had held her and comforted her when the pain of her wound was unbearable. And most important, he meant to deliver her to the safety of her brother. Of course, she had not forgotten how he'd let her almost fall off his horse when she had demanded he release her. Or the way he had clamped his strong hand over her mouth at the Stewarts'. He was an overbearing brute, to be certain, but he had not harmed her.

"My uncle means little to me." She offered him a slight pat on the arm to ease his obvious concern. "But I fear he would punish Robert for befriending you."

He severed their gaze and straightened, moving his body further away from hers. "Nae more talkin'."

Kate's nostrils flared as she inwardly scolded herself for fancying him to be anything more than an obstinate worm. She prayed the man didn't have a wife waiting for him in Skye. Poor wretched thing she must be if he did. "Though I owe you my life, I find you immensely dislikable."

He arched an eyebrow at her and gave her a measuring look. "Come, Campbell," he challenged with a slow, rapier smirk. "Be the first of yer ilk braw enough to tell me what I've done to provoke yer scorn."

"Your kin," she accused without hesitation, "murdered my father and left my brother and me orphaned to a man who did not want us."

The laird's hard expression faltered, but his voice was firm, his gaze steady on hers. "'Twasna I who killed him."

Kate nodded. "I'm thankful for that."

Jamie watched them curiously from a few feet away, momentarily distracted from his examination of a particular patch of powder-blue blossoms. The lass was bonny, aright. Fer a Campbell, that is. But did she think she could make his laird like her by staring up at him with that trusting look in her eyes? He reined in a bit closer. "You willna make him like ye. His mind's made up. He hates ye," he said.

Callum would have whacked the young warrior right off his horse, but he could not tear his eyes away from Katherine Campbell—a discomfiting condition he'd suffered from more than once since first laying eyes on her. He dipped his gaze from her large coal eyes to the luscious contours of her clenched mouth. Hell, he didn't know which was more dangerous of the two. Fortunately for him, she turned away, her spine stiff.

"Then my enemy and I have something in common," she replied coolly.

Callum shifted uneasily, wanting to say something. But what? Could he deny Jamie's charge—or her own? They were enemies, her name as hated as his was worthless.

He bent forward slightly and inhaled the scent of her hair. He shouldn't want her. But he did. And every time he looked at her, each time her body yielded against him, he wanted her more.

Her braw spirit tempted him with unbidden images of her in his bed, just as fiery. She could wield a sword, that much was evident by the throbbing in his thigh, but hell, her tongue was even sharper. Twice he was torn between grinning at her saucy mouth and kissing the belligerence off her lips.

He was daft. She was a Campbell, and he could not wait to be rid of her.

Chapter Six

⁓

THEY RODE THROUGHOUT THE NIGHT without stopping and traveled alongside the still waters of Loch Leven the next afternoon. They passed grand mountain ranges whose summits were hidden by swirling clouds and vast verdant fields where grouse basked beneath the sun. Kate took in every detail of the new landscape around her. With such raw splendor surrounding her, her awareness of the man behind her intensified. The sleek strength of his arms around her waist. The knotted steel of his thighs beneath her. Had these MacGregors somehow convinced Robert not to kill them? She simply could not believe her brother would consort with MacGregors. Had they come to Glen Orchy to kill her uncle? Why had they protected her? Had Robert asked them to do it? Had he somehow discovered his uncle's true intentions for her? And why would he risk his life by trusting MacGregors?

Dear God, had her brother betrayed them? Nae! She would never believe it. She pushed the thought out of her mind and replaced it with a dozen others. There were so many questions, and she was too sleepy to think on them all now. She leaned against the chieftain's chest, mindful of her sore shoulder, yawned, and made a mental note to question him about it more later.

Callum's muscles flexed involuntarily when her body sank into him. The lass was bone weary, and he didn't fancy the notion of her sleeping on him again. They would have to stop. Sleeping outdoors anywhere but in Skye was unwise, but he would rather travel a few more leagues north, into friendlier territory. There were some who knew him by sight and would risk all for a chance to take his head. 'Twas not safe to stop, but more dangerous was the pleasure he took from her ease with him, the softness of her curves, the scent of peat lacing her feathery curls when they blew across his face. He shifted back, separating himself from her.

He reined in his mount at the crest of a windswept ridge and scanned the dense patches of pine nestled in the glen below. "We'll stop there fer the night."

Stopping beside him, Graham studied his profile with concern creasing his brow. "Ye look pained. Yer wound needs closing."

The only sign that Callum had heard him was the tightening of his jaw. His commander was correct. His leg was stiff, and every time the lass in his lap inhaled, it felt like she was digging a dagger into his flesh. The slice had to be closed before fever set in. He'd had many injuries put to the fire in the past, but the mind simply could not prepare for the brand.

When they reached the trees, Callum set Kate down first and then glared at her after a painful dismount.

"I apologized for wounding you!" she charged, though

he hadn't said a word. His brows dipped over his eyes, but she didn't shrink away from his blackest scowl. "You should have called out! I didn't know you had come to aid me."

He peered down at her for a moment, looking like he wanted to say something. But then he turned without a word and snatched Angus's pouch from the warrior's lips.

"We need a fire," he called out to Jamie and limped away.

Callum stopped when he reached a tall pine, leaned his back against it, and tipped the pouch of brew to his mouth. When he spotted the lass storming toward him, he raised his eyes to the heavens.

"Why did you not have your friend's wife tend to your leg?" She reached for the hem of his plaid to take a peek at his thigh. He swatted her hand away.

"Get some rest, Katherine. I willna—"

"It's Kate."

He stared at her with eyes a heart-stopping shade of stormy blue, then took another swig of whiskey.

"I willna have ye sleepin' on me, *Kate*." He closed his eyes, letting the potent brew warm his muscles. When he opened them again, she was gone. Against his will, his gaze scanned the campsite until he found her again, sitting on the ground a few feet away, her knees drawn up to her chest. She watched Jamie start the small fire between them and shook her head when Angus offered her some of Mae Stewart's black bread. Callum studied the shape of her face, the bonny luminance of her deep, dark eyes, the sensual fullness of her mouth. Fire flushed through his veins. Damned whiskey. He ran his hand over his stubbled jaw. He would never compromise his convictions by bedding one of his enemies. No matter how enticing she'd felt nestled between his thighs for the past day and night. When she rubbed her arm, he felt a sharp sting of pity for her. She had not complained once about her wound, though he knew it pained her. He quaffed another long drink from the pouch, determined to douse the embers of desire and mercy she ignited in him. If he had any sense at all, he would leave her here in the morn.

Her eyes shimmered like the gabbro of the Cuillins when Jamie's flames finally sprang to life. As if sensing his silent vigil, she shifted her gaze to his. Callum's knees buckled beneath him. Of course, his weakened state could be blamed on the whiskey he'd consumed and not on the tender look she aimed at him. Damn her, where was the seething contempt in her eyes? She was a Campbell, for hell's sake! Why was she looking at him like he was anything but her worst enemy? If she hurled a few oaths at him, cursed his clan to hell, he might not find her so pleasing. His back slid down against the trunk, and he landed with a heavy thump that rattled his teeth. God help him, he felt like grinning at her.

"A few more swigs of me brew and ye willna feel a thing," Angus chuckled. Callum leaned his head back, preferring not to watch Graham's sword heat to bright orange.

"You are not going to . . ."

Callum heard Kate's voice and closed his eyes again. He liked the sound of her, the dulcet huskiness that carried an undercurrent of strength so deeply rooted, she did not even fear the Devil.

"You cannot mean to sear his flesh with *that!*" she

screeched, causing Callum's shoulders to bunch up around his ears.

"Sit ye down, lass," Graham said softly. "There's naught else to be done."

Callum looked at them and blinked at the three scalding swords in Graham's hands. One. He dragged his hand across his eyes. His friend held only one sword. One glowing, sizzling iron rod that would soon . . . He guzzled more brew and braced himself for what was to come.

"Well? What are ye waitin' fer?" he demanded a moment later when Graham simply stood there staring down at him.

"I'm thinking I should tie yer hands first," Graham admitted.

"Do it."

And still Graham hesitated. Callum MacGregor was mighty indeed. If he swung that fist and made contact with Graham's face, the commander was sure he would not awaken for a se'nnight. Years of hard labor and torture had made Callum stronger than any man Graham knew, but 'twas the torture he had endured and the scars that still marred his body that made Graham hate the task at hand.

"Graham," Callum warned impatiently.

The blade descended. For a moment, the entire world went black. Callum clenched his teeth and threw his head back, but he did not make a sound.

Kate stood aghast, unable to move while the sickening smell of burning flesh wafted through her nostrils. Graham dropped his sword and strode away, swearing as he went. The instant he was gone, Kate bolted forward.

When Callum opened his eyes, he was not sure if he

couldn't form a rational thought because of the pain rip-ping through his entire body, or because of the beautiful goddess kneeling before him, looking like she was about to weep all over him.

Without warning, she snatched the pouch from his fingers and dumped a goodly amount of its contents over his leg.

Callum reacted instantly. His eyes widened and blazed with both fury and agony that made him writhe. He clutched her shoulders and fought the urge to fling her across the campsite. "Christ!" he shouted between gasp-ing breaths. "What the hell did ye do to me?"

"The whiskey will cleanse the wound," she explained, but Brodie yanked her from Callum's arms and hauled her to her feet.

"Ye will stay away from him." His dark hair eclipsed even darker eyes that impaled her while he pulled a dag-ger from his belt. "Have ye no' done enough damage to him? Will ye no' be satisfied until ye have killed him?"

"Nae!" Kate took a step back, feeling her mettle begin to fade for the first time. These men surrounding her were warriors of the most savage ilk. Their laird meant to de-liver her to safety, but they looked only too eager to hang her from the nearest tree. "I did not mean to cause him in-jury. I saw him riding toward me and I thought he was coming to fight on the side of the McColls."

"Why in hell would we fight on the side o' the bloody McColls?" Brodie raised his voice at her. "Are ye daft?"

The mighty chieftain hiccuped. " 'Tis understandable. She's a Campbell."

"Aye, she's a Campbell." Angus agreed and spat in

disgust. "Stick a knife into a MacGregor's guts as quick as her men kin would."

"Treacherous she is."

That insult was enough to strengthen Kate's mettle back to full force. "I did not stick a knife into his guts, but his thigh. And as for my men kin, at least they are not cowards who slice men from behind like your kinsmen did to my father. They do not go around raping and pillaging innocent people and starting wars that last for centuries."

"We didna rape anyone innocent," Angus argued.

"Shut up, Angus." Callum groaned against the tree. He rubbed his forehead. "And what in blazes is in this brew? I feel like my head's floatin' off my shoulders." He attempted to stand, held on to the tree for a moment until the ground stopped moving, then tried again. He nearly fell on top of Kate. Grasping her waist to right himself, his heavy body almost caused her to fall with him. He groaned when a bolt of pain shot through his leg.

"And we wouldna kill a Campbell from behind." Brodie moved closer to them, his voice hard as steel. "We would look him in the eye and—"

"Brodie, step back before I take my sword to ye," Callum warned, trying to fight the effects of Angus's whiskey.

Angus caught his laird when Kate took a step toward Brodie and Callum teetered on his feet.

"Look him in the eye, you say?" she asked quietly, her voice seething with emotion. "Do you take that much joy in killing that you want to see your victim's last breath?"

"If they're Campbells, aye."

Kate shook her head with disgust. "I see now why my

uncle's hatred for your clan is so profound. Why he always warned us about the MacGregors. You defy kings and kill earls for little reason other than you enjoy it."

"Little reason?"

They all turned toward Callum, who was hanging over Angus's shoulder and looking more lucid than he did a moment ago. His eyes glittered against the firelight when they locked on Kate. His nostrils flared with anger. He did not blink. He seemed not to breathe. "Did I hear ye right?"

The forest went deathly still; even the crickets seemed to hush awaiting Kate's reply. She looked at the other men around her. Each wore the same expression of cold, hard contempt. Her heart leapt with fear. She did not doubt in that moment that should she say the wrong thing, they might just kill her after all. "I didn't mean . . . I know it must be difficult to lose the right to bear your name, but surely you understand that—"

"Nae, ye dinna know anything aboot losin' yer name," Callum cut her off. He pushed himself off Angus and closed the distance between them in two strides. "Ye know nothin' aboot us save half-truths that took place over half a century ago. Ye have no' lost yer land, or yer—"

"I lost my family."

His jaw tightened around something more he wanted to say. The fury in his eyes faded, leaving him with a resigned look as his gaze dropped to the pulse at her throat. Kate had the urge the lift her hand to shield her flesh from him. For he looked as if he could stop the beating of her heart if he but thought about it.

"Then ye have good reason to hate us, Katherine Campbell." He began to turn away. "Try no' to ferget it."

"You make the task easy, MacGregor," she hurled at his back. "If I had my sword I would show you."

"Ye're a Campbell." Callum tossed her a dry smirk over his shoulder. "I wouldna expect anything less from ye. Angus," he snapped. "Come here."

The largest of Callum's men took a step forward just as his laird's knees buckled under him.

"Ye fokin' poisoned him," Brodie accused the burly warrior while Angus dragged his unconscious laird back to the tree.

"'Tis the whiskey," Angus defended. "Auld Gillis said 'twas stronger than any man. I'm guessin' he was right."

Kate watched Callum slump to the ground and begin to snore. Even in his dead stupor he appeared to be brooding. By the saints, his conviction to hate her was even stronger than her uncle's was to hate the MacGregors. She wanted to hate him, too. She did hate him! But when he let out a low moan, she found herself moving in his direction. She almost reached him when Brodie stepped in front of her, blocking her path.

"Ye'll be away from him now." His voice was low, warning her not to argue.

"But I—"

"Sleep over there." He pointed, then cupped her elbow to move her along.

"Let her be, Brodie. She's not going to stab him in his sleep, are ye, lass?"

Kate looked up into Graham's warm gaze and shook her head. He smiled, revealing a dimple as devastating as Callum's sword.

"Callum could use a woman's gentle touch during the night," she heard him tell Brodie as he led the grumbling Highlander to the fire.

Kate turned back to their laird. She had no intention of touching him. She simply wanted to make sure his wound had been closed properly. *Savages,* she thought, cringing again at the memory of his sizzling flesh. Sitting beside him, she carefully lifted the edge of his plaid off his thigh, then nearly retched. The skin was black and blistered, but the wound was sealed. Her gaze drifted over the rest of him. Heavens, he was big, his legs well muscled and long. She blinked away, covering his thigh, and looked at his hands instead. She remembered how skilled they were at wielding his great claymore against the McColls and, she realized now, her uncle's men. She'd been so busy praying for her own life, she hadn't even looked up to see who he was killing. They were born enemies, but she could not forget the strength in his arm or the murderous glint in his eyes when he stopped a McColl blade from cutting her down the middle. He had the look of a savage, garbed in his plaid and leather wrist cuffs instead of clean breeches and polished boots like her uncle wore. But he hadn't tried to ravish her. In fact, his touch was so gentle when he held her in his saddle, the very thought of it drew a sigh from her lips. She closed her eyes and settled against the tree beside him, thanking God that it was Callum MacGregor who found her, and not the monster who had murdered her father.

Chapter Seven

⁓

DUNCAN CAMPBELL SLOWED his mount as he approached Kildun Castle. Something was amiss. Silence clung to the land like scum on a pond. Beneath clouds of rolling charcoal, the high battlements stood empty. He looked around and wiped the sheen of sweat from his brow. He was alone. He'd cursed his men the entire way back to Inverary for falling so easily to McColl blades. He hadn't been there to see how it had happened. Why should he have risked losing his life to raiders? But now, with a growing sense of panic knotting his innards, it dawned on him who his men must have fought. He had feared the MacGregors would go to Glen Orchy to take revenge on his niece for what he'd done to one of their women a fortnight ago. He wanted to get Kate away before they found her, believing she would be safe in Kildun. The rebel chieftain would never return here. He had been so sure of it.

When he reached the lowered drawbridge, he dismounted and drew his sword. The wind howled through the deserted entryway, sending a chill over his flesh and the acrid scent of blood to his nostrils. Images of another day much like this one flooded his memory. Fearing what he would find when he reached the bailey, and fighting the urge to run the other way, he stepped cautiously past the gatehouse.

Over a hundred of his men scattered the bloodstained ground, flies swarming around their hewn bodies. Dread and fury produced a faint groan from the back of Duncan's throat. He had seen this kind of destruction six years ago—when the Devil had left Kildun. Duncan had never forgotten that day. It was forged in his memory, branded into his dreams.

Alerted by the screams of his comrades, he and twenty of his men had rushed down the narrow stone stairs that led to the dungeon. When he arrived there he wanted to flee back up the way he had come. He had covered his mouth to keep from retching. Dismembered bodies littered the stony ground, all of them ravaged by a single sword. Duncan's eyes followed that blade, glinting red in the torchlight, as it descended on Donald Stuart, his father's first in command, and near cut him in half.

At first, Duncan had feared God had finally sought vengeance against his father's sins and had set Satan loose upon Kildun. Blood dripped from the creature's long, limp hair barring his face. His eyes shone beneath like brimstone against the torchlight, striking terror in the hearts of the men around him. The beast's shoulders were slightly hunched forward and massive, providing him with unearthly strength.

Just beside him, one of Duncan's men screamed and fell to the floor. Duncan's body shook as he gripped his hilt with both hands. He'd managed to swing his blade, but it whooshed across empty air. Something whistled just in front of him an instant later and another guard crumbled to his knees, clutching the fatal gash across his belly.

Ten breaths had passed while Duncan stood alone in the paralyzing silence of his father's dungeon. Someone whimpered. A lass's voice. Duncan's eyes darted to the eastern wall, knowing who it had to be. Still, he staggered backward when he saw that MacGregor was gone, and with him the chains that had held him. Young Margaret MacGregor's confines lay crushed on the ground in a heap of twisted steel.

Impossible—Duncan remembered thinking—until the murderer stood before him.

"Fer now, ye will live to tell yer faither I will return fer him."

Duncan took another swing at him, determined not to die cowering at a prisoner's feet. His blade was met in midair by a crushing blow that sent fire up his arm. Mac-Gregor's sword ground against his until the tip was only inches from his eye.

Strewn over her brother's shoulder, Margaret MacGregor cried out, halting the blade's deadly course.

"Dinna force yer death. It will come soon enough," MacGregor had promised him before he fled, taking his sister with him and vanishing into the mists.

Duncan wished the bastard had killed him instead of leaving him to face his father. It was the first time Liam Campbell had ever struck his son. Would that he had never stopped. It would have been more merciful than the contempt hardening his father's eyes from that day hence.

Duncan surveyed the gruesome scene around him

now. The Devil had finally returned to Inverary, and with the same fury. A sound from beyond the western curtain wall startled him. He spun on his heel, his sword at the ready to send the MacGregor straight back to hell this time.

He waited, hearing naught again but the wind. He inched forward toward the heavy portcullis that led to the inner bailey, drawing up his nerves to face his most formidable enemy once again.

Instead, he came upon his nephew, tied securely with rope, to the half-raised thick iron gate.

Robert Campbell stared down at his uncle and felt a tight knot rise in his throat. His great relief at being rescued vanished from his eyes as he noted the absence of any man at mount beside his returning uncle. The knot thickened, threatening to suffocate him if the strip of plaid tied over his mouth was not removed posthaste!

It took far too long for the earl to lower the gate and cut the cloth away from his face. "Where's Kate?" Robert erupted.

Duncan did not answer him right away but looked around the deserted grounds, then continued cutting the rest of him loose. "Did he kill everyone, then?"

"Nae, anyone who did not lift a weapon was put in the dungeon," Robert told him quickly. "They need be released. But first, Uncle, where is my sister? Why does she not ride with you?" Panic and nausea vied for his attention. Robert refused them both. The moment one hand was free, he used it to grip his uncle's doublet. "Give me your reply!"

Eyes of forged steel finally fastened on his, narrowing slightly and stilling any further movement from Robert, despite his freedom. "Why do you fear for her so, Robert? You do not even consider that I might have left her unharmed in the care of my guardsmen in Glen Orchy?"

Robert had spent days helplessly secured to a wrought-iron gate, praying for an act of God to free him so he could save his sister. He prayed now again that it was not too late.

"Because the men you took with you to Glen Orchy are all dead, as these men are. I beg you tell me my sister is not among them."

Now Duncan gripped his nephew's tunic and yanked him closer. "How do you know the others are dead? It was the MacGregor, was it not? And you told him where to find me." His eyes seared into Robert's. "You chose to give them my life in exchange for yours," he accused, then pushed his nephew away. "Here you are alive and well while your sister is their captive. You are a coward, Robert." He nodded at his own words while Robert went pale. "Your grandfather would toss you from Kildun."

"I did not tell them where to find you," Robert flung at him before turning for the stable. "You did."

"I?" Duncan stormed after him and stopped him by closing his fingers around Robert's wrist. "I told no one but you where I was going!"

"And Graham Campbell," his nephew informed him. "Or rather, Graham Grant, commander of the Devil Mac-Gregor's men. Aye, they made certain I knew whose eyes I was staring into ten breaths after we were led past the gates by the traitor that *you* took in as your kin after I arrived here."

"Nae." Duncan reeled back, stunned. He shook his

head, refusing to believe he had been so easily fooled. "Graham Campbell drank with me, sat at my table."

"And with me," Robert agreed, his voice trembling with fury at the man he had come to think of as his friend. "He deceived us all. He led us outside the protection of the castle on the pretense that a band of MacGregors, led by the Devil himself, had captured you and were holding you just beyond Loch Awe. He led us directly into the swords of our enemies, at least two hundred strong." Robert's gaze swept over the bodies around him. Bodies he had been left to stare at for days. "We did not stand a chance against the wave of destruction which came upon us. Quickly our men were slain. Without mercy or pause were their bodies torn asunder and trampled." He returned his gaze to his uncle, checking back the emotion in his voice. "The Devil and his men came here to kill you, but you were gone. Grant told him you were in Glen Orchy. They were on their way there when they left."

"And they left you alive." Duncan's tone dripped with the accusation of betrayal.

"The fighting was over. My sword had been wrested from my hands. After the MacGregor instructed the bulk of his men to take your cattle to his holding, he ordered Grant to hang me, charging you with doing the same to his kinsmen."

"And hang you he did." Duncan smiled dryly. "But MacGregor let you live. You were fortunate. When the Devil strikes, he leaves no Campbell alive."

Robert's eyes narrowed on his uncle. "How then did you escape him?"

Duncan lifted his shoulders in a hesitant shrug, but he looked away from his nephew when he spoke. "I had gone for a morning ride after helping your sister with her swordplay. When I returned, your father's land looked much like this. Katherine was gone."

"And Amish and John?" Robert asked, drawing both hands down his face in an effort to calm his frantic heart. "Were they killed, as well?"

"I don't know what became of them. They were not among the dead."

"We must send word to the lord protector."

Duncan shook his head. "Cromwell will do nothing. He sent over four hundred men to hunt the Devil after he killed my father. Most of those men were killed by Highlanders who side with the MacGregors. He will not tax his army so again. That is why he leaves the duty of killing the outlaws to the noblemen of Scotland."

"But you are his vassal, uncle. Your entire garrison was killed. Surely he will send reinforcements."

"It will take time."

"Then I will find her myself," Robert vowed.

"Where do you propose to look first?" Duncan did naught to conceal his mocking smirk. "This man holds no patch of ground in Glen Orchy, Glenstrae, or Rannoch. He left the banks of Lammond long ago and disappeared into the north. Since then, he has been as difficult to capture as the mists that hide him. If Cromwell's army could not find him, you certainly won't."

Robert's expression hardened, reminding Duncan of the lad's father when Colin had set out to find the MacGregor after he had escaped. Liam Campbell had been pleased. At least, he had accused, one of his sons did not shyt his breeches in the face of a common outlaw. But

Duncan had known the truth of it, even if his father was too blind to see.

Colin had been well loved by their father. He was tall and well muscled compared to Duncan's scrawny physique. His dark good looks had also earned him the favor of the castle wenches at Glen Orchy. Robert's resemblance to his father was a bit unnerving. Their eyes were the same, light brown flecked with gray and green and glinting with determination. But the similarities between father and son ended with their physical appearance. Robert Campbell was no coward.

"I know in which direction to ride," Robert said stiffly.

"And when you come upon him," Duncan challenged, "how will you succeed in gaining your sister back when you could not even keep your sword in your fists the first time you faced him? I fear you will not escape his wrath a second time."

"I do not care if he kills me. I will free my sister from him first."

"Braw words." Duncan searched his nephew's eyes and was pleased at the raw resolve lighting their depths. The Devil had to be stopped, but Duncan had decided long ago that he would not give his life simply to avenge those who perished at the fiend's hands. His father might have thought him a fool, but he was not fool enough to think he could live through an encounter with Callum MacGregor. Nae, but he enjoyed taunting the beast. The law was on his side when it came to hanging the rebellious Highlanders and branding their women. But he had not thought the Devil would ever return here. MacGregor had to be completely mad to slaughter Kildun's garrison a second time.

"Callum MacGregor needs to be dead."

"If he has harmed my sister, he will be."

"If?" Duncan tempered his query with a withering sigh. He would never make the same error his father had made in allowing doubt to grow in the heart of his kin. Robert had to know and understand well that the Mac-Gregors were their enemies. Doubting the like gave room for pity, and pity bred sympathy. Nae, Duncan would nurture Robert's fury and mayhap the lad would succeed in ridding them of the Devil once and for all. "Lad, I've no doubt he will violate her. Let us pray he does not kill her." He smiled tightly when Robert rushed for the stables again. "We will need more men!" he called out.

His nephew slowed to a halt and looked over his shoulder at him. "You said it would take time."

"Not if they come from Scotland," Duncan promised. "I can assemble at least one hundred within a few days. But Robert," his uncle added when Robert turned to face him fully. "When we find the bastard we will employ a more effective strategy than charging his holding."

"What do you mean?"

Duncan looked toward the castle doors, returning once again to that day—and the only thing that had stopped MacGregor from killing him. "He has a weakness. And I know what it is."

Chapter Eight

"GOD CURSE YOU!"

Kate's eyes darted to the right to see who had hurled the offense, but the dozens of faces staring back at her all looked equally guilty.

Beside her, Callum lowered his gaze, avoiding the accusation and anger thick in the air. He knew he was not welcome in Roderick Cameron's village. They were afraid of him. 'Twas why he had dismounted before he entered the village and commanded his men to do the same. Leading his warhorse by the bridle gave him a less intimidating appearance.

"Go back to the hell that spawned ye!"

These people wanted peace, no matter what it cost them.

"Why do they hate you?" Kate tugged on his plaid. "I thought you said their laird was your friend."

When Callum lifted his eyes and met her incensed gaze, the sudden urge to smile near overwhelmed him. It astonished him that even while he was being so painfully reminded of what he had become, the indignation Kate felt over his rebuke could soften his black heart.

"They dinna all hate me. 'Tis only the MacGregors who curse me."

She stopped walking, stopping him, as well, with her hand still on his plaid. Her eyes opened wider, and Callum allowed himself a moment to bask in the knowledge that she truly didn't know who he was. As far as she was concerned he was simply a MacGregor laird, guilty of the same as any other. And some traitorous part of him gloried in it. She didn't know of the blood that covered his hands. That covered all of him. He should tell her the truth, but the truth was too harsh and ugly, and it would change the way she looked at him.

"Your own kin hate you? Why?" she demanded to know.

A glossy curl obscured the alluring curve of her cheekbone. The tilt of her chin tempted him to lean down and kiss her until she went weak in his arms.

"Many of these people have changed their names and live here now as Camerons. They want the world to ferget us. I keep reminding the world that we still exist."

"How do you remind them?"

"By keeping our name alive and avenging the wrongs done to my kin." Hell, she tempted him as no one had ever done before to give account of what his name meant to him.

Her expression on him softened briefly, and he was the one who felt weak. "You sound more like their hero than their enemy."

For an instant, he wanted to stay in that moment forever. But the lives he'd taken for his name, and in the

name of vengeance, were too great an iniquity to be forgiven. He ground his jaw and picked up his steps again.
He was an outlaw, a murderer, the most feared MacGregor in Scotland, and the one with the largest price on his
head. He was not a hero.

"Come," he said, grasping her hand as he cut toward
the stone keep overlooking the village. "I must be granted
permission before we go further."

They were met just outside the fortress by Roderick
Cameron. He was an imposing man with thick gray hair
plaited on either side of his weathered face. The plaid
draping his expansive shoulders and belted low on his
waist was fashioned of many colors. His eyes were the
shade of a stormy sea, but when they settled on Callum
they softened with fondness.

"How d'ye fare, MacGregor?" He slid his gaze to Kate
and smiled in a way that told her he thought Callum was
faring rather well. He swept his arm across the threshold
to usher them inside the keep. "Enjoy the comforts of my
home as is afforded to friends."

Callum placed his hand on the chieftain's shoulder. "I
must refuse yer generous offer. I would chance nae further peril to yer people. I wish only to see the woman."

"Verra well." The Cameron held his palm up to stop
two of his men when they stepped forward to accompany
him. "This way." He led Callum and his small troop toward a cottage at the farthest edge of the village.

Kate fell in behind the two lairds and found her pace
even with Graham's. All around her, the inhabitants
stepped outside their doors, drawn by the presence of the
tall, dark laird accompanying their own. Kate regarded

none of them, for their stares were hard, fearful, and mistrusting.

She knew both the Campbells and the MacGregors had their enemies, but she wasn't sure whom these people regarded with more contempt, her or Callum. "What wrongs have been done to them, and how has he avenged them?" she asked Graham softly, though her gaze remained fastened on Callum's back.

"I fear ye're about to find out, lass."

She tilted her face up to look at him just as they reached the cottage. Graham swept his cap off his head and moved to the side of the entrance, after Callum and Roderick disappeared within. His hand reached for Kate when she moved to follow them.

"Mayhap 'twould be best fer ye to wait here with me." His words were firm, as was his hand on her arm, but the gentle entreaty in his green eyes told her his request was given for her own good.

Kate brushed his hand away and stepped inside. A small fire burned beneath a trivet in the center of the outer room. Firelight mingled with that of the sun's rays spilling across the rushes from the window.

Callum stood with the Cameron and another man, slightly smaller in stature, his palms resting on the shoulders of a boy with large, doleful eyes and a dirt-streaked face.

"'Tis yer laird, boy," the man said, looking as wide-eyed as his son. Kate could not tell which of the two chieftains the man referred. "Pay him the homage he deserves." He pushed the child to a kneeling position in front of Callum, but Callum raised his palm to stop him.

"Tell me aboot the attack."

The man pushed his son away with a quiet order to leave the cottage. He waited until the boy was gone before he spoke. "'Twas a band of Menzies who did this to m' Rhona."

Callum's jaw twisted around a low curse battering against his teeth.

"We've had nae quarrel with the Menzies fer years." Cameron assured him. "These men acted on their own. No' under any command of their laird."

"They marked m' wife's face in accordance with the law!" The man stepped closer to Callum, his eyes gleaming with defiance and fury. "They are Argyll's dogs, fer they spoke of their reward as they burned oot her eye."

A sharp gasp drew the men's attention to where Kate stood at the door, her face ashen and her hands trembling as they twisted the woolen folds of her skirts. "What has my uncle to do with this?"

"Yer uncle?" the man asked, sounding as horrified as Kate looked. His expression changed quickly to loathing as he drew a small dagger from a fold in his plaid. "Have ye come to finish what yer kin began, then?"

Before he took a step in her direction, Callum blocked his path and snatched the dagger from his hand.

"I will avenge m' wife," the man insisted.

Callum's rigid gaze stilled the remainder of his protests. "No' on her." The thread of warning in his softly spoken words was unmistakable. "Bring me to yer wife. I've tarried here long enough."

The man did as he was commanded without sparing Kate another glance. "M' Rhona is here," he said, pulling away the curtain that separated the outer room from the sleeping quarters. "Her sister is changin' the dressin' to her wound."

Kate watched him lead Callum inside. The Cameron did not follow. When they were alone, the older chieftain turned to her, a deep frown drawing his gray brows over his eyes.

"A Campbell," he whispered.

Kate turned to him, still horrified that her uncle was responsible for branding a woman. "You needn't worry that I'll tell my uncle you are friends with Callum."

He stared at her, looking somewhat perplexed by her casual use of the laird's name. Then he shrugged his massive shoulders. "I dinna care what ye tell him, lass. The MacGregor saved my life."

Kate smiled, glad to hear it. "He saved mine, as well."

Now the Cameron stared outright at her, his jaw going slack an instant before his scowl returned full force. "The Devil has never spared a Campbell's life, let alone saved one. Surely he has ye too frightened to speak the truth."

Kate's feet took root in her spot. *The Devil?* Nae. Och, God, nae! Fear and anger warred within her, stopping her from running out the door or charging through the curtain. It was Callum who killed her father! Her grandfather! He had lied to her. He was the Devil MacGregor! *He has never spared a Campbell's life.* Dear God, was Robert dead, as well? She swayed on her heavy feet, feeling ill, her breath growing tight. She had smiled at the murderer, likened him to a knight of old! Now his cold regard made perfect sense. He had no heart.

The curtain snapped open. Callum stood in the doorway. His expression bore the remnants of horror but hardened with each breath into a mask of barely contained control. His eyes blazed with fury, hatred, revenge. Kate took an involuntary step backward when he stormed across the rushes. It was easy to see now how he had gained such a worthy title.

"Devil," she whispered as he passed her, heading for the door.

His scorching gaze swung to her, halting her drumming heart. He moved toward her before she could run, and closed his fingers around her arm. Without a word, he dragged her back to the curtained doorway and then left her there gaping at the sight within. She heard his determined footfalls as he left the cottage. His coarse command for his men to await his return two leagues outside the village faded against the gurgled wheeze of a woman's breath and the mournful sobs of her sister as she applied more ointment to the charred flesh beneath her fingers.

Chapter Nine

KATE STARED SILENTLY into the growing flames, fed by Brodie's careful attendance. Vaguely, she was aware of Jamie covering her shoulders with a thick plaid of coarse wool. Sitting beside her, his dark eyes flickering against the firelight, Angus held out his pouch of brew to her. When she refused it, he tapped it against her arm.

"Drink. There's a deep chill in the air this night. The whiskey will keep ye warm."

Indeed, the cold seeped into her marrow, but the weather was not to blame. Callum was out here, somewhere, alone. Roderick Cameron had told her where Callum had gone. What he intended to do. She was not afraid for Callum's life, or for the lives of the men who had branded Rhona MacGregor's beautiful face. Nae, if their judgment was about to come upon them, it was a righteous one. The chill that iced her blood came from the memory of looking into their executioner's eyes. He was going to hunt them down. He would show them no mercy, for there was none in him to give.

He never left a Campbell alive. Her grandfather. All the men of Kildun's garrison.

Her father.

She looked up at Graham when he folded his legs and sat opposite her.

"Is my brother dead?" Her quavering voice shattered the silence around them.

Graham pulled off his cap, tucked it into his plaid, and raked a golden lock of hair out of his eyes. "Nae." He shook his head when Angus held up his pouch. But for the pop of a thin branch burning in the fire, quiet had once again descended on the campsite.

Please God, Kate wanted to believe him. If the Devil killed Robert, too, she would cut his throat while he slept.

"Is it only Campbells he kills?" she asked coolly.

Jamie shifted closer to the fire. Brodie spat into it and then lay down, closing his eyes for the night. Graham's gaze, though, never wavered from hers.

"Nae, lass. He kills friends of the Campbells, as well."

Kate's blood drained from her face at the indifference in the commander's voice. Her uncle deserved to be flogged for his part in Rhona MacGregor's branding, but how could life mean so little to these men? She knew she could never understand, for she cared even for the lives of her cattle. "Why? Why all the killing? I know our clans have been warring for centuries, but what is behind it all? A woman? What offense did my clan commit so long ago that cost my father his life and still brings such scorn to all your faces?"

No one answered her right away. Brodie opened his eyes and cast her a narrowed look before closing them again and shaking his head.

Graham poked a long stick into the embers, his handsome face growing pensive. "Would that this war was about a lass," he said. "Fer nae matter how fine she was, it would have ended before it ever touched Callum and Maggie." He caught a small piece of dried meat that Angus tossed him and took a bite. He chewed for a moment, then continued. "This war began three centuries ago. Callum was born with its purpose already flowing in his veins."

"Aye, I know of the battles," Kate told him. "But I don't understand what sort of men would fight them for so long?"

Graham's eyes glittered at hers across the firelight. "Men who are the sons of kings," he said, his words weighted with the measure of respect and affection he felt for them of whom he spoke. "Ye want the full tale of it, then?" When she nodded, he pulled in a deep breath and threw the remainder of the meat into the fire, as if the telling of it ruined his appetite. "The MacGregors are a royal race, descended from King MacAlpine. Their territories were once vast and held by the old ways—by right of sword. A fierce and mighty clan, they fought at the side of Robert the Bruce. But they were betrayed, and their land in Glen Orchy was given over to the Campbells, who had gained influence in the royal court." His voice was soft and deep, compelling even Brodie to sit up again and listen. "The MacGregors found themselves reduced to the position of tenants on the lands that were once theirs."

"Taken from us by cunnin' and devious schemes that continued until yer ancestors had gained it all," Angus added solemnly and produced another pouch from a heavy fold in his plaid.

"The MacGregors fought back, of course," Graham said. "Naturally, they directed their attacks against those who had wrested their land and their livestock from them. They were brutal and feared by all. They killed and slaughtered many until their oppressors were forced to obtain royal assistance in putting an end to the troublesome tribe. Given noble titles and the right to hunt their enemies with dogs, the Campbells and some others provoked the MacGregors into more acts of violence, and the formidable clan was only too happy to oblige."

"Driven from Glen Orchy, the MacGregor chiefs lived at Stronmelochan at the foot of Glenstrae," Brodie added. "While the Campbells expanded eastward into Breadalbane."

"Aye," Graham agreed. "'Twas up to the Glenstrae MacGregors to carry on the resistance, but their chiefs were hunted down and murdered, their sons along with them, and their land taken, also. When the Protestant parliament, many of whom are Campbells, declared it illegal to be a Catholic, many Highlanders joined the Gordon clan chieftain in his fight against the realm. But the chieftain was beheaded, and the clans who backed him were pursued with fire and sword."

"To this day, we are considered papist heretics," Jamie muttered quietly.

"After a particularly bloody battle at Glen Fruin, a half century ago, the clan was proscribed," Graham continued. "The name MacGregor, abolished. They are forbidden to bear it."

Kate nodded, knowing a little about their proscription

and what it meant. "All lieges are prohibited from bearing them aid," she said, repeating the creed she'd heard
her uncle say many times.

"Aye," Graham confirmed and then added, "They have
been stripped of every basic human need, including the
right to bear arms and the right to gather together in one
place. They are hunted, men, women, and children alike,
and their heads are used as pardon fer the most vicious of
crimes. Care of the aged and the sick is still refused to
them. Even the sacraments of baptism, marriage, and burial are denied. And yet the MacGregors remain, despite
everything."

They were to be forgotten.

Jamie tore a hunk of bread away from his loaf and offered it to Kate, breaking her thoughts. She'd known the
MacGregors were forbidden to bear their name, but she'd
believed they had forfeited that right by defying every decree set forth by the realm. She had no idea their proscription had stripped them of so much more. Did her kin truly
have so much to do with the annihilation of an entire
clan? It was difficult to believe. Why hadn't Amish or
John ever told her any of this? Mayhap they were afraid
of contradicting her uncle. They never judged the Mac-
Gregors, even knowing they killed her father. She closed
her eyes and inhaled, gathering the strength to ask her
next query and the courage to hear the reply.

"Is this why Callum killed my grandfather? What did
my father do to deserve his wrath?"

"I do not know anything about yer father, lass," Graham answered her and untied his belt, settling more comfortably into his plaid. "But Callum did not kill yer
grandfather."

"But everyone knows the Devil—"

"They know only what yer uncle believes to be true. Mayhap yer father and yer grandfather fought. We Highlanders know Colin Campbell did not agree with his father's tactics against the MacGregors. Mayhap he—"

Kate rose to her feet and held up her palm to stop him. She was not about to listen to such treachery against her father. "Has the Devil convinced you of this?"

"Nae," he said, never flinching at her challenge. "Callum does not pretend to know what happened. But he did not kill Liam Campbell."

"How do you know?" Kate demanded.

"I know because I was with Callum in Skye when he learned of yer grandfather's death. He near went mad again."

"Again?" Kate asked, barely able to breathe.

"Aye. The revenge was his to take. He earned it." Graham did not give the full meaning of his words time to seep in before he spoke again. "When Callum was a lad, yer grandfather and his army rode into his village and killed everyone in it, including the laird Dougal MacGregor and his wife. The chieftain, 'twas rumored, had begun a new rebellion and had been known to declare his name openly. Yer grandfather had them all slaughtered, save fer Dougal's young son and daughter. To them, he delivered a harsher punishment than death. Callum and his sister grew to maturity below the belly of Kildun Castle, where they paid fer their father's crime."

"Maggie was but five summers auld when they took her." Jamie's voice was low and riddled with anger Kate had not heard in it before.

She stared at him through a heavy haze of tears. She

wanted to shout at them all that what they told her was false. Her grandfather would never have done such a vile thing. Her father surely knew naught of it. He had children of his own! He would have done something. My God, *had* he done something? Did Colin Campbell kill his own father, mayhap in the heat of an argument? Nae! Never! She refused to believe any of it. She did not come from such merciless ilk. She wanted to tell Graham, but the sob poised behind her lips stopped her from opening her mouth. She willed her feet to move. She needed to be away from them, away from the contempt she saw in their eyes when they looked at her. Now she understood it better. She turned, ready to make her way to a tree closer to the shadows. But she stopped, unwilling to run away from them as her uncle had. What could she say to them? If all this was true, what could she possibly say?

"I am sorry for what my kin have done. I know it is not enough, but I would have you know it just the same."

Graham smiled, turning to watch her as she settled down for the night a few feet away from them. "That's the first Campbell who has ever apologized to a MacGregor."

"Aye." Brodie nodded, then smiled with him. Angus chuckled, thinking the apology was even more satisfying than his brew.

"Is it aright if I like her?" Jamie asked in all seriousness, and he knew that it was when the others burst into hearty laughter.

Chapter Ten

KATE WAS AWAKE when Callum returned to them early the next morn. How could she sleep when images of women's branded faces and children living out their lives in a dungeon invaded her every thought?

Quietly, she watched him dismount and look around, making certain they were all there, safe. His men still slept, rolled in their plaids, scattered around the dying embers of their campfire. When he saw her, he dropped his gaze to the ground, then turned to tie his reins to a nearby tree.

"Did you kill my father?" she asked him, needing to know the truth. Her grandfather may have deserved Callum's wrath, but her father did not.

"I never knew yer faither."

God, she needed to believe him. "Are you injured?" she asked, rising to go to him. Blood stained his plaid and smudged his jaw, but it was clearly not his own. For while his voice fell heavily on her ears, the unbending steel of his emotions remained.

"Dinna concern yerself with me, Kate," he answered before turning to leave, this time on foot into the trees.

She watched him go, and though she knew he had been victorious in his endeavors the night before, he walked with the weariness of a man defeated. Was he simply a heartless rebel, bent on killing Campbells because he felt they'd treated his clan unfairly? Or was the Devil a man with a greater cause? *Keeping our name alive and avenging the wrongs done to my kin.* She recalled his words at the Cameron holding. God's mercy, he fought to avenge too much. She picked up her steps and followed him, wanting, needing to know if her grandfather had truly kept him locked away in a dungeon when he was a child. And if so, how far would he go to right *that* wrong?

Coming upon him a few moments later, she studied him from between the tangle of branches that separated them. He stood naked and alone at the edge of a loch, its surface set aflame by the morning sun. His plaid and tunic, along with one crumpled boot, lay in a heap at his feet. His left boot flew over his shoulder and just missed Kate's head when she left the sanctuary of the trees, her gaze fastened on his bare back. Though every muscle that fashioned him was honed and defined by years of toil and battle, it was not the sheer beauty of him that drew her closer but the ugliness of long, jagged scars covering one end of his expansive shoulders to the other.

They were deep, angry imperfections carved into stone. The sight of them brought tears to Kate's eyes. How old was he when he had received them? Had it been her grandfather's hands that had produced them? In that moment, Callum MacGregor became more than an avenging warrior to her. He was a man who had lived through the merciless torture of a barbarian. His purpose was made even stronger by his pain.

Paralyzed by the poignant power before her, she watched him stalk into the sun-dappled current like Poseidon returning home from war. She had felt his body against hers, hard as granite. But never had she seen a naked man before, and never one so finely made. She did not blink as the water caressed his shapely calves, then rose upward to his thighs as he waded deeper into the loch. Mesmerized by his sheer masculine glory, her gaze continued up over the perfect roundness of his buttocks. Her mouth went dry, and her heart pounded so loud in her chest she feared he might hear it.

He tilted his face toward the sun. The splay of muscles in his upper arms rolled under his skin as he spread his arms at his sides, skimming his palms over the cool, satiny surface. It was then, while she stared almost longingly at the length of his fingers, that she noticed he had removed the leather cuffs that normally covered his wrists. She lifted her hands to her mouth to still a sob welling in her throat. Pocked skin, almost worn down to the bone, bore evidence of the irons that had held him captive.

"D'ye have somethin' ye wanted to speak to me aboot? Or were ye plannin' on just starin' at me while I bathed?"

Kate thought hard about running then. But it was too late; he was already turning around to face her. She was thankful, at least, that half his body was covered in water. That is, until his eyes found hers.

How could they chill her blood and sear her flesh at

the same time? They drew her in, inviting her onto a battlefield for which she had never practiced. Looking into them, she wondered what victory would gain her if she was braw enough to engage.

"Would ye care to join me?"

Her heart near beat right out of her mouth with the thought of it. She felt her face burn and almost turned away, but he seemed to be enjoying her discomposure. She suspected he was quite used to terrifying everyone around him. But she was not everyone.

Folding her arms across her chest, she forced herself to look him straight in the eye. "Nae, I would not care to join you. But I do appreciate the consideration you afford me by bathing. It would be better for us to speak when you are not covered in blood."

He said nothing but continued to trace the curves of her body with his bemused gaze. Kate thought he might be trying to provoke her anger. She was certain he had no idea how he was making her insides tremble.

"Well?" he asked after another moment passed with her staring at him.

She blinked. "Well what?"

"What is it ye want, besides me to look more appealin' fer ye?"

"I can assure you I care not how you look, MacGregor," Kate argued, irritated now that he had turned her meaning into something entirely different. "Were you beaten for your pride?"

He nodded, and though the slight humor hovering around his lips was arrogant indeed, Kate was dreadfully sorry for her words the moment she spoke them.

Finally she lowered her eyes. "I did not mean—"

"Speak yer mind, Kate Campbell," he drawled and lay back into water, exposing his sculpted chest to the sun. "If my scars please ye, then say it and let us be honest enemies."

Kate took a step forward. Her hand came to her chest. "Please me?"

He lifted his head to squint at her. "Aye."

"They horrify me!" She watched him paddle away from her on his back and was tempted to reach her hand out to bring him back. "Why didn't you tell me you were the Devil MacGregor?"

"Ye didna ask," he called back.

Oh, the man was completely insufferable. Kate looked around for a rock to fling at him while he swam farther away. "MacGregor," she called out. "Did my grandfather truly . . ." God, she couldn't bring herself to ask him, to even think of it. It didn't matter. He had no intention of answering her. She moved closer to the edge of the loch.

"Did you kill him for what he did to you?" She gritted her teeth when he continued to swim away. "I am trying to talk to you!" she shouted.

Still nothing.

"If you would just . . . MacGregor!" she called out louder while he drifted. "I believe you did not kill my father. Are we to remain enemies simply because of our names?"

"'Tis the only reason we need," he called back, sunning himself.

Kate's blood boiled. She was tired of hating him. Or trying to. And besides, if what Graham told her was true, her reasons to hate him were completely unjustified. But Callum's weren't. She took another step forward. She didn't want him to hate her, no matter what had been done to him. He was swimming farther away from her, and the more he swam, the angrier she became. She refused to fight with him ever again, and she was determined to prove it to him, even if it killed her. Before she could think clearly enough to stop herself, she unfastened her kirtle and kicked it away. She stepped into the loch and swam toward the belligerent chieftain in her shift and hose.

He heard her splashing behind him but did not bother to turn around, which infuriated Kate all the more. When she was close enough to reach out and touch him, a strange comfort washed over her. She had traveled in his embrace since the moment they met. His closeness was becoming familiar to her, enjoyable, safe.

"Why are you running away from me?" she asked, frowning at him, and at the dull pain beginning to throb in her shoulder.

He turned and opened his eyes to look at her. His long hair swept over his forehead, gleaming black down his shoulders. Droplets clung to his long lashes, giving more potency to his hard blue-green gaze. "I'm no' runnin', lass. I'm floatin'."

"Do I frighten you, then?" she charged, fueled by his nonchalance. For in truth, she knew she was the one who was afraid. Not of his strength that could overpower her so easily, but of her own maddening attraction to him.

"How could a wee thing like yerself frighten me?" He turned and swam away again.

Kate swatted the surface and gritted her teeth. "You're afraid of Campbells, then!"

It was definitely the wrong thing to say, she realized when he pivoted around and impaled her with his angry glare. He rose out of the water, looming over her and blocking out the sun. She had to fight to keep herself from withering in her spot. "Woman," he said very slowly, the word rumbling on that bear's voice. "I've crushed more Campbells than ye'll ever know, and I'll go to my grave with a Campbell's heart clutched within my fingers."

Kate tipped her head back. The intensity in his gaze held her still, but her heart roared within her chest. His face was so hard, so unforgiving. She wanted to look away, for she knew now the passion that burned within. How deeply was his hatred emblazoned on his heart? He'd had a lifetime to nurture it. He would die hating her. Nae. She did not want it to be so. She raised her eyes to the dark, damp strands of his hair falling around his shoulders, the faint trace of blood not completely washed away by the water. She should fear him, but there was more to him than anger and malevolence. She had sliced open his leg, and he had not sliced off her head in return. Even when she fired his fury, he had not put his hands to her. His eyes were sharp and hard, but sometimes, when he looked at her, his gaze grew tender, as if he could not sustain his resolve to hate her.

"Will that heart be mine, my laird?" she asked quietly.

"It might," he answered, pulling her gaze back to his.

"Nae." She shook her head. "If you hate me so much, why did you save me? I do not believe you would hurt me."

Callum wanted to mock this trust she so freely granted him. Trust that poured from her lips, from her eyes every time she set them on him. Trust he did not deserve. But instead, he found himself enraptured by it. "Ye dinna know anything aboot me." His voice rumbled like thunder, a low growl of warning, and something else . . .

"I know what people call you," she said. "But mayhap they are wrong. Mayhap you are more like Sir Gawain or Percivale than Satan."

Callum reached for her then and slid one arm around her waist. Drawing the lower half of his body flush against hers, he leaned toward her, his long, sable lashes swept downward. "Ye dinna know me, Kate." His velvet baritone was an erotic caress as seductive as the smirk that curled his lips when she struggled to free herself. "Or what I'm capable of doin'." Her flesh felt warm and soft beneath her wet shift, igniting a fire that blazed through his veins. He kept her still while he spread his palm over her belly, then upward, slowly, deliberately between her breasts and over her collarbone. Her lips parted on a sigh that mingled their breath even as she fought him. Hell, how easy it would be to take her. He lowered his head and covered her mouth with his. Her protests ended instantly, provoking him to taste her more fully. He swept his tongue inside her, then out again as he slanted his lips to take her at an even deeper angle. His kiss was fierce, possessive, his tongue probing, stroking her with sweet, hot, melting desire until she groaned and looped her arms around his neck.

When Callum felt her tongue flick against his, he grew hard against her. He could tear the thin barrier between them away and with one forceful surge impale her to the hilt. He wanted to show her that he was not the gentle man her eyes hoped for. He was no knight on a quest to save bonny damsels, though, by God, she was the most beautiful of them all. He could take her now, shatter her fanciful notions of him. God knew he could do it, for she tempted him beyond reason. But he knew the harsh reality of the world, and what would become of her if he took her. For her own good he had to keep her heart out of his hands.

He broke their kiss, letting his mouth hover over hers. "I am the MacGregor," he whispered on a growl that sounded harsh to his own ears. "The most feared enemy of yer clan. Dinna ferget it, Kate."

With every ounce of control he possessed, he released her and leaned back in the water. He was a murderer, aye, not a violator of women. "D'ye want to know why I saved ye?"

She shook her head no. But he saw the new spark of fear in her eyes even before he gave her his reason. He forced a thin smile. She deserved to know what a ruthless bastard he was, though at present he hated himself more than when he was Liam Campbell's prisoner. "Ye are more valuable to me alive than dead."

Kate's arm stung, along with her heart. She felt tears slowly rising to the rims of her lashes and grew angry with herself for letting him see the effect of his words.

"I want yer uncle's head," he continued, "and when he comes fer ye, I will take it with nae mercy—his and those of any others who come with him."

Kate's heart lurched. Terror washed over her, as frigid as the water beginning to numb her limbs. Her uncle had already proven her value to him when he fled against the McColls. He would not come for her. But her brother would. Robert would search for her. "You said Robert was your friend."

"Nae, I never said I was friend to any Campbell."

He was going to kill her brother! She had to do something. She could not allow Robert to die for her.

"I fear you've made a terrible error," she said, doing her best not to weep. It would do no good against his hardened heart. "My uncle will not come for me."

"Aye, he will." Slowly, Callum treaded toward her again. When he reached her, he lifted his fingers to a tear spilling down her cheek. "I know he will, because I would come fer ye." She broke away from his touch and swam back to the shore. He watched her snatch her kirtle from the ground and then flee, satisfied that he crushed any hope she had placed in him.

"Aye, Kate, if ye were mine and someone took ye, I would follow him to the ends of the Earth until I got ye back."

Chapter Eleven

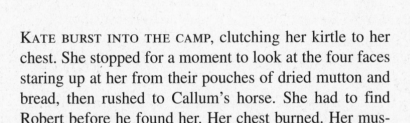

KATE BURST INTO THE CAMP, clutching her kirtle to her chest. She stopped for a moment to look at the four faces staring up at her from their pouches of dried mutton and bread, then rushed to Callum's horse. She had to find Robert before he found her. Her chest burned. Her muscles felt frozen, save for the throbbing in her arm. She tried to pull herself up into the saddle, but a bolt of pain shot through her and almost made her retch.

A large pair of hands caught her by the waist and steadied her.

"Now, where do ye think ye're going, lass?" When Graham turned Kate around to have a look at her, his expression changed to concern. "Hell, yer wound is bleeding. What in blazes did ye do?"

"She looks like she had a bath," Angus offered, coming up behind Graham to see what the fuss was about.

"Did Callum toss ye into the water, then?" Jamie passed the others and rushed to her side.

"Jamie, why the hell would he toss her into the water,

ye lackwit?" Brodie smacked the younger warrior on the side of the head, hoping to knock some sense into him.

Jamie glared at him. "Because she's a Campbell, why else?"

Kate shook Graham to gain his attention from the others. "You knew I was bait to bring my uncle to Callum. I must go to Kildun!" Her teeth began to chatter, and Jamie near barreled over Brodie to retrieve a plaid from the ground to cover her.

"We cannot let ye do that, lass," Graham said gently.

"But he is a loathsome coward," she argued, trying desperately to make them understand. "My brother will be the one to die!" She leaned against Callum's horse when another wave of pain washed over her.

"Who is a loathsome coward?" Jamie asked, thoroughly confused.

"Callum is," Brodie answered.

Jamie's shoulders straightened. "I take offense to that."

Angus snickered, then guzzled some brew from another pouch he had hidden beneath his plaid.

"Kate." She heard Graham speak her name. She dabbed her head with the back of her hand, wondering when the air had turned so warm. "Yer wound has opened, lass."

"Hell, she's bleedin' all over m' plaid," Brodie complained, sincerely upset.

Angus belched, then swiped his hand across his mouth. "Since when d'ye mind someone else's blood on yer plaid?"

"Please!" Kate shouted at the men. "You do not understand. My brother . . . he will look for me. You must let me go! I will not let him die because of me!"

Callum was securing his plaid over his shoulder when he stepped out from within the trees. He stopped as her plea reached him and pierced him like an arrow. He'd meant to frighten her, to open her eyes to the truth, but her desperation to save her brother's life was too familiar to his own. Despite the darkness that consumed him, he clung to one love. That of his sister. He defied the law in honor of his name, but he had given up his soul in exchange for Maggie's life. He would not force Kate to do the same. He was glad he had listened to Graham and not killed Robert Campbell.

Callum called her name. She turned, along with the others, as he picked up his steps again and moved slowly toward her.

"I willna harm yer brother." Aye, 'twas his voice he heard promising to spare the young Campbell's life yet again. His voice that sounded uncommonly gentle to his ears. "I willna kill him. I swear it," he repeated, reaching her.

"Even if he comes to fight you?" Kate questioned, needing to be certain.

"I vow he will walk away unscathed." His gaze dropped to the blood seeping through her shift. "Come." He pressed his hand to hers, thankful that she did not pull away. Her confidence in his word produced a warm smile he could not resist giving her. "Yer wound needs tendin'."

Her expression went from appreciative to terrified in an instant. "You will not attempt to burn it, will you?"

Callum bit down on his words. He would not lie to her. He closed his fingers around hers instead. "I'll no' do anything that'll pain ye overmuch."

He turned to Angus. "Give me yer brew."

The hulking warrior gaped at him. "All of it?"

A seething glare from his laird stilled the remainder of Angus's protests, and he handed the pouch over.

Callum cut a quick glance to Graham next. The commander nodded, knowing what needed to be done. He pulled a small dagger from his belt and headed for the cooled campfire, motioning for Jamie to gather more leaves.

"She needs to come oot o' her undergarment. She'll catch a wicked fever soaked through like that," Brodie muttered with a tight smirk when Callum walked past him.

His cousin spoke true. She needed to change into her dry kirtle before she was unable to do it herself. Of course, Callum was not opposed to undressing her. But his control was already on the brink of shattering from just looking at her in her wet shift, her dark waves clinging to her fluid curves.

"I would know what you mean to do," Kate demanded weakly while he led her toward the trees.

He knew exactly what she meant. She was worried about how he was going to tend to her arm. He did not think it wise to tell her just yet. Best to keep her mind off the blade, mayhap even rile her a bit. "I mean to offer ye the privacy ye denied me while ye get oot of that shift."

"You did not seem too bothered by my watching," Kate couldn't help but parry, as ill as she felt.

"Aye," he conceded with a long, repentant sigh while he placed her behind the nearest tree. "Devils have nae honor."

"But knights who offer a lady her privacy do."

He stared after her, unable to look away as he had promised. Knights. He almost laughed. What did he know of them? Those noble heroes who brandished their swords against injustice. His blade was stained only with vengeance. The lass was daft. But hell, he felt more human around her. More like a man than a monster.

"You're looking!" Kate shrieked at him from her hiding place.

Grinding his jaw, he turned swiftly away. He was enjoying very manly thoughts when she came up behind him a few moments later and tapped him on the shoulder. He turned and looked down at her pale face with the residue of longing still heavy in his gaze.

"Drink this. It'll keep ye warm." He pushed Angus's pouch between them before he was tempted to drag her into his embrace and do the like himself.

She accepted the whiskey and drank. Immediately a crimson blush streaked across her cheeks, just before the color changed to a greenish hue.

"Ye've fergotten to apply yer ointment," he stated firmly, taking hold of her shoulder.

"I—och hell . . ." She squeezed her eyes shut and trembled all the way down to her toes. "I could not apply it to my back." She swayed on her feet, but Callum caught her and sat her down gently on the ground.

He eased her kirtle off her shoulder with careful fingers. "'Tis no' so bad," he said, squatting over her and examining the wound. When she tried to look, he cupped her hand in his and brought the pouch to her lips for another drink. When he returned to his ministrations, his hands shook and he cursed himself. He'd tended to hundreds of wounds to keep his men alive. This was no different. But it was. Kate's skin was cool silk, milky white, and no matter how hard he tried, his littlest finger kept brushing against the swell of her breast while he tried as gently as he could to remove the packing Mae Stewart had used on her.

Kate remained still until she saw Graham approaching with a glowing dagger pointing straight at her. "Nae!" She struggled to gain her feet, but Callum's hold on her remained firm.

He lowered his lips to her ear, closing his eyes when her intoxicating scent wafted through his nostrils. "Come, Katie lass," he whispered. "Ye have faced doun the Devil. Ye willna turn Campbell on me now, will ye?"

She clutched fistfuls of his plaid and smothered her face into his chest when Graham came closer. "Do not burn me!"

Warding off Graham momentarily, Callum held her, knowing firsthand how badly this was going to hurt. "Another drink, Kate. It needs be done. I willna have ye die on me."

"Aye, I'm of more value to you alive." She pushed away from him, glared at Graham, then squeezed her eyes shut.

She did not remember Graham leaving, or if she screamed. Just Callum's arm around her, cradling her while he sealed her wound shut with Graham's blade. She was certain he asked her forgiveness a time or two while the hot metal seared her flesh. She was also acutely aware of the warmth of his muscles and the controlled strength he used to hold her still. So close, she took in the angle of his jaw tightening beneath a dark dusting of facial hair. His mouth, so firm and decadently shaped.

"You kissed me in the water."

"Aye."

"Think you might ever do it again?"

He stopped tending to her arm and looked down into her drowsy gaze, wanting to kiss her now. "I'm afraid I might."

"Will you make certain you are dressed next time?"

Her words were slurred enough to make Callum smile as he went about finishing his task. "If I must."

"You really should smile more."

When his brilliant blue eyes settled on hers again, she tried to show him how it was done, slanting her lips just before she belched loudly enough to rival Angus on his drunkest day.

"There, you see? Just like that." Her eyelids drifted closed, but she fought to stay awake. "Aye, you are quite a handsome man when you smile. Though you are handsome when you frown, as well, Clalum MacKreglor. Damn it, that hurts." She cried out softly when he poured some of Angus's brew over her shoulder, as she had done to his leg.

"I'm done, Kate." Tenderly, he adjusted her kirtle so that the fabric did not touch her flesh. His fingers grazed her face and then paused when she moved closer to his touch.

"Thank you for not killing my brother."

Callum did not move his hand away but stroked her temple with the backs of his fingers.

She opened her eyes, addling him thoroughly. "I see two of you." She smiled again but then grew serious.

"Clalum?"

"Aye, lass?"

"If you did not kill my father, then who did?"

Chapter Twelve

KATE WOKE UP many hours later, propped against Callum's chest while he kept his horse at a slow pace and his arms closed loosely around her. Her head ached from front to back. The bouncing up and down did not help, and she silently cursed his horse and every other horse in creation while they trotted along a rocky incline. She was trying to find a more comfortable position when she remembered that her knight was her captor and she was nothing more to him than bait to catch a jackal. She tried to sit up, but her head felt like it was going to teeter off her shoulders and career to the ground.

"How do ye fare, Kate?"

The deep voice behind her ears boomed through her head and made her cringe.

"Must you shout?"

"I'm whisperin'."

"Do not whisper so loudly, then," she groaned. "I feel like I'm dying."

Behind her, Callum nodded sympathetically, familiar

with the agonizing aftereffects of Gillis's brew. He laid his hand on top of her head and eased her back against his chest. "Just be still."

Kate knew he did not like her, but once again, he was comforting her. His hand, one that had killed more Campbells than she cared to ponder, was so achingly gentle when he touched her that it almost made her doubt the conviction of his hatred. She did as her captor ordered and leaned against him, squinting in the daylight at the land around her.

Slopes were fast becoming mountains that rose like great granite curtains around her. When she inhaled, her nostrils tingled. The air was getting thinner. She had never traveled outside of Glen Orchy before, and she began to realize just how much she had missed. The Highlands were an uncharted place, vast and wild with untouched foliage and men who hid atop jagged cliffs, unseen in the mist. It was an untamed land of bursting color. The heather grew here in lush splendor, decorating the braes in rich purple majesty. But there was something more. 'Twas gray. The color of strength. An endless line of mountains rose boldly toward a vast blue sky that hovered so close one would wager his best horse that he merely need lift his hand to the sky to touch it. It was as if the very heavens descended upon this land. Kate decided the Highlands were the most breathtaking, soul-stirring place in creation.

Somewhere overhead, a hawk released a cry that echoed for leagues through deep glens and over rolling moorlands. Kate closed her eyes and snuggled deeper into Callum's body.

Hard, tight muscles caressed her back. The weight of

his shoulders slowly relaxed over hers, enfolding her. Thighs nestled and caressed her now instead of feeling like stones against her hips.

Callum sighed when Kate let out a wee snore under his chin. He had always considered himself hard, not pillow soft or cushioned with clouds. But hell, he was fast becoming this woman's bed! She was a Campbell. And a nuisance. He tightened his arm around her and stroked her belly with the pad of his thumb. Acts of both protection and possession, he realized, praying for God to grant him strength to keep his wits about him. Protecting her was one thing, but possessing her would be deadly. Deadly for them both. Still, when the wind blew her curls against his face, he closed his eyes and inhaled. He had always thought nothing in the world could ever smell better than the Highlands. He was wrong.

He accepted a wedge of cheese from Brodie, who rode up beside him. They chewed in silence for a few moments before Callum turned toward him. "Brodie, stop starin' at me and speak yer mind."

Brodie shrugged his shoulders and tossed back the strands of dark hair that fell over his eyes. "I was just thinkin' how even-tempered ye have become since takin' the lass." He let his eyes rove over her form. "'Tis plain to see that she pleases ye," he continued, even though Callum glared at him. "I was wantin' to know if ye are thinkin' o' claimin' her."

"I'll claim nae Campbell," Callum answered him, tight-lipped.

"She fancies ye, laird," Brodie went on. "Listen how she purrs like a kitten all wrapped up in yer arms." The way Callum tightened his hold on her did not go unnoticed by Brodie. "Have ye no' considered a way to torture the Earl of Argyll before killin' him?"

"Nae, but I'm sure ye have thought of naught else," Callum replied. Brodie was a most ruthless warrior, loyal in battle, but a bit overly bloodthirsty.

"The lass." Brodie smiled, pointing his chin at her.

"What aboot her?"

"Bed her, and bed her thoroughly. What could be worse fer The Campbell than to have a MacGregor growin' in his niece's belly?"

Callum went still on his mount. He hadn't thought of anything but bedding her for the past se'nnight. 'Twas true, 'twould be satisfying to tell Argyll that MacGregor seed grew in his niece, before Callum killed him. And if he took her to his bed, there would be no marriage between her and the English lord of Newbury. Aye, that thought pleased him well enough. But there was something more to consider.

"And what would become of her when she's returned to her brother carryin' my bairn? Ye saw what was done to Rhona MacGregor just fer bearin' our name."

"Aye, there is nae mercy fer sympathizers," Brodie agreed quietly, then eyed Kate pressed so intimately against his laird. "Mayhap, then, 'tis best ye dinna give her back. Fer I fear it may be too late."

~

Since she had slept most of the day, Kate was wide awake when Callum and his men settled into their plaids that night. Lying down was fruitless. She blamed the stars for keeping her eyes open, the sound of the leaves rustling for keeping her ears alert. But it was the man sleeping across the campfire who made her heart feel restless. No matter how she tried, she could not stop thinking about his kiss. Lord, but he was dangerous. She hadn't been able to move in his iron embrace while he touched her so intimately, as if he owned her. And then she didn't want him to let her go. He'd ravished her, all right, but she couldn't seem to muster even the slightest bit of anger over it. His mouth took her with ruthless mastery. His hot tongue sliding over hers made her so weak and willing, it frightened her thinking how far she would have let him go had he not stopped on his own.

God's mercy, he had warned her twice to remember who he was, and she needed to do just that. It was one thing to liken Callum to a champion of his people—for saving her from death—but caring for any MacGregor was considered treason. And the Devil was the most forbidden of them all. She sat up, cursing her wakefulness under her breath, and turned toward the sleeping laird.

Callum was not sleeping but sat propped against a tree, his legs outstretched before him and crossed at the ankles, his eyes on her.

She cast him a diffident smile. "Sleep eludes me."

He did not move, but his expression appeared to soften beyond the glimmering firelight.

He was a stranger to her, and yet the chill of midnight tempted Kate to move closer to the familiar warmth of his body. She drew in an uneven breath instead. "I fear I will never sleep at night again if I keep sleeping in the day."

"A burden, to be sure," he agreed, his voice light and teasing. "But if the restive sparkle in yer eyes tells the tale true, 'tis one less troublesome than the one I will be sufferin' again on the morrow."

Kate's eyes flashed at him, and a hint of a smile etched her lips to match his. "Suffering indeed. If you had to endure the tedium of traveling with an insolent ogre day after day, you, too, would bless unconsciousness when it came to claim you."

His eyebrows rose with surprise, but instead of scowling at her as she expected, he grinned and set her heart to pounding. "Have ye always been so braw, Kate Campbell?"

"Nae," she assured him. She tucked her legs beneath her and turned her gaze to the flames. "When I was a child I was very much afraid of thunder. The ground rumbled much the same way when the Highlanders raided. But Robert always promised to protect me. He was quite gallant, even as a boy." She smiled, remembering. "My father often mused that my mother should have named her son Galahad."

"One of King Arthur's knights who fought against the Picts."

Kate slanted her gaze at him. "You know of them?"

Callum nodded, "Graham once spoke of them. Men whose armor shone with the radiance of righteousness."

"Aye." Kate met his steady gaze. "They believed in what they fought for. Robert used to tell me it is not the victory but why a man fights the battle which makes him a hero."

Callum regarded her in silence. A play of the light across her eyes it was not: he saw himself, and who he might have been, in their shimmering reflection. He cast his glance downward. "I have naught in common with such men. 'Tis late." He folded his arms across his chest and closed his eyes. "One of us needs to sleep, else we'll ride my horse into a tree."

Kate lay back down and stared up at the treetops. A moment of silence passed before she broke it again. "Robert used to tell me tales when I could not sleep."

"I am no' yer brother."

She sighed and turned to her side to find a more comfortable position, then . . .

"My faither was a hero. He led the *Griogaraich* against his enemies with Hamish Grant at his side fer many years before he was killed. When we were lads, Graham and I once . . ."

Kate closed her eyes and let the sound of his rich, lilting voice carry her away to her dreams.

Chapter Thirteen

WHEN THEY STOPPED at an inn two nights later, Kate was so deliriously happy at the thought of sleeping in a bed, she didn't notice the possessive way Callum kept his fingers clenched around her wrist after they dismounted.

Callum had agreed to stop here because they were at the edge of MacDonnell country, and though none were permitted to aid the MacGregors, most Highlanders did. His men could use a hot meal, and mayhap if Kate slept in a bed this night, she would cease falling asleep in his arms. Every time she pressed her cheek against his chest, as if she belonged there—or when she looked into his eyes like he was her champion—she tempted him to forget all he lost in her grandfather's dungeon and imagine that something new and wonderful was still possible in his life. Hell, he was going daft, and the dulcet sound of her breath, the achingly sweet comfort she found in his embrace were to blame. He had to find a horse for her to ride and get her out of his arms. And fast.

But this night he kept her close to him because even

though the innkeeper, Ferguson MacDonnell, was his friend, the price on a MacGregor head was too high for some to resist. And since Kate traveled with him, she was considered his. Her life, forfeit.

He could have entered the inn with caution, but if there were enemies inside, their fear of him would keep Kate alive. So, feeding what they knew of The Devil, he brandished his sword and kicked open the door. He stood beneath the entryway like a wraith freed upon the swirling mist. The inn grew silent while he raked his powerful gaze over every face, warning death swift yet painful should any come against him.

Angus let out a loud belch, stepped around his laird, and entered the inn first. He sauntered over to a large trestle table where a group of ruffians sat, their cups paused in midair at their lips. He hovered over them with dark, bloodshot eyes. "What ails ye, ye bunch o' sorry knaves? Have ye never seen a MacGregor before?"

"Aye, we have," said the leader of the group. "But none as ugly as you, Angus MacGregor."

"Archie MacPherson, I thought ye were dead." Angus laughed and grabbed hold of the man's forearm to haul him out of his seat and into his arms. " 'Tis good to see ye, old friend."

Flanked on all sides by Callum and the rest of his men, Kate watched, relieved that the men were not enemies, for one would have to be a fool to cross the mighty brutes surrounding her. She was also surprised to find more friends of the MacGregors. It pleased and comforted her to know they were not hunted everywhere.

Now that the threat of bloodshed was over, she relaxed and took in the sights around her. The inn was more like a tavern, with rooms above stairs to accommodate patrons and the wenches who served them with coy giggles on their lips. The scent of ale and sweet wine flooded Kate's lungs and made her gag at first, but then, oddly enough, the place began to smell cozy.

"M'laird, welcome," a small man with a bulbous nose and thick, unruly red hair greeted when he reached them. He turned his pale green eyes on Kate, giving her a hungry looking over that made her shift closer to Callum.

His response was to toss his arm around her and drag her to him. "MacDonnell." Callum's voice was an octave above a growl. "If ye dinna quit starin' at her, I'll be forced to stop ye myself."

The innkeeper's eyes darted back to Callum. "My apologies," he said, offering a swift, repentant smile. "I didna mean . . . I'll have me Robena prepare a room fer ye right away."

"That will be two rooms, innkeeper," Kate corrected him as he turned to find his wife.

"My apologies again," MacDonnell offered her, then glanced back at Callum. "I thought she was yers."

"Nae," Callum said then tugged her back to him when she tried to pull away. "But we'll be needin' only one room."

"I am not staying in the . . ." Kate's vehement refusal faded from her lips when Callum set his cool cobalt gaze on her. She felt like she'd been hit with a large stone. She cursed herself and squared her shoulders. It astounded her that she could battle a whole legion of sword-swinging McColls but one look from this man could set her heart to racing.

"Is she under yer protection, then?" MacDonnell asked, unsure of what to do.

Callum nodded. "Aye, she is."

To be used as bait, Kate corrected him silently. His ransom until he had her uncle. She said nothing in front of the innkeeper, but she planned on setting Callum Mac-Gregor straight the moment they were alone.

Which was about to be any moment. Kate swallowed audibly when Callum clutched her hand and pulled her toward the stairs.

"Make certain you request extra bedding from your friend the innkeeper," she demanded on the way up. "I wish him to know that you will be sleeping on the floor and not in the same bed with me. I am not a trollop."

Callum ignored her. When he reached the room, he flung the door open and stepped inside, leaving her to follow.

Kate glowered at his lack of chivalry and stepped past him to survey the small room. As she had suspected, there was only one bed. Callum knew his way around the inn, that much was obvious. She eyed the old fur blanket on the bed and wondered how many times he had tumbled a maid upon it. The thought of it brought heat rushing to her face and a sharp prick of anger to her heart.

"I'll have Ferguson's wife bring ye somethin' to eat."

"And where will you be?" Kate asked, turning to him.

"Below stairs, sharin' a drink with my men."

Her brow rose sharply. Of course, he didn't want her around while he guzzled his brew and dragged any number of willing wenches to his lap. Well, she certainly was not about to spoil his eve. Let him bed them all, what did she care?

"I dinna want ye—"

"Och, I know perfectly well what you want," she accused him. "Just do not bring your women back here with you. The door will be barred."

His only answer was a slow smile that dared her to do it. "Dinna leave this room," he warned as he left, shutting the door behind him.

Kate stared at the door, and then snapped her mouth shut. Did he truly believe he could order her about because she was his captive? He was a fool if he did. And an even bigger fool to believe she would obey him.

An hour later, seated at a long table with his men, Callum lifted a tankard of ale to his lips. Many of the inn's patrons had retired above stairs, but the tavern was still crowded enough for Callum to almost miss Kate's entrance. Graham sat beside him, telling him about a wench he planned on meeting later that night, but Callum did not hear a word, so arrested was he by the sight of Kate standing in the doorway. A snood of dyed ruby ribbon was fastened beneath her hair and tied in a bow on top. Long, lustrous blue-black curls fell down her back, almost to her waist. She wore a kirtle of indigo wool, given to her, no doubt, by Ferguson's wife. A shawl of deep ruby draped her shoulders. It was not the sight of her drawing her full lower lip between her teeth when she could not find her captors, or even her wide, searching eyes, that made his heart pause, but the stubborn tilt of her chin when her gaze finally found his. She knew he would be angry that she had defied him, but she was not afraid. Damn him, but her fearlessness pleased him.

"Saints, she's breathtaking," Callum heard Graham say. Callum nodded as he stared at her with helpless admiration. She was the stark beauty of a winter night shrouded in the soft crimson of the setting sun.

He swallowed hard, and then his expression hardened, as well. Hell! Any one of these rogue patrons would think naught of causing her harm. Did she not understand his clan was outlawed, that the MacGregors were considered lower than slaves to many Scots? It did not matter that she looked more bonny than ever before; she was a daft fool who would get them all killed.

He almost knocked his chair over when he stood up as she made her way toward his table. She paused for a moment seeing his fierce scowl but then squared her shoulders and continued on. Jamie reached her before she reached the table and snatched her arm to escort her safely to the bench.

Kate sat directly across from the glowering laird, which earned her another deep-throated grumble. She toyed with the idea of commenting on his constant sour mood, but he looked about ready to leap over the table and throttle her, so she simply smiled at him instead, though it took enormous effort.

"Good eve, my laird."

"Return to yer room, Kate," he warned in a quiet, menacing tone.

"I cannot," she replied sweetly. "I am hungry. Dear Robena went to so much bother bathing and dressing me, I felt it unkind to ask her to feed me, as well. I would much rather dine here, with you."

Callum considered dragging her back above stairs, but doing so would most likely cause a brawl. He looked around at the patrons, his jaw tightening. Many of the men were already staring at her. They looked away when they caught his murderous gaze.

"Verra well," he conceded, motioning to a serving wench before returning his gaze to Kate. "Eat, and be quick aboot it."

"I hope I didn't spoil your merriment for the eve." Kate offered him a cheeky smile that said the opposite, then glanced up at the buxom blonde laying a trencher of steaming mutton stew before her. When the wench threw herself into Graham's lap and not Callum's, Kate didn't know whether to feel relieved or angry with herself for being possessive of him. That's why she'd defied him and came down here, wasn't it? She hated the thought of him enjoying his evening with a pretty wench. But it was clear Callum MacGregor did not allow himself much merriment.

"Just eat and dinna concern yerself with me." Callum tore at his bread and shoved it into his mouth, seeming to forget about her.

"Very well." Kate fought the urge to fling her trencher at him. She may have been wrong about him wanting a wench with his supper, but he was a callous bastard nonetheless. She decided not to spare him another thought. Heavens, she was starving! She lowered her head to inhale the delicious aromas of her supper. When a loud belch exploded through Angus's lips, she lifted her thick lashes from her food.

"What a perfect tribute to so fine a meal, Angus."

The burly brute roared with laughter, but it was the sound of Kate's mirth that made Callum lift his gaze to her once again. He stared at the slender curve of her jaw, the soft crinkle of her nose when she laughed. He felt entranced by the way her eyes danced. For a moment, he relished the sound of her joy. She made him think of hope. She made him want things he never thought about wanting before. It had taken him years to build Camlochlin. 'Twas his fortress, his sanctuary, second in his heart only to his name. 'Twas all he had and all he ever wanted, hoping for nothing more because he'd probably be dead in a few years. And he did not mind dying, so long as it was on his terms and not the Campbells', and with bravery in battle. He had never considered having a family, though he would like to have sons to carry on the MacGregor name. He had never hoped to listen to the music of a woman's tinkling laughter echoing off the steep mountain walls, satisfied in knowing 'twas he who gave her joy. He would not hope for it now.

"To Brodie." Angus raised his tankard, breaking Callum's thoughts, "May the bairn his lovely wife Netta carries fer him look like its mother and not Graham."

Graham tossed Brodie a smug wink, which Brodie answered by punching him in the arm. Soon the merriment around them grew. The men swore oaths that would have made any other woman at the table blush and rebuke them. But, damn her, she continued to laugh, addling Callum's brain thoroughly. Callum did not join in the song, nor in the raucous laughter that followed. He was, for the time being, content to sit and study Kate—when she wasn't looking at him.

He watched her so closely he did not notice the man approaching their table from behind her. No one noticed him until he slammed a coin down directly in front of her. Laughter stopped abruptly, and every eye rose to meet those of the stranger, including Callum's.

"Ye have had her long enough," the knave announced to Callum. "And ye've done naught but gape at her like a fresh-faced whelp. Now I want her."

The only sign of Callum's fury was the slight clenching of his jaw. No other muscle moved. "Take yer coin and leave before 'tis too late to do so." His voice was nothing more than a low growl. Kate found herself unable to take her eyes off him.

"Tonight I'll have a MacGregor bitch in my bed," the man behind her mocked.

Everything happened so quickly in the instant that followed, Kate had no time to react. The stranger's hand clamped on her sore shoulder, making her cry out as he hauled her to her feet. Callum stood up simultaneously, seeming to defy time as he drew his massive sword. He whirled it over his head and brought it down with such force it smashed into splinters the thick wooden table that separated him from the stranger, sending food and drinks crashing to the floor. Callum leaped over the cleaved wood and held the point of his blade against the man's throat. His calm expression had dissolved into a storm of black rage.

"Think well aboot yer next breath. It'll be yer last."

Silence descended upon the tavern, every eye pinned to the man still gripping Kate. Every eye, that is, but Kate's. Try as she might, she could not tear her gaze away from Callum MacGregor. He seemed to have grown five more inches in height. The breadth of his shoulders cast dark shadows over her and her would-be attacker. As she gazed up at him, her breath went still by the power and steady strength of his arm, the promise of destruction in his piercing glare. She knew why this man had never been caught.

"Ease yer sword, MacGregor. Ease yer sword." The stranger released Kate and took a step back. He was three shades paler than when he first arrived at the table. His Adam's apple danced, swallowing an audible gulp the moment his throat was clear of Callum's blade. Brodie crunched into a juicy pear. The sound propelled the man to turn and run. Before Callum could sheathe his weapon, the stranger was gone.

Kate blinked. A hand clasped her wrist tightly. It took a moment for her to realize it was Callum who held her, and when she did, she opened her mouth to speak.

"Bid good eve to my men," he ordered, cutting her off. Then, before she could do as he commanded, he dragged her toward the stairs.

"Let me go!" She tried to pull her hand away from him, but she didn't even slow his pace.

"That's twice I saved yer life." Callum said tightly without turning to face her. "Dinna give me yer cheek."

When he reached the room, he shoved the door open and fair flung her inside, then slammed the door shut behind them.

Kate rounded on him, her eyes sparked with fury. "You will tell me what I've done to cause your wrath against me! And do not tell me it's because I'm a Campbell. I did nothing to you!"

Callum stared at her when she shouted at him. A battle played across his features. He didn't know whether he wanted to throttle her or drag her into his arms, grateful that he was here tonight to save her. Anger lit his eyes like lightning and his jaw clenched with fury, but when he opened his mouth to tell her, he found that he had no words. He turned and stormed toward the window. When he reached it, he whirled on his heel again and raked his gaze boldly over her.

Kate went still. He was touching her. The longing in his eyes shocked her and made her tremble. Never in her life had she felt such a maze of emotions. She was angry with him, and she wanted to run into his arms so badly her legs almost ached with the need. She knew he would not turn her away again. For while his expression was hard, his eyes gleamed with warmth and the promise of complete possession. He wanted her. A flame ignited somewhere in her belly at the thought. God help her, but he was so terribly handsome standing there heaving like a dark dragon on the verge of plundering a village.

"Callum." She whispered his name, breaking the silence that seemed to stretch on endlessly. "I don't want to be your enemy anymore. I . . ."

If her plea softened him at all, he made no show of it. His expression was no more forgiving than it had been a moment before. "D'ye no' understand that my clan has been proscribed?"

"I thought we were safe here," she tried to explain, but her words faded when he took a step closer to her.

"We? Yer no' a MacGregor. Ye dinna know what it means to be one, or the dangers of being a friend to one."

"Aye, I do," she assured him, understanding now why he'd demanded she stay in the room. He had tried to protect her. "No one may aid you—"

"Upon death or branding!" Callum's voice erupted into a roar.

Kate turned away. She had to. He was telling her that

they could not even be friends, and just looking at him made her want more than that. God, protect her neck from the gallows, she wanted so much more.

"We have been declared worthless, nonhuman. A price has been placed on the heads of our men, women, and children! Our lands are free to any taker."

Tears gathered over the rims of Kate's eyes as she understood fully the depth of his pride and the reason for it. "It is as if you no longer exist." She brought her gaze back to his. "You feel forsaken, even by God. Callum, I do understand. And I am so sorry."

"I dinna want yer pity," he said, cursing himself inwardly. He should rebuke her, shake her, push her away until she was so afraid of him her fear and hatred destroyed whatever else she felt. "I'll no' allow ye to shed tears fer my clan. Ye dinna understand the danger in it."

She did understand, but at that moment she didn't care. God's mercy, she doubted even Robert would forgive her for siding with The Devil, but she wanted Callum to kiss her again. She didn't want their names to matter anymore. She wanted to touch him and forget laws and proscriptions. But could he ever forget his past and what her family had done to him?

She was sure he could hear her heart pounding. She wanted to tell him how she felt, but her mind had ceased to think of anything save the sheer size of him, the smell of sweat and fury lingering about his flesh, and the longing in his eyes for something unattainable.

He moved toward her, but a knock at the door made him pause and ushered a low growl from his throat.

Kate did not turn to follow his path to the door but closed her eyes instead and chewed her lower lip. She listened while he argued with Ferguson MacDonnell about payment for the table he had smashed. Then she near leaped out of her flesh when the door slammed shut again.

She could feel his eyes on her. Hard, dangerous eyes that had sworn vengeance upon her entire clan. Hot, burning eyes that ached with hunger for her.

"Take the bed," he snapped.

Turning to him, Kate scowled, frustrated by his deep conviction to despise her no matter how hard she tried to make him like her. "You make it difficult to ignore the true reason you saved my life."

His expression on her hardened, as if she'd just given him a great insult. "I would no' have let ye die, even if I killed yer uncle."

Kate was relieved to hear him say it. She was right about him all along. But . . . "Sometimes it's difficult to believe you care for my safety when you continue to look at me as if I were your worst enemy."

"Lass," he said, and the silken depth of raw desire in his voice made her stagger. "If I cared naught fer yer safety, ye would no' be standing there."

Kate's nostrils flared as she folded her hands into fists at her sides. "Where would I be, then?"

"Ye would be spread across that bed, beneath me."

Kate's face burned at the thought. In fact, she felt as if her entire body was about to go up in flames. "Your threats are empty," she challenged, refusing to believe he would force himself on her. "As would be your eye sockets if you dared touch me uninvited."

He actually chuckled, mocking her warning as he crossed the room.

She backed away when the distance between them shortened. "Besides," she said, hastily employing a different tactic to ensure that he remained chivalrous. "You would be making *love* to a *Campbell*."

He walked past her, a slight slant of his lips making her palms moisten and her knees go soft. "Nae, I would merely be havin' my way with one, which in our case would be just as dangerous."

Kate said nothing more but climbed into the bed fully clothed. She pulled the coverlet up to her chin and watched him settle down beside the hearth for the night.

Soft firelight danced along the walls. The room was silent save for the crackle of firewood being devoured by flames, along with Callum's crude promise drumming in her head. Fate was cruel to have cast her into the care of such a cold man, and crueler still because she liked the brute. He despised her, making it perfectly clear that his desire for her was naught more than pure lust in its most basic form.

"You've nae more need to treat me cruelly, MacGregor," she spoke softly in the darkness. "I will do my best to remember who you are from this night on."

There was a movement from where Callum lay on the floor, and then, like a mad war god rising from the bowels of the Earth, he rose to his feet and stormed out the door.

Chapter Fourteen

KATE ROAMED THE DIM HALLS of the inn, praying that no male patrons were lurking about looking for a wench to warm their beds. She held a small candle to light her way past endless doors behind which laughter and the sounds of harsh groaning echoed and made her cheeks burn.

Logic told her to leave Callum alone. He had every right to want to be as far away from her as he could get. And if she had any wits left at all, she would be glad he stayed away from her. But after the moments spent waiting for him to return had stretched into an hour, she knew her heart was the true culprit, the direst danger to her well being. She sighed tightly, trying to resolve herself to the bare fact that she was obsessed with the man accused of killing her father. *Stop it, Kate,* she chastised herself, holding the candle in front of her to illuminate a path toward the stairs. *He did not kill your father. But he is going to kill your uncle. And then they will kill him. Get him out of your mind.*

A woman's laughter seeped from behind a door to her

left, halting Kate's steps. What if he was in one of these rooms bedding some wench? Visions of his naked body poised over a heated smile assaulted her. What if he was whispering tender words of love into someone's ear while he . . .

A door opened and Kate almost fled, not wanting to see him exiting the room. The wench exiting the room was a bonny lass with flaxen hair that fell in limp coils around her cherubic face and over the mounds of round, milky breasts she worked lazily to conceal. She offered Kate a pleasant smile while she tied the laces of her gown, then hurried past her and disappeared down the stairs. Kate almost fainted with relief when Graham appeared at the doorway next, adjusting his plaid. She blushed when he grinned at her, a pair of roguish dimples slashing his cheeks, his hazy emerald gaze hooded with spent satisfaction.

"Greetings, lass," he said and leaned his shoulder against the doorframe. "I never would have believed he tossed ye out."

"He did not toss me out," Kate advised the strapping Highlander with an inquisitive smile of her own. She liked this man. His joy came easily and his brash style was strangely attractive. "Is there a line of women waiting to get into this room, Graham?" she continued when his eyes lit on her in amusement. "How many wenches have you entertained so far this eve?"

"Och, but ye have a sharp tongue, lass." He laughed, making Kate realize that she missed the sound terribly. She studied him for a moment, understanding why the women in the tavern sought his company, for he was fair of face with sunlit hair and a lithe body. Aye, he was quite handsome in a roguish way, she decided. His smile wasn't as devastating as Callum's, but it was certainly charming enough.

"What are ye doing roaming the halls at this ungodly hour?" He shoved a thin twig between his teeth and chewed on it. "It's not safe fer such a lass as yerself."

She shrugged. "Callum left the room earlier and I . . ." She bit her lip and looked at the doors framing her on either side.

Graham lifted a curious eyebrow at her as understanding washed over him. "A night's pleasure would do him good. But fear not, he is not inside any of these rooms. Fer come morn, naught will change fer him."

The candle flame quivered when Kate's hand shook slightly. She should have been relieved by Graham's words, but she felt worse than before. "What did my grandfather do to him? Tell me. Please, Graham."

Graham studied her for a moment, then drew out a long sigh. "He was shackled to a wall fer nine years, sometimes fer weeks at a time without pause, without a day in the sun."

Kate took a step back and lifted her hand to her mouth. "My God," she choked on a woeful sob. "He was a child. His scars . . . his wrists . . ."

Graham nodded. "He fought to free himself. He finally did when . . ."

But Kate couldn't bear to hear another word. She fled down the stairs, needing to find Callum. She rounded a sharp corner and almost bounced off a wall that stood in her way. The candle flickered out, and for a moment she was engulfed in darkness. Then she heard the crackle of fire and slowly turned around. She was in the tavern section of the inn. Light from the great hearth fire just behind another wall sifted through the archway, dimly lighting another path. She followed it, though a voice in her head told her to flee back up the stairs.

Callum slept in a heavy wooden chair in front of the hearth, an empty tankard strewn in the rushes beneath his dangling hand. Kate took a step closer to him until she could see his perfect features in the coppery candescence. He was a warrior, but asleep, the vulnerable tilt of his lips drew her closer. He took her breath away. She let her eyes drift over the broad expanse of his chest, the sleek, smooth sinew that shaped his arms. Her gaze traveled down the length of his body, lingering for a breath on his lean hips and then continuing, with a stifled moan, to his long, muscular legs sprawled out before him. God's teeth, there was so much of him.

Suddenly, he cried out. "Nae!" He jerked his hands forward, and Kate's eyes fell to his leather-bound wrists. Was he dreaming of her grandfather's dungeon? The terror and torment in his voice almost felled her to her knees. Without thinking, she reached for him, wanting to ease his pain and wake him from his nightmare. When her fingertips brushed his wrist, his eyes shot open. His hand snapped up and gripped her arm with such force she bit her lip not to cry out. He pulled her down, almost on top of him, and stared into her eyes with a mixture of anguish and haunting fear, the likes of which she had never seen before and would not soon forget.

"Callum," she breathed, too afraid to utter anything more.

The wall fell away from his eyes. His dream was over. As quickly as he had yanked her to him, he eased his hold on her arm. But he did not let her go. Her face was close to his, so close she could feel the heat of his uneven breath upon her lips. But it was his eyes that paralyzed her. No longer were they dark with resolve to hate, no longer were they smoldering blue orbs of forbidden desire. Kate's heart wrenched within her at the stark sorrow staring back at her, consuming her soul, as it did his.

She whispered his name again as the weight of his unguarded gaze struck her full in the heart. Before she could stop herself, she threw herself against his chest and held him.

"I'm sorry for what he did to you."

He did not answer her right away. First his arms came around her, slowly, as if he feared he might break her. He ran his palm over the length of her hair, down her back, holding her head closer. With her ear pressed so closely to him, she had no trouble hearing the fierce pounding of his heart.

"What are ye doin' here, lass?" her asked her. Then, as if he realized what he was doing, he gently pushed her away.

Now she did fall to her knees beside his chair. The shadows returned, drifting across the surface of his eyes as he stared down at her. She fought to hold on to whatever gentleness and vulnerability she had just seen in him before it completely disappeared again. She could reach him, mayhap touch him if he would only release his anger and hatred for just a moment.

"I was looking for you," she told him softly, clinging to the trace of tenderness in his tone.

His features softened again, but he looked away from

her and into the flames of the hearth fire. "Return to yer bed, Kate."

Even against the soft golden hue of firelight, his profile was all hard, harsh planes. Even his eyes gave naught away now about the torment he had suffered. Still, Kate ached to hold him. Part of her knew it would be like reaching her hand toward a ravenous lion. Her fingers could very easily be bitten off. Och, but to touch such a magnificent beast, to touch him and not be eaten alive.

Slowly, casting off her fear, she lifted her fingers to his wrist and touched the leather cuff that covered scars too horrible to look upon. He turned and looked at her and her heart stopped, ready to be devoured. She drew in a deep, quivering breath and straightened her fingers to stroke his wrist. "Do you wear these to remember?"

"Nae, I wear them to ferget."

Kate squeezed her eyes shut, hoping to trap the tears she would shed so unabashedly for him. But they came nonetheless. She expected him to pull away, but he turned his hand in hers until their palms met. Then he closed his fingers around hers. His touch was gentle, whisper soft.

"Cease yer cryin' fer me. It willna change a moment of the past."

But she wished she could change it. Even more than that, she wanted to change his future. She wanted him to let go of his hatred and . . . and what? Kate bit her bottom lip, keeping her eyes fastened on his fingers. What did she want? God's fury, what did it matter? He was a Mac-Gregor and she a Campbell. Their destiny was already written in the law, carved into his flesh. There was naught she could do to change it.

"I dinna want yer sympathy." The roughness of his voice only intensified the plea beneath.

"But it is mine to give, my laird."

Above her, Callum closed his eyes. His fingers moved over hers, stroking, caressing. Her hand was so small, so soft. He should send her back to the room before the sight and scent of her drove him completely mad. Then again, mayhap madness would be a welcome respite from the constant darkness inside him.

His heart went soft when he looked down at her bent head. She looked like an angel kneeling beside him, so ready to offer him atonement for what she did not know. "Mayhap," he murmured, "I should accept what ye offer me."

Kate did not understand what he meant, but she remembered the heated emotion in his eyes before the innkeeper interrupted them earlier that night. She tried to pull her hand away, but his fingers closed around hers more tightly. Kate's head reeled. She had the feeling of falling off one of his giant Highland cliffs, and his hand, so strong and steady, was all that could save her.

"You frighten me," she told him, still not daring to meet his gaze. "Yet I feel safer with you than anyone in my life. How can that be?"

"I wouldna hurt ye, Kate." The husky timbre of his voice felt so tender to her ears.

With breath held, she lifted her head and set her eyes on his. He held her searching gaze for a moment before she found the strength to speak again. "Do you like me, then?"

Before she had a chance to guard her heart against it, Callum's smile washed over her. It hit her full force and she felt dizzy, muddleheaded. She was almost glad that he smiled so rarely, for surely she would lose her heart to him completely, clutched in his vengeful fingers.

"Aye, I do like ye, Kate Campbell. I must be daft, but I do."

"Truly?" And then she grinned at him and watched, delighted and tingling all the way down to her ankles as his smile widened into a torturously resplendent grin of his own. A new spark of hope lit Kate's eyes. "Does this mean you will forget about killing my uncle?" When his grin vanished and he turned away, she tugged on his hand. "They would never stop hunting you."

"'Tis late," he said and stood to his feet. "We're leavin' at first light, so ye best get some sleep."

He pulled her to her feet and took up his steps behind her when she headed back toward the stairs. He couldn't take his eyes off her. The gentle sway of her hips as she climbed the steps drove him to distraction. She was the granddaughter of the man who destroyed everything Callum was. He should feel naught but contempt for her. Instead, he found himself aching to hold her again. To tell her of the dreams he had given up years ago. Kate Campbell was carving her way through his flesh as deeply as the gouges that encircled his wrists, and he had to stop it. He would never allow her to reach his heart the way the cold, cutting metal of Liam Campbell's shackles had. Still, when she turned to look at him over her shoulder, he felt his heart quicken.

She entered the dimly lit room first and then turned to him while he bolted the door. "Callum, I . . ."

"What?" He looked at her, taking in the spark of apprehension she tried to conceal beneath her veil of dark lashes. He had to use all his strength of will not to gather her up in his arms and kiss her senseless. When she took a step toward him, he gritted his teeth and held up his palm. "Would ye set yer life to ruin, Kate?"

She shook her head, ignoring his attempt to keep her at a distance. "I would talk to you, comfort you from your memories."

His smile mocked her, but the sorrow that haunted him was evident in his husky voice. "I fear nae one can do that. No' even ye." But she could. She did, even now.

"When I was little I was told that hatred was poison." She moved closer still, until her intoxicating scent filled his lungs. He clenched his fingers in an effort to stop him from taking hold of her. "I see the truth of it now." Her fingers shook as she raised them to his face, touching him, stroking him as if he were a beast she meant to soothe. "I would stop it before it kills you."

"Kate." He uttered her name as if it pained him to speak it. As surely as her sword had pierced his flesh, her trusting, worshipful eyes caused him to take leave of his senses. He had been a villain for so long, he no longer knew what it felt like to be anything else. Until she looked at him. "Ye shouldna care aboot such things."

She nodded and began to turn away from him. "But I do."

His fingers closed around hers and he pulled her back, capturing her waist with his other arm. He swept her off her feet before he even kissed her. Covering her small hand with his, he brought her fingers back to his face as he lowered his mouth to hers.

Chapter Fifteen

~~~~~~~

HIS KISS WAS HOT, passionate, his tongue a fiery brand exploring the deepest recesses of her mouth. He was hungry and hard, and Kate felt a thread of fear course through her. When his hand cupped her buttocks and razed her against his stiff erection, she arched her back to end their kiss. He bent with her, cupping her body with even more intimacy. His ragged breath along her throat thrilled the fear right out of her. His large, rough hand untying the laces of her gown made her forget everything but the feel of him, the scent of him. She didn't want to think about consequences. She didn't care about them.

Her breast came loose, and he moaned, taking it in his hand. The raw desire in his hooded gaze when he broke their kiss to draw her nipple into his mouth made her groin ache for something she didn't understand. Something only he could satisfy.

He carried her to the bed, gently biting her nipple until it grew as tight as the rest of her. They fell to the mattress. His body covered hers, but his weight did not crush her.

She opened her mouth to him again and clenched her fingers in his hair, pulling him closer while he kissed her. His hands tore at her gown, pulling the thick folds up over her knees. Then his fingers slipped beneath. His breath was ragged, heavy with desire. Kate went rigid when his palms grazed her inner thigh. His hand lingered there while he spread the pad of his thumb over the hard nub of her passion. Red-hot pleasure bolted through her and she squeezed her legs together. He spread her apart again with his knees, slid his hand behind her rump, and sank down onto her.

Kate knew they should stop. But the feel of his arousal between her thighs was so basely erotic, so insatiably intimate, instead of fighting him, she moved against him. He was long, and thick, and so very hard he made her melt into pool of liquid passion. He growled low in her ear and then whispered what he was going to do to her, with words that made her blush.

With one final tug, Callum pulled her skirts over her waist and rose up above her. He looked down at her, wild to taste her while his hand swept beneath his plaid and closed around his shaft. His gaze met hers a moment after his plaid rose over the tip of his swollen head. Her eyes opened wide, and she pushed herself up toward the headboard to be away from him.

It gave him a moment to consider what he was about to do, and to remember what would become of her if he did.

He yanked her skirts down and climbed off her.

Kate didn't move. She didn't breathe while he sat at the edge of the bed and rubbed his hand down his face. She didn't try to stop him when he left the room, though she wanted to. She had never been intimate with a man before, but Callum's touch, his kiss, his voice, everything about him ignited her. Every nerve in her body screamed for him, but she let him go. She had to. Not because of his name, but because of hers. He would never see her as anything more than his enemy.

She wasn't angry that he tried to bed her. Dear God, she would have let him do it if he hadn't stopped. Nor could she fault him for the anger that hauled him off her. She would never forget the disgust that twisted his features when he looked at her face. She wondered, pulling the coverlet up around her neck and wiping her eyes, if Callum would truly release her after he killed her uncle. She reasoned that if he tossed her into the pit, it was a fair trade. He wouldn't touch her again, of that she was certain. It was better that way, she told herself even while her body ached for him. Hell, but the size of him frightened her. She knew enough about mating from raising livestock to know that she could have been carrying his bairn tomorrow if he had not stopped. How would she explain *that* to her brother?

Staring up at the ceiling, she tried to remember her life before the Devil MacGregor had charged into it and changed everything. Had she been happy in her fields tending her sheep, listening to her brother's tales of brave, noble men? Aye, she had. For she'd been oblivious to the searing, aching need to be kissed by such a man. She imagined the torture of living with Callum in the future, seeing his face every day and knowing she would never be anything more than a pawn of revenge. It would be painful indeed, but she was willing to suffer it. At least she wouldn't be shackled to a wall until it became so unbearable that carving off her hands would be a better option.

God's mercy, what did she know of sorrow, of anger? Nothing! She sniffed and wiped her nose, bracing her shoulders against the soft mattress beneath her. The wonderful men in her life had taught her how to fight. Now was not the time to surrender. She must conquer her attraction to Callum MacGregor. But no matter how much he despised her, she would never hate him again. And she was going to stop him from hating her, even if it killed her.

Chapter Sixteen

WHEN KATE AWOKE the next morn, she was still alone in the room. Her pulse quickened when she sat up in her bed and stared at the empty place before the hearth. Callum hadn't returned. Was he gone? Would he have left her alone here? Had he taken Graham and the others and gone to his holding without her? She looked around the small room while her heart pounded madly in her chest. She knew he did not want her company, but would he just abandon her here in this . . . this . . . brothel? She whipped the blanket off her body and sprang from the bed. Cold rushes pricked her toes when she ran across the floor and threw open the shutters on the window.

Sunshine exploded in her eyes and spilled over her face and down her hair. She heard the shouts of men directly below and leaned out the small window to get a better view. When she saw Callum and his men, relief filled her. Brodie and Angus packed food into their leather saddlebags while Jamie surveyed a nearby patch of purple thistle.

She couldn't help but admire Callum while he bent to saddle his mount. Damnation, the more she looked at him, the more handsome he became. Two strands of his dark hair were fastened at the back of his head, while the rest fell over his plaid. He was a tumultuous, rebellious warrior, she decided, gazing at him, and though she was the object of his contempt, she couldn't help but admire his resolve to keep his name alive. Surely even Robert would see the honor in his fight. When he turned and looked up at her window, she waved at him.

"D'ye plan on sleepin' all day?" he called up to her with a fierce frown Kate was growing quite accustomed to.

She'd decided to ignore what happened between them the evening before. He didn't take her, so no harm was done. It was better if they both put it out of their minds.

Without saying a word, she disappeared from the window, combed her fingers through her hair, and snatched her shawl from where it hung over a chair. Within seconds of peeking out the window, she dashed down the stairs and out the door.

"Good morn," she greeted, tilting her face up to Callum's when she reached him, and then blushing to her roots. So much for putting their last encounter out of her mind.

A breeze blew a strand of dark hair across his face. The lock swept across his unshaven jaw and he did nothing to remove it, which only made Kate ache to do it herself. He stared down at her for a moment, long enough to make her insides melt. He possessed the confidence to conquer, the intoxicating power to thoroughly seduce her, and the strength to resist doing either.

"I purchased a horse fer ye. Can ye ride?" he asked.

"Aye." Kate's smile deepened, already seduced by his coarse charm and the full suppleness of his lips. "But I tell you, I will not get a wink of sleep."

She flashed her dark eyes at him and spun on her heel before he could reply, which would have been nothing more than a grunt by the look on his face.

Callum stood by his mount and watched the gentle sway of her hips as she made her way toward Jamie and her new mount. A moment later he swore under his breath and chased after her.

"'Tis already saddled," he said, coming up behind her. "I did it while ye slept."

"Ah, my thanks." Kate turned and graced him with yet another tender smile. "'Tis a fine horse, too." She lifted her hands to the saddle horn to mount but felt strong hands span her waist and lift her up. Her heart lurched at the gentleness of his touch.

Once seated, she stared down into his face. Something had changed in his expression. He was looking at her with such raw yearning she bit her lip and almost made it bleed. Seconds passed, and he did not turn away from her. His eyes revealed thoughts he wanted to utter, ways he wanted to touch her, not cruelly, but curiously, tenderly. Could she have been wrong about why he stopped last eve?

"Last eve was . . ." He ground his jaw then began again. "I was no' thinkin' clearly."

Kate blinked, then forced her smile to remain. "Of course, nor was I."

And then, as suddenly as his emotions appeared on his face, they vanished once again and he strode away from her.

Beside them, Jamie watched with astonishment, and then a knowing smile crept over his face.

Graham finally moseyed out of the inn a few moments later with yet another wench attached to his arm. He bid the lass farewell and joined Callum, ignoring the lethal glare his friend tossed him because he was tardy.

The troop traveled for the rest of the day with merry song echoing across the glens and lochs. The mood among the men was light on their way back to their beloved home, and Kate could not help but revel in their cheer. The land grew more beautiful with each league they traveled. The air was fragranced with heather and linseed. But the view that held Kate enthralled was that of her rescuer's broad back a few feet ahead of her. It seemed that after every fifth breath, Callum turned to look at her as if to reassure himself that she still rode with his band. She thought about riding at his elbow to save him the trouble but decided she rather liked the fact that he was concerned she would run off.

Graham took up his pace beside Kate's mount and explained to her how some MacGregors came to live on the Isle of Mist.

"We found a more peaceful life in Skye. Even the Campbells do not bother to travel so far to hunt us. After Callum escaped yer grandfather's prison, he fled to the isle and was welcomed by the MacLeods, and even the MacKinnons and MacDonalds. Many of them helped him build Camlochlin. When we heard where he was, some of us left our homes and came to live with him and fight by his side."

Kate brushed a strand of her hair out of her eyes and

narrowed her gaze on Callum's back. "Think you he will ever stop killing Campbells?"

"He already has, lass." When she turned to him he slanted his gaze to her and winked. "'Tis a start, aye?"

~

The next morning, they traveled onward to Glenelg, toward the Isle of Skye, crossing the narrows by boat. The captain, Seamus MacRae, was a slim man of medium height and with dark hair as long as Kate's, his bound at the nape. His laughter was quick and robust. Of course, that could be attributed to the three swigs of whiskey he'd consumed at the start of their journey.

"Ye brought a wife back wi' this time, eh, MacGregor?" the captain hollered over his shoulder to where Callum stood resting against the bowsprit, sharing a word with Graham. "She'll give ye bonny bairns." He lifted his boot to a crate and leaned on his bent knee to study Kate more closely. "Aye, bonny indeed."

Kate's eyes darted to Callum when he straightened and began walking toward them. Och, how she wished their names were different. A touch of flame stole across her cheeks at the notion of being wed to so fine a man. She knew in that moment that should he look into her eyes he would see the quickening of her heart. Her vision took in every splendid detail of him, from his dusty calves to the flare of his shoulders. Not a devil, but a man in whose arms she had found warmth and protection. A man whose kisses made her forget who he was, whose smile was more glorious than Lucifer's, and rarer, as well.

"She's no' my wife, MacRae," Callum announced upon reaching them. "I took her from her home against her will, and I bear the evidence of her capture upon my thigh." He pulled the edge of his plaid over his knee to expose his wound. He nodded his head in agreement when the captain grew pale and gaped at her. "She's a hell-witch, and were I you"—his gaze darkened with warning—"I wouldna stare at her so boldly."

"As ye say." Seamus took a step back, still unable to believe that a mere lass had inflicted injury to the mighty MacGregor chieftain. "I have some rope in m' quarters should ye need it."

"Aye," Kate rounded on her captor, her eyes blazing. Had she thought him warm? Fool! "You could hang yourself with it!"

Her angry retort earned her a slow, devastating smile from the MacGregor chieftain.

"Och, but she has ballocks the size of the Cuillins," Seamus MacRae laughed and turned away. "I'll leave the wench to ye, Devil. Some might say ye deserve it."

When they were alone, Callum's smile deepened, making Kate's toes curl and her teeth clench. "Ye're learnin' well, Kate."

"Learning what?" Though her question was curt, she sighed miserably immediately after she asked it. "That every moment you spend with this hell-witch is a sacrifice you suffer for the name MacGregor?" He opened his mouth to speak, but Kate cut him off, holding up her palm. "That you intend to declare your hatred of me to all of Scotland?"

She turned away, leaving Callum to stare at her profile. The wind blew her dark waves across her face, compelling him to lift his hand to her cheek. When his fingertips touched her flesh, the need to touch more of her nearly doubled him over. "Kate." She angled her head, cupping her face in his palm, and closed her eyes. "There is no' a single part of me that hates ye." His smile washed over her when she opened her eyes again, but his gaze was somber. "But yer life depends on ye hatin' *me*." He traced the curve of her jaw with the backs of his knuckles. "Or at least, convincin' others that ye do."

Chapter Seventeen

"How do we know the gel is not a sympathizer?"

Robert Campbell ceased pacing and watched his uncle leap to his feet, lean across the table, and snatch the man who spoke by the throat.

"My niece is no sympathizer," Duncan snarled.

The man nodded, then rubbed his neck when the earl released him.

Robert continued his worn path in the rushes of Hugh Menzie's great hall. He raked his fingers through the dark strands of hair falling over his forehead. He aimed a frustrated glance at his uncle, who was reclining once again at one of three long trestle tables. Neither Duncan nor the rowdy group of Menzies sharing their ale with him paid Robert any heed. It had been over a se'nnight since the MacGregors had abducted his sister, and they were no closer to finding her than they had been the day she was taken. They had gathered men from Breadalbane to Rannoch. They had enough to face MacGregor and his men if they caught up with him now.

Robert had reminded his uncle that the miscreant laird had sent almost all of his men back to his homestead. He traveled now with only four others. They had to catch up with the MacGregors before they returned to the Devil's lair, where they would face his army. But Hugh Menzie, laird of the Menzie clan, had news for the Earl of Argyll, and hence Robert found himself, at present, mumbling blasphemies meant only for the vilest tongue. He did not care.

"Uncle." He stiffened his arms at his side. "Uncle!" he called more forcefully when no one looked up. "I must insist that we leave here at once and take up our search." He almost faltered at the murderous gleam in his uncle's eyes when Duncan finally, slowly set them on him.

"We know all we need to know," Robert continued, refusing to be moved. He had cowered once already when he first faced Callum MacGregor, and it may have cost his sister her life. "The Devil attacked and killed seven of Laird Menzie's kin just a few nights past. Let us make haste while his tracks are still fresh."

"The lad is right!" a rough-looking man with hair the color of charcoal agreed. Another followed, slamming his cup on the table and rising to his feet.

Duncan's lips hooked into a sinuous smile that he cast at his nephew before he raised his cup to the others. "Let us be off, then."

~

Robert's hopes of finding Kate began to falter two days later when they hadn't found so much as a broken twig to keep them on the right path. How had the MacGregors disappeared without a trace? None of the men traveling with him and his uncle knew where the Devil's holding was. It could be leagues away, or just beyond the next hill. Surveying the rocky peaks and rolling hillocks around him, Robert could not help but wonder if they were not being watched. Could he and his meager army of forty men survive an ambush of five? Hadn't all but those five killed fifty of Duncan's men in Glen Orchy? No one would aid them if they were attacked. The Highlanders they had questioned along the way had told them nothing. Even those the earl had beaten and threatened to hang claimed to know nothing of Callum MacGregor. If his sister's life were not at stake, Robert would have admired such loyalty. The Highlanders did not seem frightened of the Devil, but of his uncle. And from what Robert had witnessed thus far, they had good reason to be.

When Graham Grant had first told him about the Mac-Gregor laird's imprisonment in his grandfather's dungeon, Robert had refused to believe him. He had barely known Liam Campbell, for their father rarely took them to Inverary. But Robert was certain no man of his ilk could be so vile. But after what he'd witnessed so far when his uncle questioned the Highlanders, he was no longer so sure. Aye, Robert knew Duncan Campbell was a warrior. The earl had reminded him of it often enough when Robert was a boy. There was no shame in shedding blood for the good of the country. But where was the honor in torturing one's countrymen because they did not give him the answers he desired?

Once Kate was returned to them safely, there would be much to consider about remaining in his uncle's service. As much as Robert hated to admit it, mayhap he was not cut out for the coldhearted, underhanded business of warring. He had certainly been deceived easily enough by the traitor, Grant. Damnation, why had he not suspected something amiss when Grant had informed him that the Devil had captured his uncle?

Like any other Campbell, Graham had known much about the centuries-long battle with the MacGregors. Robert wondered now if it was the subtle inflection of admiration lacing Graham's voice that had almost convinced *him* to admire the proscribed clan. The man pretending to be his kin had not denied that the one the Highlanders called the "Laird of the Mist" had massacred Liam Campbell's garrison. But he claimed to know for certain that the laird did not kill his grandfather, though Graham told him he would have had the right to do so. Robert had found it odd at the time to hear such unprejudiced talk from a Campbell, but Graham had assured him that his Breadalbane kin did not hold the same disdain for the MacGregors. He should have asked Graham how he knew the tale of his grandfather's dungeon was true. Instead, he let Kildun's guardsmen ride directly into the swords of their enemies.

A cold numbness trickled down Robert's spine, even now, at the memory of what had happened next. He'd been spared and brought before the warrior who led the battle. Stunned and shaken, he had turned to see that the man binding his wrists was Graham. Robert had fought against his tight hold, until he felt the tip of MacGregor's blade at his throat. But it wasn't the warm, wet metal on his flesh that halted his movements, and almost his heart. It was how badly MacGregor wanted him dead. It was clear in his eyes, in the cold snarl curling his mouth.

"Tell me where Argyll hides before I remove yer head."

Behind him, Graham had spoken quickly, dragging the chieftain's attention back to him. He spoke at first in Gaelic, causing the MacGregor's expression to darken, then informed him that the earl had gone to Glen Orchy, to the home of his dead brother.

Robert would have preferred that they kill him instead of tying him to the gate and leaving him alive to contemplate what they were going to do to Kate when they found her.

It was his fault. He had left her. He had been too eager to become a knight of the realm.

He had to find her. He prayed his sister was still alive, despite his uncle's belief to the contrary. Kate had to be alive, else not honor or even God would stop him from killing the Devil.

Chapter Eighteen

KATE RODE AT CALLUM'S SIDE as they traveled through Kylerhea toward the brae pass of Bealach Udal. She listened while Jamie, riding just ahead, pointed out the steep south ridge of Beinn na Caillich and the wild herbs and yellow and orange daffodils growing around it. The yellow daffodils are Maggie's favorite, he advised her, then waited for Kate to catch up. "I have tried to find a flower as rare as she, but my search has proved fruitless."

Kate's heart lurched at such sweet gallantry. "Margaret MacGregor must be quite a lady to invoke such tenderness in a man," she told him, wishing she knew how to do the same.

"A lady!" Brodie snorted to their right. "Why, Maggie is as much a hellion as her Devil brother."

Jamie's expression grew serious instantly. He gave his mount's flanks a hard kick that delivered him directly in front of Brodie. "I take offense to that! She is as innocent as a newly born lamb."

Brodie merely looked heavenward, and then at Kate.

"The wee hellion's protector. Some think she's a bit simple, what wi' all them years o' pain, but I tell ye, cross her and she's got a tongue as sharp as m' blade."

"Off yer horse!" Kate heard Jamie's demand and Brodie's subsequent laughter as she turned to follow Callum when he passed her.

The laird had cantered to the top of the low summit and was looking out over the landscape when Kate reached him. She came up slowly, mesmerized by the perfect image of some battle-hardened king of old returning home to his kingdom.

"Your sister has a champion."

Callum smiled, bemused by her fanciful notions and determined to rid her of them as he turned to look over his shoulder at Jamie. "'Tis his duty to guard her, nothing more."

Och, but was he so consumed with one thing that he failed to see something as large as one of his men in love with his sister? Or could he simply no longer recognize love at all?

"Does my uncle know where your home is?" she asked as they climbed the next pass.

"We dinna hide. If Argyll wants to find me, 'tis easy enough."

"And you hope that he will. Because of me." When he nodded, she drew out a wistful sigh. "Pity, it would be enjoyable here without him." She cocked her brow at him when he cast her a bewildered look. "What?"

"Ye possess a way about ye that makes significant things seem . . . no' important at all."

"You mean our names?" She dismissed his impression of her with a shrug. "They are only as important as others make them. I refuse to waste another moment being afraid of the consequences of associating with you. You will find that I don't frighten easily."

Beside her, Callum smiled, already knowing her declaration to be true.

"Take you, for instance. My uncle tried desperately to make me fear the terrible Devil MacGregor, but I barely spared you a thought."

"No' a thought?" He flashed her a winsome grin that made her senses reel. Nothing she had seen thus far matched its beauty.

"Barely one." She did her best to keep her composure and offered him a teasing smile of her own. "Of course, I did not know it was you at the time."

"And now that ye know me, d'ye find me worthy of more than a passin' thought?"

She blushed, hating herself for doing it. "I think of you from time to time, I admit."

His grin softened into a smile so intimate, so shockingly sensual her mouth went dry. She licked her lips to keep them from sticking together. His eyes followed the path of her tongue. His expression darkened with desire. He wanted to kiss her, and she wanted him to. Dear God, she knew she would go willingly to him if he but spoke the request, hanging be damned! She wanted to taste his mouth, his breath. She wanted to be in his arms again, to feel his hardness against her breasts, his skillful hands holding her, exploring her, caressing her while he told her . . .

"Are there many people in Camlochlin?" she asked, forcing from her mind the foolish notion that he would ever care for her.

"There are enough." He watched her guide her horse up another steep incline, making certain her mount did not slip. "There are more of us in Rannoch."

But Kate did not hear him. From the top, her gaze spread over the breathtaking panorama of a world set apart from the rest. Black mountain ranges, their jagged peaks swathed in silver mist, cut across an endless horizon as if painted there by a mad artist bent on intimidating visitors. She could have been looking at the sacred isle of Arthur Pendragon's burial place, for Skye appeared timeless, ancient, untouched.

"It is Heaven," she spoke on a shallow breath, not wanting to move from her spot, wanting never to leave this place.

"Nae, but 'tis as close as I'll ever come to it."

She turned to him, disquiet marring her brow. "Can you not forget what haunts you, even here?"

He shook his head and continued onward. "'Tis here where I remember."

⁓

They traveled for the rest of the day in silence, save for Angus's gravelly voice filling the braes with old Highland ballads and Brodie's intermittent groaning.

As they passed through the small village of Torrin, the black mountain range—or the Cuillins, as Jamie had called them—loomed closer in the distance, a force of nature as harsh and unyielding as the warrior chieftain riding toward them. They skirted round Loch Slapin and followed a path that brought them directly below the mountain brae.

Kate doubted any view could be more splendid than

the one she had seen at Glen Arroch. But she was wrong. The road they traveled rose above a sun-dappled loch toward the honeycombed cliffs of Elgol. Every step was more treacherous than the one before it, but the view alone was worth every heart-stopping turn. Following closely behind Callum, they winded around another curve, at whose edge Kate was forced to stop. She was certain they had arrived at the end of the world or the beginning of time, for the brutal grandeur that unfolded before her stilled her breath. The entire horizon was a chiseled masterpiece of jagged, shadowy mountaintops and white, swirling mist. Her heart wrenched at the intense loneliness of such a savage landscape. Who could survive here, and who could survive without it once they had seen it?

They continued on while salt tang filled her nostrils and the sound of crashing waves below played like music on the moist breeze. This land was as tumultuous as the sea and just as dangerous, with mossy peaks and crannies, and slippery slopes that promised certain death with one wrong turn.

Finally the cliffs fell away, leaving the troop on a grassy crest overlooking a remote haven nestled beneath the giant slopes of Sgurr Na Stri and the craggy bulk of Bla Bheinn to the north. Directly below them were rolling moors carpeted in lush lavender heather. Sheep dotted the sunlit vale, and cattle grazed amid cozy thatched-roof bothys strewn across the grass. To the west of the glen, a wide loch spewed small frothy caps along a pebbled beach where children played.

"Camlochlin Castle." Callum reined his mount closer to Kate and pointed down into the glen.

The fortress must have been built of the same stone as the mountain behind it, for it blended into the landscape so neatly she doubted she would have even noticed it there had Callum not pointed it out to her.

Kate longed to push on ahead and enter this vast, separated land Callum called his home. The men did not move toward it, and just when she was about to question them about why they were not rushing home, the sun began its short descent. Golden rays of light were captured in the mist above the mountains. The sky exploded into flames of bronze and yellow, while the curtain wall before her grew even darker, casting shadows over the land. Splashes of gold fell upon the loch, turning white caps a frothy ochroid.

"I want to go there," Kate breathed on a longing sigh, then turned to Callum. "Now."

Callum held her gaze with his own and wondered at the way she worked at chiseling away his defenses. He'd never planned on bringing a woman here to share his life. He had neither the time nor the heart for such watery notions. But if he was going to entertain thoughts of taking a wife, she would be a woman who loved his home as much as he did. A woman who could see beyond the veil of the unyielding and the impenetrable and appreciate the beauty of a land that spoke to the heart alone. Aye, and mayhap she would even be able to see something good in him beneath the beast he had become.

He swallowed back the unwanted desires Kate Campbell stirred in him, but they returned full force when she slanted her smile at him and then kicked her mount into a full gallop.

The men followed her down the steep heather incline,

but before Callum let loose his reins, he watched the back of Kate's slight form racing toward his home as if it were her own.

With a heart that felt lighter than it had in years, he set his eyes on his castle and his heels to his mount. Within seconds he thundered past Kate and his men as if they were pausing to admire the scenery.

The celebration of their return began even before Kate and the others reached the castle, when Angus popped the cork off a fresh pouch of brew and, in an uncommon gesture of generosity, passed it around. After a long swig of the potent spirit, Kate shuddered all the way to her kneecaps, then set her eyes on Camlochlin's laird. He had reined in just before entering the pasture and then turned his horse back toward the others, his smile wide and beautiful, his long hair streaming across his shoulders.

There was happiness in Callum's life, and it was here. Kate was thankful for it. She wanted to be a part of it.

Aye, Callum was happy to return home, but 'twas the joy in Kate's eyes and the tenderness of her smile that exhilarated him.

He lived his life with a single purpose, to avenge what had been done to him, his clan, his sister. He'd hated who he had become—until he saw himself through Kate's eyes. He despised the memories that haunted him, but just looking at her made him forget. At first he had fought her effect on him because she was a Campbell. Then he fought it because she could never be his—and live. Hell, leaving her in that bed at the inn had nearly driven him mad. But they were far away from the world now, far from the law. Somehow she had come to mean more to him than revenge, more than a quick tumble to quench his desire. His heart longed for the redemption she offered him. His body ached to hold her. He looked over his shoulder at Camlochlin. His sanctuary. But so much was missing from his life. He had no notion of how to find what would make him whole again, or even if 'twere possible. He was an outlaw, a murderer, a monster. But Kate Campbell saw something more.

He flicked his reins.

When he reached her, he leaned forward in his saddle, coiled his arm around her waist, and heaved her onto his lap. He offered her no explanation as he gazed deep into her questioning eyes. He could barely think at all. Instead, he stroked the soft contour of her cheek, then slipped his hand behind her nape and bent his mouth to hers. She did not resist him. He knew she wouldn't. Her lips parted on a sigh of sweet surrender that made his whole body go rigid and melt at the same time. His tongue swept deeply, intimately into her mouth, tasting her and letting her taste him in return. Plunging his hand within her hair, he tilted back her head while the other drew her closer. He kissed her with exquisite thoroughness, ravishing her softness until she fell back, limp in his arms.

He lifted his head and slid his gaze over her glorious face while she hiccupped and smiled at him. And all at once he knew 'twas not only her heart with which he should have been more careful.

Chapter Nineteen

CALLUM COULD NOT HELP but smile as he stepped into Camlochlin with Kate clutched to his arm. He should be angry with Angus for feeding her Gillis's poison, but he liked the way she pressed herself against him. He knew she held on so tightly to keep herself from stumbling, for the whiskey was potent indeed. But her rather submissive position would also work at easing some of the tension sure to come when he told Camlochlin's inhabitants who she was.

He looked around at the squires and vassals rushing to help his men disarm. Baths were already being prepared to wash away weeks of dirt and grime, and somewhere close by, Callum heard Old Keddy the cook shouting for a dozen fat hens to be slaughtered in celebration of the laird's return. Brodie's wife, Netta, heavy with child, came barreling down the long stairway and near leapt into her husband's arms. Graham was besotted with kisses from Rabbie the tanner's twin daughters, Glenna and Lizabeth.

Callum drank in the sights and sounds of his home like a man parched by the sun. He knew the face of every man, woman, and bairn who greeted him. Familiar scents of smoky peat and burning tallow wax fragranced his nostrils. He drew in a deeper breath, letting it comfort his restless spirit. Aye, Heaven.

His gaze dropped to Kate. 'Twould not be Heaven for her. When his kin learned that she was a Campbell, and naught but a captive to him, they would treat her unkindly. Some might even try to cause her harm. At the thought of it, his heart seized with the need to protect and shelter what was his. But she was not his, his mind reminded him.

"Who's the lass, then, Laird?" someone called out as if to drive the truth of it home.

Best to get it the hell over with, Callum thought, involuntarily pulling Kate closer. "This is Katherine Campbell," he shouted so that all could hear. People stopped what they were doing and gathered 'round him, some already whispering offense at her name. Callum's expression went hard. "She'll be brought nae harm here, understood?"

The mumbling soon died down, but there were questions aplenty. Callum felt Kate slip against his arm and wondered if she was even aware of all the faces staring at her.

"Did ye snatch her from her home, Laird?"

"What d'ye plan to do wi' her?"

Hell, she wasn't completely oblivious to what was being said, Callum realized when she lifted her head from his arm.

"She looks dimwitted. Is she simple, then?"

"Nae," Callum replied succinctly while he carefully fit his hand over Kate's mouth. He'd felt the slight tightening of her shoulders and knew she was about to let his clan find out what a fearless little hellion she was. No MacGregor took kindly to being insulted, and especially by a Campbell. "She's drunk."

Suddenly he jerked his hand back and shook it as if he'd been burned. "Christ, ye near took off my finger!" he bellowed at her.

"She bit him!" someone shouted. A dozen men moved forward ready to protect their laird. The rest simply stood there gaping.

"Stand doun," Brodie warned, stepping in front of the men before they reached Kate. "'Tis no' the first time she's wounded him, and I'm guessin' 'twillna be the last."

"Aye." Kate's glassy eyes blazed at Callum. "And if he ever muzzles me again"—she paused to lift her fingers to her lips and burp—"I shall do more than bite him."

"She's a fiery wench," a male inhabitant called from the crowd.

"Will ye be claimin' a Campbell, Laird?"

"Nae, I willna be," Callum called out over the sudden throng of dissatisfied voices.

"Of course he won't," Kate responded in kind. "I am already betrothed to a lovely man." She tossed Callum a pert smile when he scowled at her.

"A *lovely* man?" Even Angus had to question that.

"He's English," Callum explained.

"I love him!"

Callum didn't actually smile in front of his clan, but his eyes warmed considerably at Kate's announcement.

"Good, then ye'll be pleased when yer brother returns ye to him." He did not give her the opportunity to reply but called to one of the lasses hanging off Graham's arm. "Glenna, take her to a room."

He watched Kate reluctantly leave the hall, turning over her shoulder to glare at him one more time. Hell, she was spitting mad.

Callum grinned.

Brodie snickered while Angus pushed through the dispersing crowd and headed for the buttery.

Callum looked around the hall as the people returned to their duties. He hadn't seen her among the faces, and he turned toward the doors to check the barn.

"Brother?"

He heard her voice, slight and soft behind him, and his heart slowed as he turned.

Margaret MacGregor's frame was small, almost frail compared to her brother's brawn. Her back was slightly hunched. Her short, pitch-black hair pointed out in all directions and was littered with straw.

"Greetins, fair lass." Callum bowed slightly to his sister. When he stood to his full height a moment later, his eyes grazed over the top of her head. "I see ye were lyin' in the barn again."

She did not return his smile, but Callum knew she was happy to see him by the tears glistening over the tips of her long, dark lashes.

"Did you find him?"

"Nae," Callum told her, knowing who she meant. "He fled."

She nodded and scratched her small, dirty nose. "Why did you bring her here?"

"She is his niece."

His sister looked toward the stairs, pondering his words. After a moment she turned her enormous blue eyes on him, knowing his reason. "So he will come to ye."

Callum nodded and looked away. For she saw who he was. She had seen what became of him when he gave up his soul to take her from hell. She hated the thought of him killing anyone, even a Campbell. "It will end with him, Maggie."

She lifted one small hand to his face and the other to the tears streaking her cheeks. "Nae, it will end with ye," she said, wiping her face.

Callum took her hand and kissed it. He did not bother telling her that was what he meant. When Argyll was dead he would stop warring with the Campbells. He would explain it all to her later.

"Jaime's been pickin' flowers fer ye again," he said, wanting to lighten the mood of their reunion. He crooked her arm through his and led her toward the great hall. "When last I saw him, he was headin' fer yer chambers with an armful of daffodils. Those are yer favorites, nae?" he teased and was rewarded with a scowl as dark as his own.

"Ye know they aren't, Callum. Why did ye not tell him that my favorites are orchids?"

"Orchids dinna grow well in the north."

"That is why I like them best. They are delicate."

"Like ye," Callum said, smiling at her.

Margaret quirked her lips, looking much like the imp their mother used to call her. "What flower would ye pick for Katherine Campbell?"

Callum snorted. "I wouldna pick flowers."

"Ye let her take a bite out of ye." Maggie looked up at him, then cut him off when he opened his mouth to speak. "Ye fancy her. What flower would ye pick for her?"

"Tulips," he mumbled, ignoring her knowing smirk. "Come, let us get somethin' to eat."

She shook her head. "I'm not hungry. You go, brother, and then please share a word or two with Keddy about keeping ducks off the supper trenchers."

"He's already agreed to keep mutton off them," Callum reminded her.

"I know, but it upsets Matilda." She smiled when he finally promised to speak to the cook.

Chapter Twenty

KATE SAT AT THE EDGE of the bed and watched in silence while Glenna hurried around the room, plumping cushions and opening shutters to air out the room. That the Highland woman did not utter a word to her during her work was uncomfortable enough. But worse, every time Glenna looked at her, her eyes seethed with anger.

Kate knew why. She was as unwanted a guest at Camlochlin as the English were in Scotland. Damnation, she was tired of people despising her because of her name.

Her head was beginning to pound. Hadn't she vowed never to drink Angus's whiskey again? Och, she was no good at keeping promises. But Callum surely was. Unfortunately, the effect of Angus's brew had worn off enough for her to recall Callum's smug reply to her when she said she loved lord whatever his damned name was. She also remembered the way he had kissed her before they entered the castle. She touched her fingers to her lips. It was even better than before, if that were possible. His mouth had caressed hers, his gaze so gentle and full of meaning.

Almost as if he . . . *Och, stop it, Kate. You were drunk, you fool!*

She slammed her palm down on the mattress, and Glenna looked up from filling a basin with fresh water and glowered at her.

Kate offered her a repentant smile. "I was pondering something. I did not mean to startle you."

"I'm no' afeared o' Campbells," Glenna snapped.

"Of course not. That isn't what I . . ." Kate shook her throbbing head and began again. She'd never fought with a woman before and didn't fancy the thought of having her eyes clawed from her head. "You fancy Graham," she said instead, hoping to steer the young maiden toward more pleasant conversation, since she was finally talking. "He's quite handsome and—"

Glenna dropped the basin to floor. In truth, she delivered it to the rushes with a vigorous smash.

"Keep yer hands off him. He'd never touch the likes of ye."

Kate's mouth fell open, but before she could form a fit reply, someone else spoke behind her.

"Glenna, go fetch some rags to clean up your mess. Graham is already occupied with Lizbeth, so there's nae need to make haste."

Kate turned to the dulcet voice as Glenna strode out of the room. What she saw nearly made her recoil.

"She believes Graham is in love with her." The woman hunched beneath the doorway turned to watch Glenna leave. She sighed and shook her head with pity. "And they say I'm dense."

Kate was still reeling from the sight of her when the woman—or was she a child?—she was certainly small enough to be one—turned to her. Whatever she was, she was surprisingly beautiful. Kate wasn't certain if it was the dirty streaks covering parts of her round face that made her eyes glimmer like clear blue ice, or if it was their size that made them so stunning.

"I am Margaret. But I prefer to be called Maggie. I already know who ye are."

Kate's stomach twisted with sorrow and then shame. God's mercy, this was Callum's sister. Her hair was a mass of dark tangles and her spine, misshapen and bent like that of an old woman. Was her grandfather responsible for this? Kate could barely stop the disgust in her heart from spilling forth. Unfortunately, Maggie took notice.

Those brilliant eyes narrowed on Kate, and then, with a scowl as fierce as her brother's, Maggie turned to leave. "My brother awaits ye in the great hall after ye freshen up."

Stunned and saddened by Margaret's appearance, and sorry that the poor lass had misread her contempt, Kate bolted to her feet and rushed after her when Maggie left.

"Please, wait!"

Maggie didn't even pause in her steps but continued straight down the hall and into another room. Kate followed her, coming to an abrupt halt at the entrance.

The room was large! There was a heavy wooden bed against the south wall big enough to fit three people, but by the crisp look of it, no one slept in it. Daffodils, fresh and old, festooned every table, every window niche. The walls were painted with lush green vines, and in the corner was a small tent fashioned of dyed leather, long sticks, and heavy rope.

Maggie pushed the flap away from the opening of the tent and disappeared inside.

For a moment, Kate had no idea what to do. The room, the tent, Maggie's appearance . . . everything overwhelmed her. But she had to apologize for hurting Maggie's feelings. She went to the tent and knelt beside it.

"Please come out," she prodded gently. "I didn't mean you any insult."

"Callum awaits ye in the great hall. Off with ye."

Kate wrung her hands together trying to find a way to make her come out so that she could speak to her. "I . . . I feel as if I know you already." She leaned closer to the flap. "Jamie has told me much about you."

Maggie's face appeared where the flap was, momentarily startling Kate. "What did he tell ye?"

"That you like yellow daffodils."

Maggie rolled her eyes heavenward. "Mother Mary, I do not like them. I like orchids." She crawled out of the tent and sat facing Kate. "I told him I like daffodils because he picks so many for me."

Kate had the sudden urge to smile, but first she needed to apologize. "It was a long journey here. I did not mean to treat you unkindly."

Maggie studied her for a moment, and then arrived at some conclusion that softened her features with a smile. She lifted her fingers to wipe a smudge of dirt from Kate's brow even while her own face was streaked with it. "Ye were not hurt, were ye? Callum would never let ye be hurt."

"I was not hurt," Kate assured her. She could not keep herself from thinking about the years Maggie had spent in a dungeon, and what had happened to her there. Amazingly, though, there was tenderness and innocence in Maggie's eyes that Callum lacked. "You said you already knew who I was. Then you know I'm a Campbell?" Kate added hesitantly. When Maggie nodded, Kate pushed on. "And you don't hate me?"

Maggie patted her cheek, then stood up. "My brother has enough hate in him for both of us. D'ye want to come to the barn with me?"

The change in topic was so abrupt Kate didn't answer her right away. Then, "The barn?"

"Aye, it's verra peaceful there."

Kate smiled and rose to her feet, accepting Maggie's outstretched hand.

Though her body was bent, Maggie MacGregor had no trouble almost racing down the stairs, still clutching Kate's hand, of course. The delicious aroma of food wafting through the air made Kate's stomach ache. Panic filled her suddenly when she realized that Maggie was leading her to the great hall. Hell, Callum and his entire clan would probably be there and she had not even washed her face. It didn't matter that they had all seen her less than an hour ago. Surely they expected her to wash the grime from her body after traveling for so long. Och, she must look like a village wench! She ran her free hand through her hair and yanked at some of the tangles, but it was no use. She was a mess. She also realized that this was the first time in her life she was concerned with her appearance. The idea pleased and disturbed her at the same time. It was wonderful to want to look pleasing, and even more wonderful to have someone to look pleasing for. Sadly, the man she wanted to please didn't even like her. But he certainly had not kissed her like a man who held her in contempt . . . unless he was just so happy to be home.

His home. God's teeth, what would her uncle think if he knew she was in the MacGregor holding? She looked around, soaking up the thick tapestries that provided warmth to the castle. The long corridors were illuminated in the soft glow of sconced torches. The furniture was plain but tremendously big. Exactly what a wondrously big man like Callum would choose, although poor Maggie likely ceased to exist when she sat in one of the carved walnut chairs sprinkled throughout the halls.

The two women rounded a corner that opened into an endlessly long great hall with a vaulted ceiling that rose upward two full landings. Kate's face paled when she saw dozens of ladies, all with clean, untangled hair and unwrinkled gowns, seated at the long trestle table with Callum's men. The light from the central hearth did not help her position, either. Every eye seemed to fall on her curiously being led by the hand by a wee hunched-back woman. Self-consciously, Kate ran her hand over her gown to smooth it and then wondered if breaking free of Maggie's surprisingly strong grip and running for the doors would make her look even more foolish.

She spotted the object of her affliction and forgot everything else. Callum MacGregor stood a good head taller than the other men, save Angus. His long, dark hair was neatly combed and hung loose over his shoulders, the shadow of stubble gone now from his ruggedly chiseled features. He wore a loose-fitting white tunic unlaced at the neck and tucked at his waist beneath his folded plaid. He stood with Graham and a female of ample bosom and sultry green eyes.

Kate tightened her grip on Maggie's hand, not wanting to go any further.

When he looked up from the flaxen-haired wench's coy smile, Kate knew it was too late to flee, though she was no longer sure she wanted to. Callum looked pleased to see her. That is to say, he was not scowling. His eyes swept over her, his gaze a tender caress. But Maggie had stepped in front of her, and Kate wondered if he was looking at her or his sister.

"Greetings, Callum!"

Callum lifted his goblet and finished off its contents in one swallow, then returned his sister's greeting.

"Did ye drag Kate oot of her room before she could bathe?"

Kate's smiled vanished. If Maggie weren't holding her hand so tightly she would have fled the hall and Camlochlin itself.

"She does not need to bathe," his sister huffed. "She needs friends, so I am going to introduce her to Matilda and the others."

Callum looked over her head at Kate. "Mayhap Kate would like somethin' to eat first."

Kate was torn between smiling like a dreamy dimwit into his beautiful eyes, or smashing a trencher over his head for not even caring if she was in love with an Englishman.

"Later." Maggie tugged on her hand, pulling her away from Callum. "I'm sure she will not want to eat Keddy's supper after she meets Henry and the others."

Kate felt Callum's eyes on her, but she did not turn around as they exited through a small door at the other end of the hall. They entered the kitchen, and Maggie threw the burly, chubby-faced cook a glare as menacing as her brother's on his angriest day. Kate plucked an apple from the chopping table just before she was hauled through another door. She completely missed Keddy's scathing glare.

A cool, salty breeze whipped through Kate's hair when they stepped outside. But for the distant roar of whitecaps

forging toward the shore, the only sound in the utter still-
ness of the surrounding mist was Kate's own breath.

"It is beautiful here," she said, gazing at the twilight
wonder around her. "But we should go back inside. It's
too difficult to see."

Maggie yanked on her hand. "Follow me."

A few more steps and Maggie pulled on another door
just off the eastern wall of the castle. The wood creaked,
weathered on its hinges. Kate followed her inside what
she assumed was the barn, if the sounds of squawking
made by various farm animals were any indication. Finally Maggie released her hand and reached up to retrieve
a small lantern hanging low on a wooden rafter. She lit the
candlewick inside, and Kate drew in a short gasp. It was a
barn, but like none she had ever seen before. Fresh hay littered the floor, and bags of oats and nuts hung from hooks
on the walls. There were no cages to house the animals.
Instead, they roamed freely, nibbling at scattered corn-
meal and sliced apples strewn along the floor. There were
not many animals here. A duck was either very happy to
see the two women or quite displeased, for she waddled at
them honking loud enough to wake the dead. A pig followed the duck in hot pursuit, snorting just as loudly. An
old horse crunched on a carrot in the corner, and he, too,
looked up when Maggie and Kate entered. A gray and
white cat leapt from the rafters and startled Kate.

"Bertrid, this is Kate, my friend," Maggie informed the
purring cat and then sat down on the floor. "Well?" She
glanced up at Kate. "Are ye not going to say hullo back?"

"Greetings to you, Bertrid," Kate replied politely, feeling silly. She felt a tug on her skirt.

"Come doun here. 'Tis less threatening to them. They do not know ye yet, Kate."

Kate bit into her apple and glanced around at the corn strings decorating the barn from rafter to rafter. Crisscrossing the corn were strings of blackberry, elderberry, and various nuts. Animals were carved into the wood, and dried daffodils fragranced the air. It was positively enchanting. "You did all this?"

"Jamie did it for me. Now sit."

Kate obeyed and waited for the next introduction.

"This is Henry." Maggie became the perfect chatelaine as she introduced the snorting pig to her newest friend. "He likes to be pet behind the ears. And that's Matilda. She honks aplenty, and though I vow she rants louder than Angus, 'tis but her declaration of love. That's Ahern. He was Callum's best warhorse. He once belonged to the Earl of Argyll, but Callum took him when we left. Ahern is verra braw, but he's old now."

By now, Henry the pig had curled up into in Kate's lap like a well-loved puppy, and to her surprise Kate felt a sense of calm wash over her, be it from the comforting, gentle tones of Maggie's lilting voice or from Henry's slow, rhythmic breathing. She liked it here, and she was glad to be away from all the eyes in the great hall.

The barn door opened, and Matilda spread her wings and honked out a few more oaths as wind blew the hay on the floor into circles around the small group.

"We are fine, Jamie," Maggie called out without turning. Then she looked at Kate through the corner of her eye and explained in a low voice, "My brother always sends him to watch over me as if I were a hapless child."

Kate was about to turn around to greet him when she heard Callum's thick, velvet voice behind her.

"Yer brother only wants to be assured of yer safety. Should we flog him fer that?" His tone was light, and when he reached them he folded his long legs and sat down in the hay beside Kate.

"Och, ye've been flogged before and it did not help a bit," his sister replied tartly.

Kate shot her an incredulous look. How could they jest about such a thing when Callum bore those terrible scars all across his back? She felt his gaze on her and turned to find she was right. His eyes flickered in the light like embers. When he spoke, the husky cadence of his voice made Kate's spine tingle.

"How d'ye like my sister's friends?"

"I think I like Henry best." She lowered her gaze to the sleeping pig in her lap.

Callum watched her stroke the swine and imagined what it would be like to have her touch him with such care.

"Ye have no' met Sarah yet, then?" he asked, rising to his feet again. He crossed the barn and bent into the shadows. When he came into the light again, he was carrying a small lamb in his arms.

Unabashedly, Kate watched him. She loved how he walked, proud but not arrogant, with the grace of a king and the quiet strength of a leader. He squatted before Maggie and handed the lamb to her, then sat down near Kate again.

"She's a bonny babe!" Kate cooed and slipped her fingers beneath Sarah's woolly chin. "What big brown eyes she has."

Maggie seemed to melt, caressing the lamb to her chest. She closed her eyes and lavished Sarah's head with kisses. "Sarah must stay here now since she was trampled by the other sheep," Maggie told her, her kisses unceasing. "Keddy wanted to make stew of her."

Kate gasped.

"Aye," agreed Maggie. "But I bit him and asked him how he liked it."

Biting her tongue to stifle a giggle, Kate was thankful for the dim lighting. She was sure Maggie was perfectly serious, and Kate did not want to insult her by laughing.

"I will never eat even a morsel of meat," Callum's sister declared lovingly.

Callum grumbled something, but his sister seemed not to notice as she threw herself down in the hay and lay there on her back with Sarah atop her belly.

An hour later, Kate and Maggie both lay on the barn floor. Callum had requested that they return to the castle, but both women refused. Sprawled on their backs and staring up at the low rafters, they talked quietly while Callum sat propped against one wall, his long legs stretched out before him and crossed at the ankles. Both of them giggled when he began to snore.

"Did Callum tell ye about our imprisonment?"

The question was so sudden and unexpected that Kate took a moment to answer. Then, "Nae, he has not spoken of it."

"He never does." Maggie looked toward him. "I do not remember much before we were taken captive. They put the sword to my papa, and then did bad things to mama before they killt her, too. Callum tried to fight them, but he was just a lad. Och, he grew strong later, though." She paused. Her eyes drifted off to the past for an instant, and then she blinked and began to breathe again. "He did everything they demanded, but they still beat him."

Lying still beside her, Kate turned to gaze upon Callum's sleeping face while his sister spoke.

"He is so stubborn, though." Maggie yawned and her eyelids grew heavy, but she continued speaking. "Each time they beat him he vowed to kill them. They mocked his promise, until one morn when he pretended to be asleep. A guard stepped closer to him and my brother killt him with just his forehead. Callum knew they would kill us because of what he had done."

The barn was so quiet Kate heard the sound of her drumming heartbeat. She wanted to scream for Maggie to cease, but she could say nothing. She poured her eyes over her knight, aching to climb into his lap the way Henry had climbed into hers. She wanted to kiss his face and soothe his cold heart. But he would never let her. The thought made her moan.

"They came for me first. But Callum broke free." Though Maggie's voice was but a whisper, Callum's eyes opened as if he were hearing her words in his sleep.

He rose from his place against the wall and stood over them. "Come, to bed with ye now," he said gently and picked Maggie up in his arms.

"Och, but were they not surprised at that, Callum? Were they not surprised at how ye killt them all?" Maggie said, and then closed her eyes.

Callum's expression twisted with some emotion so painful Kate doubted she would ever recover from seeing it.

As she settled into bed that night, Kate's thoughts were plagued with images she prayed hard to forget. But first, she prayed that the two people who lived through the horrible tale could forget them, as well.

Chapter Twenty-One

⌒

THE MORNING SUN BLAZED like a dragon's breath through the wide, unshuttered windows of Kate's room. Golden light splashed over her hair while Maggie brushed it until Kate's scalp began to ache. Callum's sister had insisted on bathing her new friend after they shared a hearty meal of cooked oats. Kate's skin still tingled from the scrubbing she received at Maggie's strong hands, but it felt wonderful to finally smell better than a fortnight's worth of dirt.

She had so wanted to brush Maggie's hair, but the lass refused. But after Kate commented on how Jamie might be tempted to plant a kiss on her cheek if it was clean, she did agree to wash her face.

At Callum's request, a handmaiden named Aileen had delivered an earasaid and an armful of kirtles and shifts to Kate's room earlier, all of which were tried on until Kate finally chose one with a sleeveless bodice of sapphire wool. The cut was low, the laces ending just beneath her breasts. She wore a cream-colored shift beneath with long bloused sleeves. Maggie had helped her don her earasaid of patterned scarlet and saffron, pleating it around her waist with a belt and wrapping the spare material around her shoulders. She'd secured the plaid with a round brooch of hammered bronze.

"Kate?" Maggie asked now, brushing one of Kate's curls around her finger. "Is yer uncle very skilled with a blade?"

Kate heard the distress in her voice and knew what Maggie was really asking her. "I've never seen him in battle, but he often boasted of his skill." When Maggie expelled a little groan, Kate hastily continued. "Whereas I have seen Callum wield a sword, and I do not believe any man could stand against him."

"Are ye verra frightened for yer uncle, then?"

Kate shifted in her seat. She was not worried for him at all. In fact, she did her best not to even think of him. But she couldn't tell that to Maggie without the girl thinking she was as coldhearted as her grandfather. "I don't want Callum to kill him," she finally said, leaving it at that.

"Nor do I."

Kate turned to her, surprised. "How is it that you suffered with your brother at the hands of my kin and you don't wish them dead, as Callum does?"

Maggie's huge eyes shimmered with tears when they settled on Kate. "How much longer will my brother live if he keeps killing them? Sooner or later they will come for him. Just like they did at Kildun."

Kate nodded slowly and turned back around. Her heart beat madly in her chest. She knew Maggie was right. She had even tried to tell him at the inn. This war would never end if the killing continued, and Callum would surely die. "We must stop him."

"How?" Maggie asked. A dash of hope tinged her voice. "D'ye think he will listen to ye? He did say he would give ye tulips."

"Tulips?" Kate turned to her again with a befuddled look. The lass had the most peculiar way of switching topics right in the middle of a conversation.

"Aye, he would pick tulips for ye."

Kate almost laughed. "Your brother would never pick flowers."

"That's what he said, but then he said tulips. I think he fancies ye. So will ye speak to him?"

"Aye." Kate nodded, rising from her chair. Tulips? Whatever made him choose that particular flower? She touched her fingers to her mouth. And why would Maggie think he fancied her? He had kissed her, aye. He had even wanted to bed her. But it was lust—he had all but told her so. He could never bring himself to care for a Campbell. Could he?

"Kate?"

"Aye?"

"What are ye waiting for?"

⌒

"I don't think this is a good time," Kate whispered out of the corner of her mouth to Maggie as they headed down the stairs.

"Why not? You look verra bonny in yer earasaid."

"Look." Kate pointed to the faces staring up at her from the bottom landing. There were only one or two at first but, emboldened by the rest, more of Camlochlin's inhabitants gathered at the foot of the stairs until Kate and Maggie faced a small crowd of mumbling Highlanders. Kate paled, noticing that each face bore the same expression of hardened contempt for her.

"Where is Callum?" Maggie demanded, recognizing the anger, as well.

One man stepped forward from the crowd. He wore a heavy woolen tunic beneath his plaid. His legs were bare, his boots dusty and tattered. "Why d'ye stand beside a wretched Campbell as if she were yer friend, Maggie? Send her back from whence she came."

Maggie stepped around Kate's shocked face and wagged her finger at the man. "Iain, ye'll not speak of her that way. She is my friend, Campbell or nae. And Callum's, as well."

"Our laird would ne'er befriend our enemy," someone shouted.

"Aye, he had to rob her to force her uncle to face his fate."

"Toss her oot on her arse!"

Kate took a step back as the crowd grew larger. Many of them were shouting now, demanding that she leave Camlochlin and ignoring Maggie's small fist when she shook it at them. Someone took a step forward, and Kate backed further away until her heels bumped the stairs. Then she heard the shout of a loud, resonating voice, and every head in the hall turned in the direction from which it came.

Graham stood in the doorway leading to the great hall, arms at his sides, ready to draw his sword. Beside him, Angus appeared bigger and more menacing than ever. Brodie was there also and slid his dagger across a small whetting stone clenched in his fist. Jamie stood at his side, his usual innocent expression exchanged for one far more threatening.

"What in blazes is going on here?" Graham demanded. "Did I hear ye all right? This fair lady is not welcome in our home?" The crowd was silent for a moment, and then someone muttered the name Campbell and the rest began to nod.

"We dinna care what her name is," Jamie warned in a low growl. "Callum's orders are that nae harm be brought to her. Now step back."

Maggie tugged at Kate's sleeve. "Jamie's verra braw, nae?" She let out a little sigh and then went back to glaring at the crowd.

"The MacGregor's taken leave of his senses to bring a Campbell here," another thick Highland voice called out, and the others agreed until their voices rose again. Brodie and Jamie hurried to Kate's side while Graham unsheathed his sword, prepared to fight.

He did not have to. Dead silence fell upon Camlochlin after the doors behind the angry crowd slammed shut. Slowly, the sea of heads turned toward the entrance. The only sound to be heard was that of Brodie's muttered oath at the sight of his laird.

Callum paused at the doors for just a moment, taking in the scene before him. 'Twas clear by the expressions on Brodie and Jamie's faces, and by Graham's unsheathed blade, what was going on. When he took a step forward, the crowd moved backward like a great waning wave. His eyes, so piercing and deadly, slid to Kate. "Are ye well?"

She nodded, unable to do more. He spoke quietly, but

he looked more dangerous than he had the night at the inn when he cleaved a table in two. He moved slowly, his hands at his sides. Every face found by his wintry gaze paled before turning away. He circled the crowd until he came to stand before Kate. When he took her hand in his, his frown deepened at her trembling.

"My senses"—he raked a lethal glare over each face until he found who he was looking for—"left me long ago, Alasdair. And while I'm more inclined to kill Campbells, I'm no' entirely opposed to killin' MacGregors if the need arises." His burr was thick with suppressed fury, and if Kate was not so terrified for them all, she would have sighed at the sound of him, the safety she felt being with him.

"I've kept ye all protected here. But I warn ye if one of ye speaks unkindly to her, ye'll leave Camlochlin. One way or another." He turned to face her, and Kate was sure he hadn't meant to let his eyes drift over her features so tenderly. They were supposed to be enemies, and after meeting Maggie and hearing of their life in her grandfather's dungeon, Kate understood why Callum would never give her his heart. But here he was protecting her from his own clan. Did he do so because she was more valuable to him alive, or for another reason entirely?

The crowd dispersed with one final and far less dangerous glare bestowed on them by their laird. Brodie sauntered away, digging his sharpened blade into a pear as he went. Angus and Graham left the castle to practice their swordplay, the larger of the two throwing his head back to laugh when Graham threatened to whack him all the way to England.

Maggie tugged on Kate's earasaid and whispered in

her ear when Kate bent to her, and then announced that she was going for a walk. Her brother motioned to Jamie to go with her, a command the young warrior was only too eager to obey.

"Ye look verra bonny, this morn," Kate heard Jamie tell Maggie while he strode out the door behind her.

When they were alone, Callum's gaze drifted over Kate from foot to crown. "Ye look fine, as well." He lifted his fingers to the shiny curls draping her shoulders. "And yer hair." He paused to frown and dropped his gaze to the floor as if fighting some deep emotion. Kate rejoiced when he lost that battle and returned his gaze to her tresses. "Yer hair is pleasin' to look at," he finished quickly.

Kate curtseyed and did her best to conceal her amusement over his loss of composure. "Thank you, Callum."

She tilted her face to study his profile as they began to walk together toward the great hall. He was so tall, so broad compared to her. When he slid his eyes to her and caught her obvious awe, she blushed a true shade of crimson.

"I'm still angry with you," she said in defense of the teasing smile slanting his mouth.

"Truly?" He traced her profile with his bemused gaze. "Ye look rather joyous to me."

Kate shrugged her shoulders. "That is because soon I will be reunited with my beloved betrothed."

"Aye." Callum nodded. "His name has slipped from my memory. Lord Newton of Manchester, is it?"

Kate almost paused in her steps. Hell, what was the name she had given him? It wasn't Newton, was it? "His name is of no importance," she said haughtily, not about to confess that she didn't remember. "There is a more pressing matter I wish to discuss with you."

"Ye have my ear," he said, keeping his gaze ahead.

"It is about my uncle." She cut him a quick side glance, expecting him to scowl or mayhap storm away. He did neither. "I am concerned for you."

"Ye insult me."

"I don't really care." Och, he was scowling now. "Insult will not kill you; Cromwell's army will."

Callum's mouth hooked into an arrogant half smile that made her insides burn. "If his army finds me and comes here, they will die at the hands of MacGregors, MacLeods, and MacKinnons. I intend to kill Argyll, Kate. Nae one will stop me. No' even ye."

"What about Maggie? She does not want you to kill him, either."

He was quiet for a moment, but then he shook his head. When he spoke again, the hard edge in his voice told her this conversation was about to end. "My sister knows who I am."

What in damnation did that mean? "Will you at least consider—"

"Nae."

Och, but he was a stubborn man. "You are making it terribly difficult to like you, MacGregor."

"You like me well enough, Campbell."

She heard the smile in his voice and turned to look up at him. Her steps faltered at the warmth of his gaze. His mask was gone, momentarily tantalizing her with the bare truth of his emotions. His expression darkened with unspoken yearning so replete she drew closer to him, wanting to fling herself into his arms.

" 'Tis a burden, to be sure," he said, "but I am willin' to suffer it."

Kate's brow rose sharply, the slow curl of her lips a direct challenge to his beguiling grin. If he insisted on keeping up his air of detachment, which his eyes told her was a facade, she was not going to make it easy for him. With her heart racing, she reached for him, fitting her hand into his much larger one. She hid her satisfaction when his composure seemed to desert him again, and she leaned in closer to him.

"Though your suffering might be great, I will grant you no pity."

Instead of pulling away, he twined his fingers through hers, binding her to him more intimately. "Ye're a fierce opponent, lass. I'll grant ye that." He took his time looking her over, letting his smile carve into a slow, seductive smirk. "But I'll no' be beaten by a Campbell."

Blast him, but he would not give up! "Aye, as your scarred leg can testify," she replied tartly.

He actually threw his head back and chuckled. Kate stopped walking and gave his hand a tug. Now he stung her pride. If there was one thing she was good at, it was wielding a sword.

"Why do you laugh, Callum? Do you not think I fight well?"

"Aye, I'll admit ye fight well, fer a lass. I saw ye fight against the McColls."

"For a lass?" She snatched back her hand and folded her arms across her chest, drumming her fingers on her elbows. "I could beat you, Callum MacGregor."

Humor danced across his handsome features. Even

though it made Kate angry that he found her amusing, she couldn't help but smile at the sight of his arrogant mirth.

"Let me out of this heavy plaid and meet me outside."

"Och, nae, lass. If I injured ye, I'd never fergive myself."

He was an overbearing ruffian, indeed. But his gentleness with her was what made her move toward him. She missed his arms around her. Blast him again for not missing it, as well. She took another step closer until their toes touched, then tilted her head to meet his gaze. His mouth was so close when he bent his head to her that she felt his breath warm against her lips. "Are you afraid of me, then, MacGregor?" she whispered against his chin and cautiously laid her hands on his chest.

She felt his body respond almost instantly. His muscles tightened. His heart accelerated. Kate rejoiced. She did affect him! It was enough to make her want to kiss him again, though in truth, she had thought of naught else since the first time he laid his mouth on hers. He lifted his arms, ready to enfold her. His breath pulled on a low, ragged groan as his hands touched her back and sank into her curls.

She stepped back, using all her will to do so. She wanted more from him than his kiss, and if she had to battle him to get it, she would. "To the yard, then. And make sure your sword is ready."

He watched her disappear above stairs and ground his teeth at the wonderful agony hardening his loins. "Och, lass, my sword is ready. That's no' a problem."

Chapter Twenty-Two

CALLUM WAS NOT A MAN to waste his time while he waited for Kate to meet him in the practice yard, and that was why Brodie found himself beneath the tip of his laird's sword three different times in the space of two breaths. When Callum finally spotted Kate making her way to him, he waved his cousin away, stabbed the ground with his blade, and leaned on the hilt to admire her. Her skirts flared around her ankles, narrowing at her hips. The bodice she wore revealed her feminine beauty. Her hair, he noticed with a smile that darkened his eyes with desire, was still unbound, whipping across her fearless smile.

"Are you ready for me?" she called out before she reached him, then waved happily to Brodie and Angus, before accepting a lighter sword from Brodie.

"Aye." Callum's eyes drank in every inch of her while his lips curled into something feral. "I'm ready fer ye."

When she faced him, he shook his head at her and

stepped back. "Wait, lass, ye'll wear some protection. Brodie, go fetch—"

Kate's sword glittered in the sun as it descended upon Callum's head. His reflexes were instantaneous, and, yanking his blade from the ground, he deflected the blow, paused, and sent her a stunned glare. She grinned in return and parried his next swing.

"I'd prefer it if ye wore some armor, lass," he said and swiped his blade across her belly.

She leaped backward, easily avoiding the blow. "It hinders me. And I would prefer it if you were not so careful with me." Slinging her sword over her head to gain more momentum, she swung left, then right, then chopped at his flanks. "I can . . ." Her sword met his in a clash of sparks. ". . . defend . . ." She sliced low at his legs. ". . . myself."

"The lass is beatin' his arse!" Angus roared with laughter, then yelped when Brodie cracked him broadside against his temple with the flat of his sword.

"D'ye intend to run me through, Kate?" Callum inquired with a provocative growl that sent fire down Kate's spine.

God's blood, she had to focus her thoughts on fighting him and not on the wickedly erotic grin on his face, the fire in his eyes. He was excited, his senses heightened. He was thoroughly enjoying himself. He looked so physically arousing, she found herself wondering what it would have been like to bed him that eve at the inn. She swung. And missed. His arm shot out and coiled around her waist. With a flick of his wrist, he spun her on her heels and hauled her back against his chest. One hand splayed across her belly, holding her close, while the other held the edge of his blade pressed to her throat. "Yer no' concentratin', Katie lass."

The throaty tangle of his voice against her ear made her nipples spring to life and press against her shift. She fought the titillating effect of him behind her and rammed the hilt of her blade into his ribs.

He released her and bent over slightly, holding his side. Kate leapt away and blew a lock of hair off her cheek.

"I intend to lay you flat on your back, Devil." She gripped her hilt in both hands and readied herself for his next assault. She countered his advance with a strike to his thigh, which he blocked almost too effortlessly. He shook his head, lowering it just a fraction to impale her with his gaze.

"And what will ye do to me when ye get me there, woman?" His voice thickened around that one word, as if to remind her that he could take her, dominate her, possess her. His lusty smile told her he wanted to do just that.

She brought her blade down hard. He leaped to the right, whirled on his boots, and whacked her backside with the flat of his blade. His grin widened when she glowered at him. He moved backward without even bothering to swing while she advanced, slicing at him viciously. "Did I say somethin' that distracted ye again, lass?"

Kate quirked her brow at him, beginning to understand the tactic he chose to employ. The rogue would resort to anything! Devil, indeed. Well, she could be just as devious. "Aye, Callum, the thought of me atop you distracted me." She sliced over his head, and almost took it off. "Or mayhap"—she moved forward, their blades clanging hard with each matched blow—"I would prefer you on your knees."

She attacked. And caught him.

He touched his fingers to the blood staining his shirt-sleeve, then let his smile shine on her fully. "Well done."

"Och, Callum, forgive me!" She lowered her sword, dreadfully sorry that she'd wounded him—again. Before she had time to leap away, he was upon her, clipping the sword from her hands.

"Never show mercy to yer enemy, Katie." His heavy voice enveloped her like smoke. He spoke so tenderly her bones near melted to the marrow.

"I have nae enemy here, my laird MacGregor."

He reached her in one more stride, curled his arm around her waist, and lifted her off her feet into his crushing embrace. He dragged her mouth to his, claiming her with a long, hard, demanding kiss. His broad hand along her back molded her even closer to his rigid angles than she thought possible. His tongue plunged into her mouth, marauding her, stroking her in a dance so seductive she went weak against him. He pulled back from their kiss slowly, his eyes half-closed and burning. "I want ye."

Angus and Brodie had ceased fighting and stared open-mouthed at their laird and the lass clutched in his arms. Then Angus elbowed his smaller companion and the two moved to leave them in privacy. They stopped in midstride when Maggie's screams pierced the heated air.

Callum was the first to reach the barn. Panic coursed through him while his sister's screams echoed through a chamber of his heart he prayed every day to forget. He spotted her crouched behind a bale of hay beside Ahern's stall. She covered her face with her arms and did not look up even when her brother called her name. She wasn't injured, Callum knew by her position—by her terror. She had seen blood.

Kate rushed into the barn next, with Angus and the others. Hearing them enter, Callum turned and lifted his finger to his lips for silence, then motioned for Angus to search the barn. Something had triggered his sister's terror. Where the hell was Jamie?

Callum moved toward Maggie so softly his boots made no sound. When he reached her, he did not touch her but squatted before her. "Maggie, 'tis Callum," he said, his voice riddled with love and tenderness. If she heard him, she made no show of it but sank deeper into the shadows, a low moan vying with Matilda's honking.

Callum looked away from her only once to watch Angus hoist an unconscious Jamie out of the barn. Maggie's dear champion appeared to have fallen from the rafters. A trickle of blood covered his face, but Angus assured them with a quiet nod that the lad was still breathing.

"'Tis all right now, lass." Callum returned his attention to his sister. He knew she was in another place. And he knew where that place was.

"Callum?" her delicate voice touched him so profoundly it pulled a sob from the back of his throat.

He picked her up and cradled her body close to his chest, then turned and almost walked straight into Kate.

"Let's get her to bed," he whispered, holding Maggie closer. He closed his eyes and kissed the top of Maggie's head, then left the barn.

Chapter Twenty-Three

KATE LEANED against the doorframe of Maggie's chambers in silence. As she watched Callum bend to place his sister inside her tent, Kate's heart broke so completely for both of them that it numbed her. She felt the tears burning behind her eyes, but she was careful to hold them in check, for fear they would never stop falling. Her kin had done this—her own grandfather. When Callum rose to his feet, he turned and looked away from Kate's sorrow-filled gaze. He did not want pity. Kate knew it, but it was all she felt at that moment . . . besides the certain knowledge that she had fallen in love with the Devil MacGregor.

"She's asleep," Callum told her and ran his hand through his hair. "Hopefully she will sleep through the night."

"What happened to her today?" Kate asked when he turned to go to the window. "Please. Speak to me about it. What frightened her so, Callum?"

He looked out, remaining silent until Kate thought he would not tell her. Or he could not bring himself to. Then, with a muffled groan that seemed to wilt his broad shoulders, he finally spoke. "She is afraid of blood. It covered her, smothered her . . ." He turned to look at the tent again and swallowed back a well of emotions Kate feared he might never release. "Ye would think she'd abhor the confines of such a wee place, but it comforts her." Slowly, he faced Kate, ready to tell her what he had wished, had prayed to forget since the day they had escaped six years ago. "Liam Campbell kept my sister in a cage suspended just a stone's throw away from me." He forced himself to go on even though the horror on Kate's face clearly made him want to cease. "At first, I thought she would go mad. She was just a babe. Imagine what it must have been like cramped in a prison an inch larger than yer crumpled body." He ran his palm over the soft leather of Maggie's haven, his voice a loving whisper. "Argyll's men used to come and drag her oot and stretch her until she screamed from the agony of it." His haunted gaze found Kate's again. "I had to kill them, Kate," he said, moving toward her. "I butchered them. I killed them all with my sister clingin' to my back. I could no' stop, even knowin' what I forced her to witness."

"I understand," Kate told him softly, barely able to breathe. She suspected he was asking for her absolution. She gave it.

He took her hand and sat on the bed, pulling her down gently to sit beside him. "Nae, lass, ye dinna understand. D'ye know what she saw? 'Twas ugly, Kate. So ugly she makes herself ferget. But sometimes . . ." he paused, looking like he could not go on. "Sometimes she awakens from her dreams and she remembers."

It was then that Kate saw in his eyes the thing that

plagued him, that had utterly destroyed him. It was not the years of horror spent in a dungeon but guilt and self-reproach at what his sister had watched him do to escape it that twisted his features and dulled his eyes to a lifeless blue. "My sister would rather go back to the cage than to that one day and the blood I poured upon her. Yer uncle is right to call me a devil."

Kate walked along the shoreline, letting the frothy surf soak her feet. She barely felt the water chilling her flesh. Her thoughts were fixed on the dark, foreboding fortress before her, and on the man inside.

Callum MacGregor had survived the abyss of hell. He saved his sister from it, but what he had to become in the process near brought Kate to her knees.

Her tears fell heavy into the waves rolling beneath her feet. She could not weep this way in front of Callum, for his shoulders already carried enough, so she had left him and wept with unabashed abandon until the sun dipped below the loch. He had killed the men of her grandfather's garrison in a massacre that had made him a legend, and he believed it cost him the only thing he'd ever had the chance to love. His sister.

But Maggie *did* love him. Dear God, if Robert had saved her from such a cruel existence, Kate never would consider him anything less than the bravest of men. Maggie had many evils from her past with which to live, but Kate was certain that Callum was not among them.

Chapter Twenty-Four

CALLUM WAS NOT in Maggie's room when Kate returned. Aileen sat by the bed, working a small piece of embroidery by the light of a single candle. She looked up when she heard Kate enter.

"I'm to call Callum when she awakens," the handmaiden advised her, laying the embroidery in her lap. "Mayhap 'twould be wise if she did not see ye when she . . ." Her voice faded as she set her eyes on the tent. "Ye are a Campbell, after all."

Kate squared her shoulders and crossed the room to stand in front of her. "I will not leave. Whether you like it or not, I care for her."

Aileen peered at her through narrowed eyes, and Kate braced herself for the contempt bequeathed to her because of her name.

"Ye wield a sword right fine, ye do," Aileen complimented instead. "Even Graham is impressed with ye."

"My brother taught me." Kate began to smile, but then

her eyes opened wide. "Oh, heavens, I did not clean Callum's wound!"

"Aye, everyone's talkin' aboot how ye clipped the laird." Aileen's deep blue eyes fair glimmered in the soft firelight of the chambers. "Would ye teach me to fight like that?"

"Of course, but it was not my intention to hurt him, I assure you." Kate began looking around the room for what she would need to tend to Callum. She found a small basin of water and a strip of cloth beside Maggie's bed. "But I should tend to him. Aileen, please send him to me posthaste."

"Aye, m'lady." Aileen gathered her things, offered Kate a swift curtsey, then headed for the door.

When Aileen left the room, Kate crossed the rushes and crouched before the tent. She peeked inside. The wee lass was sound asleep, snoring, in fact. Kate gently removed a piece of straw from Maggie's hair and sighed. "Bless you, sweeting."

She waited for Callum, growing more apprehensive as the moments passed. Why did she send for him, she asked herself, dipping the cloth into the bowl. He had probably cleaned the wound himself. Why did she tell Aileen to make haste? God help her, she loved him. She lifted her hands to her throat. Loving him would most likely get her killed . . . or branded. Nae, Robert would never allow it. But what in damnation would become of her? Callum didn't love her. She was going back to Glen Orchy, or to Kildun. Once her uncle was dead she would never see Callum again. Her use to him would be over. She remembered his kisses and patted her flushed cheek with her wet hand. Callum MacGregor was passionate in his hatred—and his kisses. Her gaze drifted over the bed, and she quivered. She wrung the cloth until it was almost dry again. "God's breath, he makes me feel feverish."

"I hope the 'he' ye refer to is me, lass."

Kate whirled around, nearly knocking over the bowl of water. Callum stood in the doorway, blocking out the light from the hall. When he stepped inside he wore a smile that was becoming as familiar to her as his fearsome scowls, and even more mesmerizing. He closed the door behind him, coiling Kate's nerves into a springy mess. "Ye sent fer me?" he asked when she didn't answer his first query.

"I . . . I remembered your wound and meant to clean it."

His eyes fell to her trembling hands when she plunged them in the water again and snatched the cloth. She held it up, dripping water down her elbow. "See?"

He raised one dark brow and nodded, then crossed the room. Kate watched him check on his sister as she had. When he turned to face her, his expression unguarded and achingly tender, Kate saw the victory in this battle. She wanted it. She would have it.

"Where d'ye want me?"

"Closer." She let her heart speak for her.

"Careful, woman," he warned, his voice a deep-throated rasp. "Ye tempt me to throw ye on that bed and kiss ye until ye faint in my arms."

"I fear," she said, casting all she had left to win him to the battle winds, "if you do not kiss me, I will faint that much faster."

He was already moving toward her, helpless to resist. Cupping her face in his hands, he tilted her head upward. He gazed deep into her eyes, laying bare the tortured remnants of his heart while he swept his thumb over the delicate curve of her lower lip, parting her lips to receive him. He covered her mouth with his, caressing her, breathing her, consuming her, surrendering to her.

Kate opened her mouth to take him fully, clutching his plaid in both hands as his kiss deepened with barely checked desire. His arms closed around her, enfolding her in his protection, his strength, his desire. Here was what she longed for, to be here with him, just like this, cherished and treasured.

"I love you," she whispered when he pulled back slowly, searing her nerves with his hungry gaze. "I cannot stop myself, no matter what our names are. No matter who protests it."

He withdrew from her, and she watched in sorrow as he closed his eyes, distancing himself from her again. "It was difficult." She fought to keep her voice light. "You are not an easy man to care for, Callum. And Maggie loves you, as well. How can you not know that? Let us love you and prove you are no devil."

A low-pitched moan drew Kate's gaze back to the tent.

The flap opened, and Maggie left the comfort of her safe haven. She stopped upon seeing her brother. Kate paled at the hollow, vacant look in Maggie's large eyes. Maggie stared at Callum but didn't seem to see him at all.

A moment later, Kate knew the horrible truth of it. Maggie did see him, and she was afraid. She was terrified.

"They were dead," she said in a quivering voice that teetered on the edge of madness. "All of them were dead."

Callum did not blink. In fact, Kate was stunned to find his gaze on his sister almost as empty as Maggie's.

"His head. His head fell away."

"Kate?" At the sound of Callum's voice speaking her

name, Kate near leaped off the floor. "Ye should leave now."

"Nae."

"Callum." Maggie's voice shattered on a throaty sob. She swiped her hands over her face. "The blood was on me!"

"Aye, Maggie, I know," her brother whispered on a strangled moan of his own.

"Nae more!" she shouted. Huge tears teetered on her lashes, and her bottom lip trembled. "'Twas on my hands." Suddenly she ran to her brother and he caught her up in his arms. "Ye must cease! Please, cease!"

Callum held her, but he did not speak, and Kate knew it was his own guilt that silenced him. He had caused this terror.

"Cease, Callum!" Maggie screamed, and he closed his eyes, helpless to do anything more.

"Oh, dear God." Kate breathed, seeing the images of what happened that day. Callum had carried his tiny sister over his shoulder while he hacked at men from every direction. Nine years of torture, of watching his sister suffer, of hearing her scream, helpless to stop it. He lived in hell and had become a monster painted red with the blood of his victims.

"Please . . . nae more." Maggie's wails faded into a muffled sob. "Or they will surely kill ye."

"I'm sorry, Maggie, m'love." Callum groaned into her hair. He was only faintly aware of Kate slipping quietly from the room.

Chapter Twenty-Five

KATE CLOSED THE DOOR behind her and then sank down it. Graham and Jamie appeared over her an instant later.

"Come away," Graham urged gently while Jamie stared at the door, anguished by the sounds coming from inside, a slightly bloodstained bandage wrapped around his flaxen head. "All will be well with them."

Kate buried her face in her hands and wept softly. "If my grandfather was not already dead, I vow I would kill him myself."

Graham knelt beside her and then helped her to her feet. "Ye look like ye could use a warm cup of mead." He called over his shoulder as he led her away. "Come, Jamie, leave Maggie to her brother."

"I'll stay," Jamie called back, still staring at the door.

Graham brought Kate to the solar rather than to the great hall, since many of the men would be settling down for the eve. The only drink in the solar was whiskey, so Graham warmed it by the hearth fire and poured her a cup. Cool night air chilled the room. He pulled two oversized chairs closer to the fire and covered her shoulders with a blanket.

Kate folded her legs under her and sipped her brew. When she blanched, Graham laughed and warned her to go easy, lest she singe her insides.

"It does burn going down, doesn't it?"

" 'Tis another of old Gillis's concoctions," he told her, settling into the chair opposite her. " 'Twill warm ye fer certain."

She took another sip, slower this time, and stared into the flames. "Will it help me forget what my grandfather did to them? I do not blame Callum if he killed him."

"Callum did not kill him," Graham assured her. "If he had, mayhap he would have been satisfied."

Kate nodded, then looked at him beneath the veil of her lashes, too ashamed to look at him directly. "Did my father know of this?"

"I don't know."

Kate drank more of her brew and thought about everything. After a few moments, she spoke again. "Callum thinks he is a monster in Maggie's eyes. But she is not afraid of him, Graham. She's afraid *for* him. She wants him to stop fighting his war."

The commander swallowed a mouthful of whiskey, then closed his eyes as fire lanced through him. "I am afraid fer him, too," he admitted and leaned back in his chair. "He's determined to kill yer uncle. When he does, I fear the full power of the realm will come down upon him. Argyll knows it, as well, and taunts Callum with his cruelties against MacGregor women."

Kate shivered beneath her blanket. She knew her uncle was depraved. "He never came for us when we were chil-

dren, though he promised to. He left us for the servants
and my father's guardsmen to raise. As I grew older, he
paid more attention to me than to Robert. I found out why
last winter when he tried to kiss me."

Graham leaned forward in his chair and set his flagon
on the floor. His gaze on Kate was unblinking, his voice
low with controlled anger. "Does Robert know?"

"I never told him," Kate said. "I hope Duncan never
finds us," she added into her cup.

"Us?"

When she looked at him, Graham was watching her with
a mixture of concern and admiration sparking his gaze.

"'Tis a dangerous thing to align yerself with *us,* Kate."
Graham's expression softened when she hiccupped.
"Feeling better, are ye?"

She nodded and focused her attention on him. With the
firelight softening his beguiling features and pouty
mouth, he looked more angelic than even his younger
brother. "I'm glad to see Jamie has recovered."

"Aye. 'Twas a minor wound. He fell from the rafters
saving Maggie's cat."

"Who taught him such chivalry?" Kate smiled at Graham and cuddled deeper into her blanket.

The commander poured her more brew, his roguish
grin proving to Kate it was not him who taught his
brother such noble ideals. "Jamie is young."

"He cares so for Maggie."

"Then he is foolish, as well."

Kate regarded him while he smiled into his cup, his
dimples twinkling in the flickering light. She was quite
fond of Graham. From the moment they met he had
treated her kindly. Though he was fiercely devoted to

Callum, he had never shown her contempt because of her name. He was kind and terribly charming. With that halo of curls falling carelessly over eyes of deep emerald, and a sinful smile that could melt the heart of the most stoic matron at twenty paces, it was not surprising that almost every woman in Camlochlin sought his attention.

"Love is not foolish, Commander."

He looked up. "I was bred fer war. 'Tis the only thing lasting and constant in this life. Love is fleeting."

"I see you laughing quite often with Aileen," Kate pointed out, "Do you mean to tell me you feel nothing for her?"

"Aye, I care fer her deeply. She is my sister."

"Och, forgive my hasty assumption." Kate blushed all the way to her roots.

"My sisters Sineag, Murron, and Mary live in the bothys outside the castle with their husbands and bairns."

Kate's eyes widened. "How many sisters have you here?"

"Just the four. But I have eleven sisters in all."

"How wonderful to grow up in a large family."

"Nae." He laughed. "I learned more about women than I'll ever need to know. The rest live in Edinburgh and Moray. One has even taken a Campbell fer a husband." He nodded when Kate raised an eyebrow. "This feud began long ago, and though it wasn't our feud to fight, the Grants have always been good friends to the MacGregors. Yer grandsire was a cruel man, but not all Campbells are like him. Ye, fer one, are quite enchanting." He couldn't help but grin at the delicate flush painting her cheeks. "And I did grow fond of Robert during my stay at Kildun."

Kate's eyes grew misty upon hearing about her

brother. It felt like centuries since last she saw him. "How is he, Graham? I miss him terribly. Tell me, how did you come to know him?"

The commander dipped his eyes to his drink and then quaffed the remainder of its contents before he spoke. "I was sent to Kildun to befriend yer uncle and gain his trust."

"Why?"

"Because Callum could not infiltrate Kildun. I was to lead Argyll's men to—"

Angus and Brodie saved him from having to continue by crashing open the solar door. "There ye are, ye knave." Angus entered first, a flagon of brew clutched in his giant paw. When Kate belched and waved at them, the brutish Highlander smiled like a puppy that had just been petted behind the ears.

"I guessed Graham was spendin' his night wi' a bonny lass. I was right."

"That makes one time in yer accursed life." Brodie snickered and moseyed inside. He found a seat, fell into it, and closed his eyes.

"Brodie, why are ye not in bed with yer wife?" Graham asked him, ignoring the string of oaths muttered by Angus while he searched for a place to sit.

"Because there's nae room fer me in our bloody bed. If Netta doesna deliver soon, I'm leavin' her."

Angus howled with laughter, but Kate frowned at them all. She wanted to chastise them, and she knew she should. She just could not remember what for. She did suddenly remember her conversation with Graham, though, and turned back to him.

"Did Robert send you all to Glen Orchy?"

"Nae," Graham said. "In truth, he was against our going."

"Think ye he's still wrapped aroond that gate ye tied him to?" asked Brodie, opening one eye.

"Tied . . . to a gate?" Slowly, Kate turned to fasten her eyes on Graham. "You tied my brother to a gate?"

"Brodie, ye bleedin' whoreson," Angus barked at him. "Ye made her weep." He looked around the solar. "Where are all the fokin' chairs?"

"Angus, mind yer damn tongue," Brodie admonished him sternly.

"Well, did you?" Kate demanded, untangling herself from the blanket. She would have leaped from her chair, but she felt dizzy and clutched the arms instead to keep from spinning. "Was he not your friend?"

Graham was about to tell her when the door opened again and Callum filled the doorway. His eyes fired with something so dangerous, Graham instinctively bolted to his feet. Callum's gaze wandered over each of them in turn and then came to rest on Kate.

"Ye'll tell me where yer goin' from now on, Kate."

"And you will never speak to me again, you heartless ruffian." She yanked the blanket completely off and sprang to her feet. Then almost toppled over. Graham caught her by the elbows. She didn't take her eyes off Callum while she righted herself. "You tied my brother to a *gate?*"

"Nae, Graham did," Callum told her.

She opened her mouth to tell him what she thought of him and burped instead.

In his chair, Brodie leaned his head back, closed his eyes, and smiled.

"Which one of ye gave her the brew?" Callum demanded, suspecting Angus.

"Graham did," Kate told him. "And though he is a very sweet man, I shall never forgive him for tying my brother to a gate."

"Ye should be thankin' him, lass," Angus said before downing the contents of his flagon. "'Twas Graham who convinced Callum to spare the lad's life."

Callum shot Angus a murderous glare, which Angus answered by stepping behind Brodie's chair.

Kate blinked up at the commander and then took a step toward him. Graham moved back, unsure if she meant to hug him or rake out his eyes. She swayed on her feet for a moment, then turned her green-tinted face to Callum. "I feel ill."

Callum watched her pass out in Graham's arms, then sent his friend a scorching look before he snatched her from him and tossed her over his shoulder.

"Send Aileen back to Maggie's room," he commanded. "And if ye ever feed Gillis's brew to her again, I'll remove the teeth from yer head." He narrowed his eyes on the other two before he left. "Ye'll watch what ye say in front of her, or I'll take ye both to the fields and thrash yer godforsaken hides."

When he stormed out, slamming the door behind him, Brodie looked up at Angus and then both men roared with laughter. "Our laird is turnin' soft!"

"Aye." Graham felt his mouth hook into a smile while he stared at the door. "Finally."

Chapter Twenty-Six

KATE SLEPT SOUNDLY nestled beneath the warm furs on Callum's bed while he watched her well into the night. At first he paced before the bed, torn between his body aching for her and his heart aching to send her away. Dear Christ, she loved him. Was she daft? Didn't she understand that it was a death sentence for her? God's blood, it was his fault. He knew she didn't hate him. He had done nothing to stop her tender smiles. He let her think him a hero of sorts. He'd kissed her and more, knowing . . . He should have done all to protect her, for he was the gravest danger to her well-being. He'd even brought her to his bed! God, he wanted her there. He could not even think properly around her. And now, in her innocence, she had fallen in love with him. He might as well have killed her.

After the first hour of pacing like an anguished lion, he finally sat in the corner in a chair hidden by shadows. Flames from the hearth lit Kate's sleeping face and he watched her while another hour passed away. He already knew every contour of her features, every bonny curve that shaped her. He longed to know more of her. But the cost was too great. She had fallen into his arms, pierced by an arrow meant for him. How was he to know at the time that she would wreak such havoc on his heart? He was so sure of his defenses he hadn't bothered to guard them. And in so doing, he allowed her entrance into his hell. He had dragged her to his fortress and scribed the word *death* onto her forehead.

He clenched his teeth, his fists. He tossed his head back, needing to curse the heavens. He had hauled Maggie through the gates of damnation to save her. From what? He had become the very demons he sought to kill. And now he did the same thing to Kate. Death to Mac-Gregor sympathizers. 'Twas the motto of the realm. *God, nae.* He knew he had no right to ask the Almighty for anything. *But please, just this one thing.* "Please," he whispered. "Strengthen me."

He stood up, determined to do what he must. She was forced. Taken against her will. Aye, 'twas all she had to tell them. He had not taken her. She remained unblemished. There was only sympathy. And sympathy was easy to destroy.

He walked to the edge of the bed and squatted, bringing his face close to hers. She was his redemption for sins he thought too foul to be forgiven. But he could not accept her gracious gift without putting her in mortal peril. His hatred ran deep, with no room for love. He would make her believe it. He would do it in order to save her life.

"I'll no' love ye, Kate Campbell. No' ever." He rose to

his feet, vowing to himself that she would never know what a tortured liar he was.

~

Kate dragged her eyelids open and then slammed them shut again at the ray of sunshine blaring like a herald's trumpet through the window. Lifting her hand to her head, she released a groan that sounded to her poor ears like she was dying. And she felt like she was doing just that. She willed herself not to move, since even the merest breath shot bolts of pain to her head. Damn old Gillis and his poison. After a few moments of reeling, she slowly lifted her lids again.

God's blood, what happened to the window coverings? She shifted as cautiously as her body would allow in order to escape the blinding beam of light. Thick cobwebs tangled her thoughts and muddled her brain, and then, like a curtain being drawn, she realized she was in an unfamiliar room, a strange bed. Still too pained to move her head, her eyes darted left and right. The ceiling offered her no answers, so with great effort she sat up, still holding her head to keep it in place.

She was in a man's room, that much was clear to her. Everything in the room was carved of dark waxed wood. Even the walls were paneled with thick slabs of it, making all the furniture in the room blend into an enormous view of deep magenta brown. An intricately carved wardrobe, taller even then Callum, stood between two great chairs that could seat at least two people each. There were three tables set up to house everything from tankards of whiskey to a carved wooden chess set and assorted weapons. A silver bowl for hand and face washing rested on another table, along with a small candlestand. No tapestries decorated the walls; neither shield nor banner offered cheer. The windows were bare, and the absence of draperies around the poster bed told Kate that whoever slept here cared nothing about privacy. Yet despite the absence of color and fabric to offer warmth, the cavernous chamber heated Kate to the deepest corners of her heart. Of course, there was the giant alcoved hearth with its roaring fire to warm the bones, but Kate knew instinctively what made her feel like she belonged here all her life. It smelled like Callum, of wild heather and mist. *Aye,* she thought, closing her eyes to draw him to her. This was his chamber, his bed.

She was still smiling when Callum entered the room.

The sight of Kate sitting in his bed, her lush ebony curls tumbling around her shoulders and arms, set Callum's heart to pounding. He experienced a sudden rush of something so strong he near doubled over. When she turned her head and aimed her heady smile at him, he had the urge to drop to his knees and pay her the homage she deserved. He almost smiled.

Death to MacGregor sympathizers.

He scowled so fiercely at her it wiped the smile clean off her face. Propelling himself forward, he avoided her gaze while he crossed the chamber and stopped at the window.

"Is all well with you?" she asked, sensing by his cold, hard gaze that it wasn't. Her voice was low, pained, but Callum did not turn to look at her.

"Nae," he answered tightly. He gazed out the window at the distant heather. "There's a Campbell in my castle."

Kate's mouth fell open, and her heart drummed so

violently she felt it in her belly. She didn't hear him right. She couldn't have. "But I had hoped . . . Callum, you kissed me."

Now he looked at her over his shoulder. His eyes glimmered like cold cobalt glass against the sun. "Poor judgment on my part, nothin' more."

Kate sat, numb. Tears pooled her eyes and dripped over her lashes when she blinked at him. His eyes hardened on her. "Ye're leavin', Kate. My men will escort ye to the Stewarts' home on the morrow. Once ye arrive, ye'll tell their laird that ye escaped the clutches of the fearsome MacGregors. Tell him the truth, that the Devil abducted ye. Ask him to send fer yer brother. He will come fer ye, I've nae doubt. If ye see yer uncle alive, tell him I will come fer him."

"Why?" It was all Kate trusted herself to say. Her throat ached from the burden of smothering her sobs.

He turned back to the window and folded his hands behind his back. "I dinna need to give ye a reason."

"I want one!" she shouted at him. That her shout sounded more like a withered screech did not surprise her. Her head exploded with the aftereffects of Gillis's brew, and her heart ached to leap from her chest and into Callum's arms.

"Verra well, Kate. I'm weary of ye. I admit 'twas curious to have a Campbell in my midst that I didna want to kill. But I realize now that I canna . . ." He paused and closed his eyes, then gritted his teeth. "I canna stand the sight of ye. Leave my bed. Leave my castle. I dinna want ye here anymore."

Callum thought she would weep. He prepared himself for it. She loved him, 'twas obvious by the way she looked at him, spoke to him. She lit up like a brilliant morning sky when he entered a room, and he had just stomped the light out. He expected her to weep, to carry on the way a woman would. But when she rose from his bed and left him without a word to wither her dignity, he clenched his teeth to stop himself from shouting her name and ordering her to come back to him.

Kate ran directly to the garderobe, where she promptly expelled what was left in her stomach. Callum's cruel words echoed mercilessly through her mind. Over and over again she was forced to relive his rebuke. He had stood by that window like a warlord cast in stone, his back set straight like an arrow. God help her, but she understood why he hated her so. She did not blame him. She had hated the MacGregors, and she had not gone through one day of torture. He had every right to throw her out of Camlochlin. He had told her from the beginning that he would return her to her brother. She knew he could never love her, but she thought . . . She had hoped . . . Nae, she wept. It was her own fault for falling in love with him, for loving his home, and aye, she would declare proudly, his kin.

To Graham, who stood on the other side of the garderobe door, Kate sounded anything but proud. His heart wrenched at the rawness of her sobs, and for the first time in all the years he had known his dearest friend, he cursed the terrible beast who did this to her.

Chapter Twenty-Seven

KATE SPENT THE MORNING of her expulsion from Camlochlin alone. She refused Graham's offer to speak with Callum about his decision for her to leave. She didn't answer when Maggie knocked at her door, pleading with her to eat something. Kate didn't want food. She wanted to be someone else. She wanted to be a MacGregor. His woman, his love. But Callum had no love to give her. He seemed at times to be made only of hatred and anger. But there was more to him, she knew. There was humor and tenderness, and passion. A man whose eyes fired with pride and purpose when he spoke his name. A champion to his sister, and to her.

God, she didn't want to leave and never see his face again.

But she had pride, also, and she sat up finally and wiped her eyes. She would not spend her last day with this proud clan weeping with self-pity. She would let them know that not all Campbells were afraid to face their fate.

Callum stood on the battlements an hour later, heedless of the cold air blowing off Sgurr Na Stri. His eyes fastened on the woman in the training field with Jamie below, bracing her body as she slipped an arrow into its bow. She aimed, mindless of the satiny tendrils blowing across her face, and let the arrow fly. Callum's lips lifted into a slight smile of victory on her behalf.

He heard Graham's footfalls behind him long before the commander reached him. He did not turn around, nor did he take his eyes off Kate when Graham cleared his throat to announce his presence.

Reaching him, Graham leaned his elbows on the wall and followed Callum's gaze. "Brodie said ye changed yer mind about hunting this morn."

"Aye."

When Callum said nothing more and continued to watch Kate, Graham exhaled a slight sigh. "Yer eyes are verra telling, brother. Why do ye send her away when ye do not want her to go?"

"She's a Campbell." Callum slid his gaze to Graham for a moment before returning it to Kate. "She doesna belong here."

"That may be so, but it is not the reason you do this," Graham argued. "Are ye in love with her, Callum?"

"Nae."

"Aye, that's good to know." Graham gave him a pat on the back while he let his gaze rove over the woman below. "Because she's quite bonny and were it me, I'd not be able to think of anything but her in her betrothed's bed."

Callum whirled around and stormed away from him.

Graham heard the furious pacing behind him and smiled. Callum did care for the lass. Why, he was as jealous as a squire who just found his milkmaid in the hay with someone else. The commander decided to use that jealousy to convince his friend how foolish he was being. "I hope fer her sake her husband is not old. Someone as braw as she deserves a man who can satisfy her spirited appetite."

"What d'ye want, Graham?" Callum clenched his teeth at Graham's back.

"Want?" Graham turned and offered him an innocent shrug. "I want her to be happy. I like her. I pray to the saints the bastard does not beat her."

Callum's glacial glare was enough to make Graham clamp his mouth shut. "I know what yer thinkin', Graham. But I dinna love her, so cease yer games with me. She's a Campbell, my enemy, and she belongs with her kin."

"She is not yer enemy, Callum. She's in love with ye," Graham insisted quietly, more serious now.

"Then she's a fool!" Callum's voice exploded into a thunderous roar.

Ah, Graham thought, understanding finally. "Yer heart is set on protecting her, but think. She is *in love* with you. She is no longer safe anywhere but beside you."

Callum shook his head, refusing to be moved. "She knows the law. She will ferget me soon enough."

Graham held his palm up in surrender. "Verra well, then." He'd had enough and pushed himself off the wall. "I do not know who ye are anymore, if there's even a heart in ye left to save. But hear me, Callum MacGregor, if there be any part of ye that's still human." At his words, Callum blinked as though he'd been struck. "I'll have no part in delivering her into the hands of her uncle. And I'll pray that when she's returned she will have the sense to keep her true feelings silent. But fer hell's sake, look at her!" He set his eyes on her, obeying his own command. "She's as open and honest as a babe. They'll know her heart the moment they speak yer name."

"Then I must make certain her heart is against me."

Graham heard Callum's footfalls and turned to see where his friend was going, but Callum was already gone.

⁓

Callum charged down the stairs, taking three and four at a time. Let Graham think what he would of him, Callum was going to make Kate hate him.

When she came into his sight, his lips hardened into a tight line across his face, and his eyes glittered like a winter's night.

Kate stepped back when she saw him, then returned her attention to Jamie and motioned with her sword to continue practicing. But six feet, three inches of brawny male moving swiftly toward her was difficult to ignore. She bit her lip and almost lost a finger when Jamie swung at her.

Callum snatched Jamie's sword from his hand and shoved him away, all in one fluid motion. He rounded on Kate, a giant warrior with the cold promise of death in his gaze. "Ready yerself, Kate, or there will be one less Campbell in Scotland."

"Callum, I . . ." She began to tell him that she did not want to practice with him. She was frightened by his rage. But he swung, and the thunderclash of his blade against hers near knocked her off her feet.

At first Kate could only stare at him, in stunned disbelief that he would strike her with such force. Then he lifted his sword over his head, gripping the hilt with both hands, and she knew he was going to kill her if she did not fight back. She forced herself to stop thinking like a woman and act as a warrior. She parried another bone-crunching blow. Leaping backward, she braced her legs for his oncoming assault. Completely on the defense, she managed to block three more swings.

Just a few moments later she was gasping for breath, her hair damp with sweat and her muscles burning and quivering with spent strength. Even the McColls had not exhausted her this quickly. Then it was over. One hammering clash that rattled her teeth, and then one more that sent her heavy blade careening to the ground.

Callum advanced one step and pointed the tip of his flashing claymore at her throat. "How does it feel to be so close to death, Kate?" With the metal cold against her throat, he moved his body closer to hers and leaned down until his their noses almost touched. When he spoke, his voice lowered to a bear's growl. "Remember this day and the fear that suffocates ye. Ye might believe yer ready to face death fer noble reasons, but when the time comes, nothin' will matter but yer life. Remember this and dinna be a fool."

Kate closed her eyes, unable to breathe. He clutched her heart in his hand as he had promised. Why didn't he just kill her and be done with it? Was he so cruel that he would torture and tease her first? Nae, she had seen him comfort his sister. She saw the terrible pain in his eyes when he became Maggie's beast. He wasn't any of the things so many people believed him to be. He was proud and possessive, a defiant rebel who had given his clan a home and kept their name alive. He was a man who had become a monster to protect what he loved.

"Love is the noblest cause of all, Callum MacGregor," she said as defiantly as he spoke his name.

He shook his head at her. The flash of emotion that colored his eyes absorbed most of the hard edge in his voice. "Nae, 'tis poison to us both."

He walked away, pleading with God that she could hate him. If she couldn't, he would butcher any who punished her—and everyone else, until he drowned in their blood and ceased to exist altogether.

Chapter Twenty-Eight

KATE WATCHED HIM walk away. Every muscle in her body convulsed with the need to go after him. But she did not dare move. He had made his feelings for her more than clear. She could not bear to suffer them again.

She hugged herself to drive out the chill of a coming storm and swept her gaze across the wild moorlands and jagged mountain ridges swathed in mist. She had thought it beautiful here when she first arrived. But now Camlochlin felt harsh and infinitely lonely. It was a land as battle-scarred and unforgiving as her MacGregor. She would never touch him. Finally, she surrendered. She wanted to go home. She wanted her brother.

She scanned the surrounding hills. Was Robert close? Or at the other end of the Earth?

She was going to be taken back to Kildun, but Robert would not be there. She knew with her whole heart that her brother was searching for her. She had been so preoccupied living in her new pretend kingdom that she had not thought about what would happen if he found her.

Now the reality of it beat against her heart. If he came here, Callum would surely kill him. He had promised not to harm her brother, but Callum's hatred for her clan was too strong. He could scarcely stop himself from killing *her*. Robert would not fare any better if he found her on her way back to the Stewarts'. Chivalry would dictate that he fight for her honor. He might be able to kill one of Callum's men, but he would fall swiftly after that. Kate did not want her brother or any of Callum's men to die.

There was only one way to stop it.

~

Robert Campbell gritted his teeth as each bone-crunching blow Kevin Menzie delivered to Roderick Cameron resounded off the keep walls. One more and Robert would put a stop to it. He cut his gaze to his uncle standing a few inches away. The man was grinning!

"The Devil was here," Kevin spat, clutching the laird's plaid in his fists. "Ye'll tell us where he went, or we'll put fire to the whole fokin' village."

"I have no' seen him," Cameron said for the fourth time, blood dripping from his mouth and nose.

"He killed seven of my kinsmen!" Kevin lifted his fist to strike him again.

The blow was halted in midair by Robert's hand. "Cease this!" he shouted.

Kevin spun around, ready to strike him instead, but the murderous glint in Robert's eyes gave him pause. Then he smiled. "Or what? What will ye do? Go back to Glen Orchy and rut yer sheep. Ye have no stomach fer violence."

Robert's scorching gaze was unflinching. "Touch me and find out."

"Nephew." his uncle's voice dipped with mocking iciness as he took a step forward. Robert did not look at Duncan while he spoke, but at the Cameron laird. What honor was there in tying an old warrior to a chair and beating him senseless? "This man hinders us from finding your sister. Why do you seek to protect him? Allow Kevin to finish his questions so that we can save Katherine before the Devil kills her, if he hasn't done so already."

Robert caught the subtle look the Cameron gave him beneath his swollen eyelid. Kate was not dead. "I wish to speak to the chieftain alone."

"Nae," Duncan refused.

Now Robert turned to look at him. "Aye, or I will set my steed toward England and bring this matter to Cromwell, as it should have been done from the beginning."

For a moment their gazes locked in battle. The challenge in Duncan's cool gray eyes was unmistakable, but Robert would not be swayed. Finally, his uncle nodded and motioned for the Menzies to leave.

The instant they were alone, Robert bent to the laird and clutched his shoulders. "You have seen my sister. Tell me, was she harmed?"

"Nae."

"Where has he taken her?" When Cameron didn't answer, Robert shook him. "You give your loyalty to a man who butchered Menzies."

"Ask your uncle why the Devil killed them," Cameron replied weakly. "Better yet, go see fer yerself at Stuart MacGregor's cottage."

Robert pulled away from him and raked his hands through his hair. Hell, he didn't want to see. He'd waited his whole life to serve the realm, to fight at his uncle's side. But this was not fighting. This was something else entirely.

"Go to the cottage, young Campbell, and see what made yer sister weep."

"First you will tell me where he took her, and then I will see."

~

Robert left Rhona MacGregor's bedside, stepped out of the bothy, and summoned every ounce of strength he had in him not to retch. Instead, he set his eyes on his uncle staring at him from atop his mount.

"Why was she branded?"

"She broke the law, as did her husband and child. All Scotsmen have the authority to hold MacGregors to the law in any way they see fit. You know this."

Aye, Robert knew it, but seeing how the proscription was enforced was quite different than hearing about it. Infection festered in Rhona MacGregor's flesh. She would not live another se'nnight. And for what? Because of her name?

"You do not hold sympathy for them, eh, Robert?" his uncle asked him, his eyes as sharp as twin blades. "The Devil, and any other MacGregor chieftain, would cut off your limbs and scatter them to the four winds just to satisfy their bloodlust. This is the only way to keep them under control. It has been this way for many years. Now tell me where he has taken Katherine. I grow weary of your curiosity."

Robert strode toward his mount, spitting the foul taste from his mouth as he went. "East." He told his uncle what Cameron had said. "The Devil took her east toward Badenoch."

Chapter Twenty-Nine

"COME INSIDE WITH YE, Maggie. 'Tis goin' to rain." Callum knelt over his sister lying on her back in the cool heather not far from the castle.

She opened her eyes and smiled at him. Then she scowled, making no move to obey his gentle command. "Why did ye send Kate away? Jamie says ye hate her."

Callum blew out an explosive sigh and lifted his eyes to the hills so as not to meet his sister's accusing stare. He did not want to be discussing Kate. Not when the very thought of her made his arms ache with the need to hold her. He was doing the right thing, he told himself. Finally. "I dinna hate her," he answered. "But 'tis no' safe fer her to be here with us . . . with me."

When he looked at her again, she caught and held his gaze. Her brows quirked curiously at him. "Is it true, then, Callum?"

"Is what true?"

"Do ye think ye are so dangerous that even I fear ye?"

Her question was so unexpected, Callum simply stared

at her, unsure of how to answer. His sending Kate away had naught to do with him. Or did it? He was the Devil MacGregor, and all of hell would descend on the Campbells if Kate was harmed. Aye, what he could become frightened him. If anyone should understand that, 'twas his sister.

"Kate spoke true, then," Maggie said when the memories that haunted him darkened his expression. "Ye're no devil, brother. But ye are a fool," she scolded, though her voice was as tender as his had always been to her. "Ye took me away from that terrible place. Ye gave me back my life."

Callum had never hoped for absolution such as this. He had also never wept a day in his life, and he damn well was not about to begin now. "But yer dreams . . . the terror I caused you . . ."

"Aye," she agreed. "And each time ye leave Camlochlin to seek yer revenge, and I do not know if ye will return, the verra same terror grips me. This will end only with yer death."

He took her hand in his as understanding washed over him. Understanding he would have fought to deny, even now, if he had never seen something other than a monster in Kate's eyes. "I am a fool." He smiled, then cleared his throat when his eyes stung.

"Now will ye bring Kate back?"

"She hasna left yet, Maggie. But I canna—"

"She has so left!" she insisted, yanking her hand from his so she could slap her thigh. "She took Ahern and bade me call to the guards to allow her departure. I think Graham should have gone with her."

Callum tried to calm the fierce pounding in his chest

but failed as he leaped to his feet. "Nae! She could no' have left. No' alone!"

"I tell ye, she did," Maggie said adamantly while she rose.

"Christ!" He raked his fingers through his hair as if he meant to yank out every strand. His eyes searched toward Elgol. "When did she go?" He whirled around, dropped to one knee, and gripped his sister's shoulders. "Maggie, think hard. How long ago did Kate leave?"

"Och, 'twas long ago, Callum. 'Twas before I fed Matilda."

Since he had no idea when that was, he groaned, released his sister, then took off toward the stable, calling over his shoulder that she return to the castle. He was grateful to find Maggie finally doing what he asked when he flew past her on his mount.

Callum cursed on the wind that tore his hair away from his face while he thundered out of the glen. Why the hell would Kate do such a foolish thing? He snapped the reins, driving his steed faster. He was to blame. He had pushed her so hard she could not wait another day to be away from him. Driven by fear of what might become of her, he kicked his mount's flanks harder, urging the horse to fly.

He plundered toward Elgol just as the sky tore open above him. His eyes scanned the darkened cliffs and countryside, searching. She could not have been gone from the castle for any length of time without him noticing, he told himself, trying to remain calm—to contain his rawest emotions. Surely she could not have gone far with old Ahern beneath her. Praying she had not already reached the treacherous cliffs, Callum gritted his teeth to

keep from crying out the name that had somehow become
more important to him than his own.

Kate reached Elgol just before the heavens darkened and
poured out their wrath upon the land. She was sure it was
wrath, for the rain battered her flesh, saturating her bones
until the cold numbed her limbs. The torrent obscured her
vision and she slowed Ahern's pace, fearing she might
lead them blindly over the cliffs. A few feet up ahead, a
shadowy figure crossed her path. She pulled the old horse
to a halt and swiped the rain from her eyes. The hair
along her neck rose. A warning sounded in her head.
Someone was watching her. She cursed herself for not
bringing a sword, or at least a dagger, for protection on
her journey. She heard the sound of feet pounding the
muddy ground and turned, panic accelerating her heartbeat.

The man was upon her almost instantly. His fist caught
her in the ribs, doubling her over. He yanked on her hair,
pulling her off Ahern's back. She was too shocked by the
sudden assault and too cold to fight back while she was
dragged off the path and hurled against a wall of rock that
separated the minty fragrance of forest from the briny
scent of the sea.

Kate reeled backward and fell hard against a large
boulder, one sharp edge barely missing the back of her
head. Red, searing pain flared across her shoulder and
then sent a numbing tingle down her arm, to her fingertips. She gasped back the breath that was knocked out of
her and pushed herself to her feet to face two men, their
dark hair plastered to their satisfied faces. She clawed the
rain from her eyes, trying to gain some control over her

trembling fingers. The whitecaps behind her pitched and crashed hard against the rocks that lined the shore. Above her, the vast heavens deepened to charcoal gray and the rolling roar of thunder resonated through her bones.

"She's a bonny wench, Clyde. Are ye certain she's a MacGregor?" the first one said, sweeping his eyes over the length of her body. So lewd was his gaze, Kate almost looked away. These two would not kill her right away.

"Aye, she comes from the path to Camlochlin," Clyde sneered. "I dinna know if m' stomach can stand ruttin' a MacGregor."

Kate's fear faded into rage. She tossed each man a glare that would have made Callum proud, had he been there to see it. "Touch me and I'll rake your eyes out and toss them into the sea, you filthy son of a—"

Clyde took a step forward and cracked her hard across the mouth. She fell backward again, landing on her backside against the rock. "I see we're goin' to have to beat some courtesy into ye before we sell ye."

"What think ye we'll get fer her? She's bonny, she is." The other stared at the blood dripping over her bottom lip and licked his own mouth.

"No' much, Ewan. The barons dinna pay much fer MacGregor women, and even less if she be wi' child."

"Mayhap she's a MacLeod. Should we no' be certain first?"

Kate listened on in horror. They spoke of her as if she was naught more than a cesspit rat. This was what it meant to be a MacGregor. No honor, no dignity. No place was safe, not even here in Callum's own kingdom. Her life was worth nothing simply because they believed her name to be MacGregor.

"Ye'll tell me who yer laird is before I have m' way with ye, wench." Clyde grabbed a fistful of her hair and dragged her forward.

How difficult would it be to tell them who her uncle was? To simply deny a name?

It wasn't difficult at all.

It was impossible.

She was not a MacGregor, but it did not matter to her. Here was the noble fight of heroes. Would she cower to Callum's enemies by denouncing everything he fought to keep alive?

"Will I be defilin' m' body by touchin' ye?" Clyde demanded.

To do so meant more than just forgetting Callum's bravery and Maggie's suffering. It meant stripping away the existence of an entire clan. A clan that belonged to Scotland. And Kate was sure now that each time a Mac-Gregor was killed or denied the right to bear his name, the very hills screamed out at the injustice of it. Yet the heather still grew in all its glory, the mists still lingered over the mountaintops, exploding into golden brilliance with the setting of the sun, as if reminding her children to never give up.

Kate lifted her gaze to her captors and wiped her mouth. "It is you who defile the name MacGregor when it falls from your loathsome lips."

Clyde raised his hand to strike her again, but Kate ducked low, picked up a rock, and smashed it against his temple. Clyde swayed on his feet, then staggered backward. A look of astonishment animated his face at being wounded by this waif of a gel who now stood ready to fight.

His companion charged her like a wild boar and caught her square on the jaw with his fist. Kate crumbled to the ground, unconscious even before she reached her destination.

A peal of thunder bellowed its rage, quaking the earth and its foundations. But 'twas the sound that followed that caused Clyde and Ewan to turn. 'Twas the sound of death. Ewan wanted to run, but sheer terror rooted his feet to the ground. Blindly, for he could not tear his terrified gaze from the direction of the unholy wail just beyond the fog, he reached out to where Clyde stood equally still, and clutched his companion's sleeve.

"Good God in heaven, 'tis him." Clyde's voice rattled with the certain knowledge of his imminent death. Many had heard of the fiend, MacGregor, but not so many had actually ever seen him. Tales were told about the laird of the mist around bonfires when the moon hung low in the sky and the wind howled like the souls of his victims. As elusive as a nimbus mist, he had been hunted for years but never caught. 'Twas whispered his was the blackest soul ever to walk the Earth. But Clyde swore by his poor mother's grave that the Earth itself lent to the beast's foul existence. For the heavens blackened, and out of a rising mist he rode like a demon ascending from the sooty vapors of hell.

He did not cut them down instantly, but leaped from the heaving creature snorting beneath him. For an instant he did naught but stare at the woman lying in the sand while the rain washed blood from her face into a thin rivulet beside her.

He groaned. The sound tore the last meager fibers of

courage from her attackers. Their death was swift. Both heads fell to the ground with one mighty blow.

Callum sank to his knees beside Kate, biting back another forceful groan. Reaching his hand out, he closed his eyes and touched her throat to discover if she lived. He sighed with such relief his shoulders sagged to his chest. He scooped her up into his arms and held her close before he kissed her cherished brow. She shivered, unconscious in his embrace, and he cursed the rain for soaking her so. Ahern was nowhere to be found, but had the old horse been standing beside him, it would have made no difference. Kate was freezing, and Camlochlin was leagues away.

The cave was easy to find. There were many carved into the jagged cliff walls of Elgol. Callum built a roaring fire out of dry driftwood found deeper within the rocky crevice and some dried seaweed, which he used to cushion the cold ground before he laid Kate upon it. He undressed her, getting her out of her dripping clothes, and then he, too, stripped naked and lay down beside her. Her teeth chattered, but still she did not awaken, making Callum pray the bastards had not struck her with anything more serious than their fists.

"Nae, ye just find it pleasin' to sleep aroond me, dinna ye, Katie, my love," he whispered while he soaked his vision with her. Now that she was back safely in his arms, he knew he had to have been daft to ever let her go. He wrapped one long leg over her hips and dragged her closer against his warmth. Facing her, he used his large hands to rub the cold from each limb. He did not stop until her flesh grew warm. She moaned and nuzzled closer to him. He closed his eyes to stop the wave of emotion aching to be released, and the rush of silken heat that having her naked body against his made him feel. "Och, lass, what have ye done to this poor fool of a man? I shouldna keep ye with me, and 'tis makin' me so daft I canna think straight." He smoothed wet curls over her forehead, watching her—watching her until he knew that not being able to do so would be worse than being shackled to any dungeon wall. "God have mercy on ye, Katie, but I love ye."

Kate's eyes drifted open an hour later. Thick cobwebs settled over her like a warm woolen blanket. A very warm blanket. She snuggled deeper beneath it and faded back to sleep. She dreamed of Callum's handsome face so close to hers, sleeping beside her, his strong arms clinging to her as if his survival depended on her. Somewhere deep within her, her heart told her it did.

Chapter Thirty

KATE OPENED HER EYES. For a moment she thought she was still dreaming. But, and God help her, that face was real. The warm, spicy breath falling on her cheek was real. He had come for her, saved her from . . . She lifted her hand off Callum's chest and brought it to her swollen lip. An instant later, her gaze slipped back to him.

His bare chest.

She looked down and squeaked. She was naked! He was naked! Instinct made her jerk away from him, but his arm curled around her more firmly and then hauled her into an embrace that snatched the breath from her body. She gasped. He snored. Her bones went pliant against him. What was this? How had he found her? Why had he found her?

She would ask him why later; right now she was too occupied with the task of trying to still her beating heart, for it rejoiced with such a loud thumping she was sure it was what had awakened him. For when she looked at his face again, his gentle gaze made her tingle all the way down to her toenails. She smiled and then blushed.

Callum was sure his poor heart would never recover.

"Where are our clothes?" she whispered, lowering her gaze modestly.

"Dryin'. Ye were freezin' and I had to keep ye warm."

He still had not released her, and she did not want him to. Not ever again. "Why did you come for me?"

He pulled her closer into the steel of his arms. "I didna want to send ye away, Katie."

"They were going to sell me." She closed her eyes and pressed her cheek to his chest. "And all I could think of was you."

Callum's jaw danced beneath his flesh. God help him, how could he ever live without her? "Dinna fear, lass. They'll no' be comin' back."

Kate did not hear the terrible beast in his voice, only the hollowed guilt of a man who knew killing was the sole way to survive and wished it wasn't.

She stared up into the flames of his eyes, blue-gold kilns where his passion for life, for hope, for revenge, and for redemption burned. He had killed many. He had become something detestable, and his cause had ceased to be an honorable one in his own eyes. But nowhere in that powerful gaze was there hatred. She smiled, suddenly understanding why he had sent her away. He became a monster to save what he loved.

"You rescued me again."

God's mercy, would she always look at him as if he were a hero? Callum wondered. Even when he tried to enlighten her about his black heart, she refused to see it. "Kate." he almost didn't want to utter it. Damn it, he had to admit to himself that he quite honestly loved being a hero to her. But he was not a knight. He was not a hero. "I'm naught but a coldhearted bastard. I—"

She shook her head. "You are more than I ever dreamed of. What you do, you have been forced to do to protect those you love, to save your clan from extinction. Sometimes I can do naught more than ask the Lord what I have done to deserve meeting a man such as you, my laird MacGregor."

His gaze ravaged her with a need so profound she felt her heart stall. He brought his fingertips to her lips and angled his head toward hers. "Yer bruised." The husky warmth of his voice singed her nerve endings. "Does it pain ye?"

"Aye," she barely whispered.

He kissed her mouth softly. "Still?" When she nodded, he kissed her again, gentle, meaningful kisses that made her head spin. "How aboot now?"

"I fear it is bruised mightily, my laird." Her long lashes fluttered against his cheek. She parted her lips, waiting.

He did not make her wait, but rose up over her and watched her surrender beneath him. His breath was heavy, ragged. He looked like he wanted to say something—something that might rip his heart from his chest. He grazed his lips over hers and kissed each one with worshipful appreciation. The length and breadth of him descended full upon her. He parted her lips with his fingertips and then licked the seam of her mouth. 'Twas not the powerful control he possessed that made him so exquisitely thorough in the claiming of her mouth, but the need to savor every moment of touching her.

She opened easily to his plunging tongue and moaned into his mouth as he tasted her. She felt his rigid flesh against her untried body, but it did not frighten her. He was her knight. A savage in his own right, but his hands moved over her like silken flames, so utterly tender she thought she might go mad. When those hands found her breasts, a low sob of need escaped her. She arched her back to meet his hungry mouth sooner, and the wondrous agony of his warm lips caressing hers sent a titillating explosion of fire down her belly and between her legs.

When he broke their kiss to stare into her eyes, she smiled at him, loving him and wanting to be with him this way. "Kate," he whispered, and the desire in his eyes changed into something more pleading. "If we do this, ye'll be a MacGregor and nothin' will be able to change it."

She heard the fear for her well-being in his voice and stroked her fingers along his tight jaw. "I am already one, and nothing can change it. Nothing." She pulled him down, without having to use much force, and kissed him until he felt her whole heart in it.

He molded her breasts with delicate mastery, suckling and nibbling until he had her writhing beneath him. "Ye taste fine." Closing his lips around her sensitive crest, he sucked and brushed his tongue hard across her nipple.

Kate tunneled her fingers through his hair and held him to her. She wanted him never to stop, but the heated ache in her loins demanded to be satisfied. When he laved his tongue down her belly, Kate pushed herself up on her elbows to see just what he was going to do. His tongue fluttered over her skin, revealing his intentions. She had the urge to pull away, but the thought of his mouth *there* was too arousing to deny. Just when she thought she might swoon if she didn't feel him soon, he looked up at her from beneath his dark brows and the sexual fire blazing his eyes was enough to make Kate's legs spread wider. He dipped his face. Kate held her breath. His kiss was like a flame that spread out of control through her blood. He took his time laving, feasting on her fully. Then, taking both her ankles, he lifted her legs and opened her wider, exposing her fully to his hungry mouth.

Kate groaned and licked her lips as searing jolts of ecstasy wracked her body. She felt wicked clutching fistfuls of his hair while he pleasured her beyond endurance. Craving release, she cried out his name and watched him rise up on his knees, still holding her legs apart. Her vision drank in the full glory of him above her, so powerful, so acutely male.

She watched him enter her slowly, sensually. She was sleek enough from his mouth and her passion for him to glide halfway into her, despite her body's tight resistance. His thighs flexed on the verge of burying him into her fully. He was going to take her, and she was helpless to stop him.

She lifted her arms over her head and undulated her hips, snapping his control. The initial pain was naught in comparison to the sizzling friction of his powerful shaft dipping in and then out of her. He grew still and asked her not to move, not to speak. The muscles along his arms shuddered as passion's talons gripped him and he resisted. He released her legs and bent his head to kiss her, then lowered his weight to hers. He angled his hips and surged against her hard, hot crux.

He made love to her slowly, and with such tenderness, Kate felt as if time slowed just for them, so they could both relish every moment, every touch. Taking her fill, she slid her fingertips across the breadth of his scarred shoulders, down the dip of his spine. She looked at him to find his eyes already on her face, taking her in as if the very sight of her gave him breath. She basked in him, as he did in her with every long, deep thrust.

Her sheath tight around his length, she spread her palms over his tense thighs to feel each plunge. Pleasure heightened to its pinnacle; her muscles convulsed beneath him. He answered by driving into her with slow, deliberate strokes until her fingers clenched his buttocks and rapture engulfed her. She watched, as if in some erotic, clandestine dream, his sensuous mouth curl into the wickedest of smiles before he lifted his head and erupted inside her.

Later, she lay nestled in the place that had become more familiar to her than her home. Callum's arms would always be here to hold her, to protect her. She was certain of it, as certain as any young woman in love could be. She kissed his chest, then ran her fingers over the rippling planes of his abdomen.

He captured her hand in his and brought it to his lips. But he remained silent for so long Kate raised her head to look at him.

"What troubles you? Tell me, please."

In the amber glow of firelight, his gaze was open and his heart exposed. Would she ever get used to the way his eyes tried to speak to her from beyond the darkness that plagued him? She ran her fingers over the shadowy dimple in his chin.

"What is it, Callum?"

"The world," he told her, "suddenly seems perfect." She nodded, but an instant later he exhaled a great, deep sigh. "But 'tis no' perfect, Kate. Mayhap Ennis has it aright. I dinna know anymore."

"Ennis Stewart?"

"MacGregor. Ennis MacGregor. He changed his name."

Kate bolted upright. Callum had to smile at the beauty of her sitting there all pale and ready for a battle, her dark tresses tumbling down her bare shoulders. She was his, and it made him happier than he could ever remember being. Being here with her like this—why, it could make him forget everything else in the world.

"Callum, you would even consider such a thing?"

He dragged his gaze away from her breasts and grinned into her storming ebony eyes. "No' until that day I was sealin' yer wound and ye called me Clalum MacKreglor."

"I would never allow you to do it!" she admonished him. "I would never allow you to deny what you love."

He reached up and cupped her cheek in his palm. "Even if it meant yer life?"

Kate choked back a sob. She had become another responsibility to him. Dear God, she wanted to give him rest. She wanted to reassure him that no matter what happened, no matter what became of her, it was her choice. "I would give my life for you."

Callum closed his eyes, unable and unwilling to bear the thought. "Kate," he said, looking at her again, his voice a warm caress. "D'ye think lovin' someone makes dyin' fer them easier?"

She nodded. "Aye. Aye, I do, Callum." When he shook his head and turned away from her, she touched his jaw, bringing his gaze back to her. "Or do you think you are the only one worthy to be willing to give your life for something you love?"

Callum's heart pounded in his ears. Of course, he understood that any true MacGregor would be willing to die for his name. But he would not let her die for it.

He wanted her, needed her in his life. Every time she looked at him, every word she spoke to him, all worked at making him forget the injustices he and his clan suffered. How could he be angry at the world, when the world had given him Kate Campbell?

But she could be taken from him.

The thought chilled his soul and stirred the beast. She already loved him. She already declared herself a MacGregor. He'd made love to her, spilled his seed into her. But all hope was not lost. Nae, mayhap if he kept his heart silent, if faced with a choice for her life, she would choose to live. "I willna let ye die fer me, Kate."

Well, it wasn't a declaration of love, but he cared for her. She knew he did. She would worry him about it no more. She gave him a sympathetic pat on the hand and rose to gather her clothes. "I do not intend to die. When I return to my brother, I will—"

He snatched her wrist and pulled her back until she was sprawled over his chest. "Ye're no' returnin' to him."

"I'm not?" she asked.

"Nae." He traced her features with his smoldering gaze, then drew his fingers over her parted lips. "Ye're mine and ye'll be stayin' with me."

"But I worry for my—"

"Katie?"

"Aye?" She smiled at the sound of her name spoken so sweetly from his lips.

"Ye talk too much, lass." He devoured her mouth, capturing anything further she wished to say while his hands slid down her back and over her soft buttocks.

Chapter Thirty-One

THEY RODE BACK to Camlochlin with Kate comfortably nestled between Callum's thighs. They did not ride on the wind, but he kept his mount at a slow trot, enjoying the feel of her against his heart. It had been a long, torturous eternity since he held anyone so close to that sacred place. When he had told her he would die clutching a Campbell heart in his hands, he truly had no idea that heart would be hers. He had not been prepared, and doubted he ever would have been, to hand his heart over to her in return. Aye, he had tried to make her loathe him in order to save her life. For her life meant more to him than his home, his kin, his name. He had no doubt he would give up all for her. But 'twas his soul he had been trying to protect, also. He had lost it once because he loved. To lose it again terrified him.

Losing Kate terrified him even more.

Along the coastline on which they traveled, frothy whitecaps crashed in a rolling crescendo against the low, jagged cliffs, launching sea spray twenty feet into the air. Kate watched it, thinking how very much Callum was like the ocean, all turbulent and raging and powerful. She clutched his hand at her belly and leaned her head back against his chest, enjoying the wonderment of the day. The rains had ended and the sun shone like an orb of fire in the pale sky, but a brisk chill remained in the air, making everything smell clean and crisp and new.

A new day. Callum enfolded her deeper into his embrace and bent his face to the crook of her neck. He kissed her curls. She heard him inhale deeply, and the brawn of his body surged up against her like the waves to her left.

Kate sighed softly on an exhilarated breath. Her eyes slid to the east, where the forest had just begun to fall away in place of fallow fields where woolly cattle grazed with sluggish indifference on overgrown grass. Before her, the Cuillins rose up—a stone behemoth shielding its children beneath its vast black wings. A mist rolled over the sharp peaks and drifted downward toward the earth like a gossamer avalanche. Everywhere Kate looked she beheld power and beauty, land so achingly feral and beautiful it was almost painful for a mere mortal to gaze upon it overlong. Skies so vast she had the urge to spread her arms and bask in the freedom flying would bring. The Highlands and the people who inhabited them belonged to each other. Never was it clearer to Kate. She doubted one could survive without the other and wondered at the same time if this untamed land compelled its people to fight against attempts to subdue them, or if the people's untamed will and stubborn resilience made the land so wildly breathtaking.

"Will we have children together, Callum?" she asked wistfully, suddenly wanting to bear all his bairns here.

"Aye. I want many sons."

She turned to give him a haughty look. "Think you, you would allow me to bear some daughters?"

Humor fanned the flames of his eyes. "I would allow it only after a son."

"Humph." Kate swung around to conceal her smile, only to quiver in his arms a moment later when he parted the curls at her nape and spread his hot breath there.

"We could stop right here and continue our effort to make one."

"I think not," she said. "We are not even wed. And now that you mention it, I remember hearing Aileen and some of the other women talking at the castle, and they said that if a man wishes to have a son, he and his wife must wait until the waxing of the full moon. I think that is . . ." She counted on her fingers, then nodded. "Aye. A fortnight away."

Callum's head snapped up from its thorough ravishing of her neck, and he glowered at her raven curls. "I willna be denied fer a full bloody fortnight, Kate."

"Och, but ye will, Callum MacGregor." She imitated his thick Highland burr.

"Are ye makin' sport of my speech, woman?" he asked, sincerely surprised that she would do so.

She laughed, a rich, beautiful sound. "I find your speech quite enchanting."

Appeased, he allowed himself a smile. "There's much to learn aboot the MacGregors."

"Such as?"

"Such as the men, especially the laird, will no' be black-mailed." He yanked his plaid over his hard cock and, dropping the reins, curled one arm around her waist and lifted her gown over her hips with the other. He slipped his hand over her throat and pulled her close to rake his teeth across her skin. "I've wanted to take ye like this fer too long now," he whispered huskily in her ear, then lifted her enough to thrust his silken lance deep within her without breaking stride.

His big hands on her hips guided her up and down on his steel shaft, making her feel every inch. His low groans along her flesh sent flames up her spine. When Kate looped her arms around his neck behind her, he shoved her down hard, then swept his palm over her belly and lifted her again. He dipped his fingers to her swollen bud and stroked her until she pitched against his chest.

"I say son." He smiled into her nape and lurched upward. "What say you, Katie?"

"Twins," she bargained and then laughed with him. He grew serious an instant later when he whispered how he felt inside her. Then he showed her by cupping her from front to back in his hands and sliding her up, almost over his thick, sensitive head, then back down to his hilt.

To say that he was gentle in his lovemaking this time would be sheer folly on Kate's part. Her breasts ached, her neck felt delightfully bruised by his wicked teeth, and the backs of her thighs would surely bear the truth of his passion before the day's end.

Sometime later, when his four most loyal warriors came upon them just before they reached the crest of Camlochlin's glen, Kate's hair looked as if she had been caught in a violent Highland storm, her cheeks were flushed, and her gown twisted almost backward on her shoulders.

Brodie grinned from one ear to the other. Angus belched and nodded his head as if his approval was all that was needed to complete this pair's binding. Graham pulled up short on the reins and regarded Callum and the suddenly bashful woman in his arms with a measured look. Jamie was the only one in the group scratching his head, befuddled by their appearance.

"Where are ye all off to?" Callum looked each one of them over, adding a well-deserved scowl to Brodie's knowing wink.

"Maggie told us ye barreled out of here like there was a fire on yer arse," Graham told him, still unsure if his instinct was deceiving him. He had tumbled enough wenches to recognize when they'd been thoroughly tumbled. "What the hell happened to ye, Kate?" he asked her while she inconspicuously patted the last of her unruly curls into place.

Her cheeks went crimson almost instantly, and Graham would have smiled if the sight of her bruised face hadn't made his blood go cold.

"Graham, if ye have a question to ask, ye'll ask me." Callum aimed his fierce glare on his commander.

"Verra well." Graham switched his attention to Callum. "What the hell happened to her face?"

How had he forgotten that? "She was attacked on the road." When they demanded the full tale, he told them. "I killed the whoresons."

"Callum." The braw tilt of Jamie's chin struck Callum in the gut, and the laird arched his eyebrow and waited for Jamie to continue. "Ye canna be so careless to let her oot of yer sight again. I think I should watch over her when ye're angry with her."

Kate almost wept. She would have leapt off Callum's horse and hugged the young warrior had he not visibly cringed when Callum inched his mount closer to his.

"So ye're her champion now, are ye, Jamie? What of Maggie?"

Whatever resolve Jamie possessed a moment ago fair

dripped off his shoulders until they slumped in defeat. 'Twas too late—he had started this, and now he knew he must finish it. He swallowed audibly, then cleared his throat. "Ye know that I would never let harm come to Maggie. But Kate needs . . . She needs . . ." Callum waited patiently while the young warrior fought to girdle up his loins again. "She needs . . . someone . . . to . . . to protect her," he finally spat out.

Callum nodded and thought about it, taking his time and trying to subdue his amusement. "Verra well, Jamie. Yer duty is now to guard my sister and Kate when I'm unable to do so. But"—he leaned forward, fastened his piercing gaze on each of them, and then, miracle of miracles, began to smile—"there will be only one Sir Galahan fer this lady at Camlochlin. And that'll be me."

Jamie scrunched up his face. "Who?"

But Callum did not answer. He flicked his reins and left his men there on the crest, each one wearing the same gaping expression of astonishment on his face, save for Graham, who snatched Angus's brew out of his large paw. He held it up to the couple descending the ridge, and his lips curled into a grin. "To knights, and the ladies who love them," he toasted, then took a hearty swig of whiskey.

⌒

"It's Sir Galahad."

"Hmmm?" Callum set his gaze on his home and then on the back of Kate's head. God's teeth, he was so damned happy he was beginning to feel like a fool.

"Sir Galahad, not Galahan," she corrected him, then angled her head to toss him a mischievous smile. "But you'll do, MacGregor."

Behind them, Callum's men heard a sound they all felt quite sure they never heard before. It drifted backward and filled the glen with echoes.

"Did ye hear that?" Brodie slowed his horse, waited a moment, then slammed his fist into Angus's shoulder. "What's in that brew? I'm fearin' 'tis made me daft."

Angus reached out and near broke his cousin's nose—which would have been the third time—with a hefty swing. "Next time ye insult me brew, I'll rid ye of yer teeth, ye bastard MacGregor."

"Yer no' daft, Brodie." Jamie stared on ahead, his huge blue eyes wider than twin seas. "I hear it, too."

Angus jammed his finger in his ear and wiggled it. "I'll be damned, I hear it."

Jamie turned his awe-stricken gaze to Graham. "What does it mean?"

"It means yer laird is laughing, ye bunch of lackwits." Graham kicked his mount's flanks and raced after Callum and Kate, calling over his shoulder. "Have ye never heard the man laugh before?"

Jamie watched his brother ride away, then turned to the others and shrugged his shoulders. "Only before he aimed to kill someone."

Angus tossed him his pouch of brew. "Here, drink up, lad. Things aroond here are aboot to change, I'd wager. Ye're goin' to need all the hair on yer chest ye can gather."

Brodie laughed. "First he'll be needin' some hair on his . . ." He almost swallowed his tongue at the force of Angus's palm striking behind his head.

"Mind yer tongue," the burly warrior warned. And then Jamie took off after his laird, leaving both of his brutish friends on the ground, their fists flying.

Chapter Thirty-Two

CALLUM SAT IN THE GREAT HALL with Graham and had just shoved a slice of bread into his mouth when Brodie dragged a chair across from him and sat. Callum looked up briefly, then set about finishing his meal. After another full moment had passed, Callum lifted his gaze again, quaffed his drink, and then slammed the cup down on the table.

"What the hell are ye starin' at?"

Brodie didn't blink. Instead, he rested his elbows on the table, moved slightly forward, and peered at Callum more intently. Graham snickered and pushed his chair away from his friend's, not wanting to be in the way when Callum started trouncing the poor fool. And by the looks of it, Brodie had been trounced already this day. The bruise around his swollen eye was already turning an interesting shade of purple. Angus most assuredly, Graham decided with another smirk.

"Are ye sufferin' from some ailment we should know aboot?" Brodie asked him quite seriously and went back to studying him.

Callum turned to Graham, seeking some interpretation. When none came, he slid his gaze back to Brodie. "Do I appear ill to ye?"

"Aye." Brodie nodded. "Ye do." The corners of his eyes crinkled from his continued scrutiny. "Yer a bit flushed aroond the ears, and the way ye were howlin' ootside we figgered ye must be ill . . . or goin' daft." He sat back and added a low mumble.

Graham moved farther away in his chair, taking his cup with him. But the reaction he expected never came. Callum did not throw his chair back and yank Brodie to him by the scruff of his neck. He simply sat there, a wry quirk playing at the corners of his mouth. "Brodie, where's yer wife?"

His cousin looked around the great hall, then shrugged. "She's aroond here somewhere."

"Ye should be with her."

"I should?"

Callum nodded, "Aye, ye should."

"Why?"

"Ye love her, dinna ye?"

"Eh? What the hell has that got to do wi' anythin'?" Brodie asked him, sincerely confounded.

Before Callum could answer him, or, heaven forbid it, laugh again, Angus threw himself down into the seat nearest Brodie. "I think I broke me finger on yer face."

Jamie appeared and took his place at Callum's left. "Speakin' of faces." He reached for a hunk of bread on the table. "What happened after ye saved Kate from her attackers?"

Callum scowled at him, then went back to eating, ignoring the lad's eager eyes.

"He recited a saintly prayer over her bonny head and raced her back here, where he would have nae time alone w' her." Brodie shook his head at Jamie. "What the hell do ye think happened after that, ye whiskerless pup?"

Realization finally dawned on the youngest of Callum's warriors, and he blushed a fresh shade of scarlet. "Are ye claimin' her, then?"

Callum downed the rest of his ale, then looked up at them. "Aye, I am."

The smirk Brodie wore on his face vanished suddenly and he dropped his mutton back into his trencher. "That's why ye asked me if I loved Netta. Christ, Callum, ye dinna love the lass d'ye?"

"Should I send fer Faither Lachlan, then?" Jamie asked eagerly.

"Dinna bother," Callum said as he stood from his seat. "Our sacraments are no' recognized by the church. But I dinna need a priest to approve our union. She's mine, and I'll protect her from the law." He swept his gaze over each of them. "Do any of ye take issue with my decision?" His men shook their heads. "Good, then I'll be goin' to bed."

"Bed?" Jamie asked incredulously. "But 'tis still light oot."

Angus threw his head back and bellowed with laughter, but Callum barely heard as he picked up his pace heading for the stairs. When he was sure he was out of his men's vision, he took the stairs three at a time. Kate was in his chambers, and he'd been eager to get there since she left him for a bath. She did not need one, he reasoned. She smelled fine already.

He stopped on the stairs, lifted his arm, and took a sniff. No' too bad, he thought. At least he smelled like a man. Damnation, is this what love did to a man? Was he destined to become a smiling, blithering fool, so concerned with his odor that he would forget how refreshing fighting felt? By the time he reached the second landing his scowl turned into full-blown brooding.

His men had already noticed the change in him. Why, Brodie even thought he looked ill. With that thought souring his mood further, Callum ran his hand over his jaw, feeling for any sign of softness. He cursed under his breath and set his hard gaze on his chamber door. Kate was probably in there neatly arranging pink lilies in delicate little vases. He kicked an empty bucket out of his path. Now that she was his, she'd be staying in his chambers. Hell, he was going to have to get used to having a woman loitering around in his things. He stopped and paled as an even more horrid thought came to him. Mayhap she was polishing his bloodstained swords. God's blood! He picked up his steps and almost sprinted the rest of the way.

The door to his chambers was slightly ajar when he reached it. He was about to plunge inside and stop Kate from whatever she was doing when he heard her voice.

"Umm, does that not feel good?"

Her silky groan of delight pricked his ears and froze his blood. Heart pounding, he splayed his palms on either side of the doorframe and moved closer to the opening.

"It feels like silk. It is so smooth. I can scarcely wait until it grows."

Callum ground his teeth together, thinking of the slowest and most painful way of killing the rogue bastard in there with his woman. With his bare hands, he decided.

"Yer efforts are fer naught."

His stomach twisted when he heard his sister in there, as well, her voice pensive and soft. "It does not seem to be working. He has not tried to kiss me yet."

Kate giggled. "That's because he's afraid of your brother."

And well he should be, Callum thought, plunging into the room. He looked around, ready to remove someone's head. His sister offered him a grin from where she sat while Kate meticulously brushed her hair.

"What's . . . what's goin' on here?" he asked rather weakly, all the wind blowing out of his sails.

Kate offered him a smile that knotted his pitiful guts. "Your sister agreed to let me brush her hair. She is quite bonny, aye?"

Callum's gaze dipped to Maggie. "Aye." It sounded to his ears like a squeak, and hell, he would have scowled if he could stop the damn grin that insisted on curling his lips.

"Callum," his sister inquired. "Are ye ill?"

There. His scowl returned to him full force. He almost sighed with relief, fearing it had abandoned him altogether. Maggie laughed and he melted all over again. Was this his sister sitting here with bows in her hair where crickets had once roamed? She was clean! She was wearing a fresh gown! And all at once, before Callum could stop them, his eyes misted. He blinked a few times as if some flying mote had landed in his eyes, then went to her.

"Ye're a bonny lass." He slipped two fingers under Maggie's chin and lifted her face to his. "Who woulda thought it?"

"Och, go on with ye." Maggie waved him away. "Ye knew I was bonny all along."

He laughed, and his gaze was involuntarily drawn back to Kate. Their eyes met. For a moment Callum lost all thought. His laughter faded into a heart-wrenching smile of intimacy that sent Kate's pulse racing.

Suddenly there was a hand waving before his eyes. Callum wrenched his gaze away from Kate's and looked down at his sister. She grinned up at him, her teeth flashing. "Thank ye fer bringing her back."

Callum kissed his sister's clean head and sent her on her way. He followed her to the door and bolted it when she was gone.

Watching him, Kate was not sure if it was the mere sight of him that made her breath fail, or the smoldering intent in his gaze when he turned back to her. Her eyes glided over his form. There was so much of him, and all of it so wonderfully defined. Beneath his plaid of dyed wool, his shirt stretched across the broad flare of his shoulders. His belt hung low on his lean hips. The tattered edge of his plaid reached just above his knees, revealing a few inches of his bare muscular calves, encased in his hide boots. She searched her mind but couldn't seem to remember any man in her father's or uncle's guard who was as handsome as Callum.

"Ye didna bathe yet." The husky timbre of his voice heated Kate's blood. He stepped forward, unbuckling the belt at his waist.

"I was tending to Maggie and have not had the chance." She didn't know she was holding her breath until Callum reached her and she sighed. Hands that killed with great skill closed around hers.

His powerful fingers feathered over her flesh like a

butterfly's wings, once more astounding her that he could be so gentle.

Somewhere in the back of her thoughts, Kate realized that she should be, at the very least, apprehensive about the pure male power he exuded. She had been a virgin who had never even been kissed up until a few weeks ago. She should be frightened, coy, demure, anxious—something. But she could not pretend. Not when she was standing so close to the man she had waited for all her life. He bent his head to her and she looked up, too weak to stand. What were those breathtaking eyes trying to tell her? Or was it simply the inky darkness of his lashes that made his eyes appear to glimmer like firelight?

He lifted both of her hands to his lips and kissed them, sending currents of heat throughout her body. Without a word, he unfastened the laces of her kirtle. His breath against her cheek thrilled her; the tender touch of his fingers and the intoxicating heat from his body made her ache for him. He tunneled his fingers through the thick curls at her temples, then traced a deliciously sweet path down the sides of her face, all the while his eyes tracing her features, worshipping what he saw. She arched her head back, exposing her throat to his silken touch and then to his hungry mouth. She was barely aware of her skirts and shift falling away from her body, mindful only of the full impact this man had on her.

"Have I told you, Callum MacGregor, how right it feels when you hold me?"

"Ye dinna have to tell me," he whispered to her and carried her to his bed.

Setting her down within his fur blankets, he stepped back and simply reveled in her beauty. And then he shed his garments, and the last stone that made up the wall around his heart.

Kate held her arms out to the glorious man standing over her. She beckoned and he came to her, giving her power she never thought to possess. Though his dominating weight covered her from toe to crown, she experimented liberally, using her lips, her tongue, and her teeth over all the hard planes of his body. She was fascinated to find that she could control every deep groan this warrior uttered.

The power shifted when he grasped her hands and held them over her head. Her surrender was swift. His deft attack of warm, sultry kisses down her neck, between the satiny hollow of her breasts, and then over each milky mound conquered the arrogant victory she so fleetingly possessed. His tongue, more deadly than any sword forged, traced a heathen path over her belly, pausing to allow his lips to kiss the tingling muscles of her abdomen. Her heart went still for just a moment when she realized the destination his tongue sought. But then his face dipped, and, using a beguiling combination of tenderness and mastery, he partook of the passion's nectar she offered him. Her back arched, and violent jolts of sheer pleasure coursed through her and made her quiver to her toes.

Her tormented groans snapped Callum's control. He rose up like a languid god after devouring a bountiful feast. He lowered his hips to hers, and the touch of his rigid manhood between the crux of her thighs was so primal, so arousing, it shuddered Kate to her soul. He surged against her once, almost driving her to the brink of madness, then impaled himself in her as deeply as she could take him.

Pleasure so replete, so raw and ruthlessly erotic,

rushed through Kate's blood like a deluge. Her senses ignited until his ragged breath became her own. The scent of his desire clinging to his skin was as intoxicating as a field of bursting heather blossoms. The feel of his sculpted arms encasing her was more magical than any dream of being held in the arms of a knight could ever be.

He ground his hips against hers, withdrew slowly, then sank deep within her again. She curved her back, tempting him to suckle the ripe nipples stretching toward his hungry mouth. His appetite ripped a fevered moan from the back of her throat. Slipping his hand beneath her, his strong fingers spread over her buttocks, pressing her upward. He angled his hips to stroke the crest of her passion. His gaze fastened on her, taking in the pure beauty of her climax, and the sight of her was his undoing. He tried to wait, for he wanted to watch her like this forever, but the pleasure she took in him, the hot sheath convulsing around him, drove him wild, and finally he closed his eyes, lifted his head, and released the scalding bounty of his seed deep inside her.

Drifting off her body, Callum pulled her close against him and held her, kissing the damp curls at her forehead while she gasped with spent energy.

Later he bathed her, and it was the single most sensuous experience of Kate's life. He reveled in each wonderful inch of her body with his soapy hands and feral gaze. He scrubbed her hair and massaged her scalp with titillating thoroughness, then playfully dunked her and kissed the droplets of water off her mouth and the breath clean out of her body.

Chapter Thirty-Three

⁓

TWO DAYS LATER, Brodie, Angus, and Jamie stood outside their laird's chamber door. Brodie leaned against the far wall, crossed his ankles, and scratched his rough face with the tip of his dagger. Jamie paced a worn path across the threshold.

"Graham said to tell him posthaste."

Angus dragged his rapt attention from the door and cast Jamie a sharp glance. "Then go ahead and knock, lad."

Jamie's pacing paused and he looked up. "I will." He resumed his fretful trek without knocking. "Callum needs to know the MacLeod is comin'."

Angus shrugged his hefty shoulders. "It ain't like MacLeod's at the doors. What's the hurry in tellin' Callum? Yer gonna get yer arse thrashed good."

"Graham said to tell him." Finally, Jamie raised his hand to knock, but a low, sensuous groan drifted through the door. Jamie's fist stopped in midair.

"I wouldna knock just yet, were I ye," Brodie said with a laugh.

"Hell, this could take all day," Jamie mumbled, eyeing the door.

"Pity Brodie isna the laird," Angus quipped. "We wouldna have to wait longer than a dozen breaths before 'twas over."

"And I'd still have ye beat by ten," Brodie returned with a grin.

"I'm knockin'," Jamie said, ignoring them both. "He'll want to know aboot the MacLeod."

Angus grinned harder and folded his arms across his brawny chest. "Ye have much to learn, pup. Nae man wants to be interrupted while he's enjoyin' a woman. As ye're aboot to find oot."

"I'm no'—" They all heard the door open, but it was too late for Jamie. "—afraid of him."

Callum stood there naked but for his plaid wrapped around his waist, his face darkening with murderous intent. He didn't know who to glower at first, so he glowered at all of them. Angus looked down the long hall, wondering how quickly he could get to the stairs and save his arse. Jamie backed up when Callum took a step forward.

"What the hell are all three of ye doin' standin' ootside my door?"

Brodie pushed himself off the wall and looked up and around like a dimwit who'd wandered into the hall and found himself lost.

Jamie cleared his throat. "Graham sent me to give ye the news."

"What news?" When Jamie told him, Callum still wasn't satisfied. "And it took all of ye to tell me this?" The slight smirk on Brodie's face told him the truth of it.

He and Angus had followed hoping to see Jamie get thrashed for disturbing their laird.

The menacing glint in Callum's eyes when he set them back on Jamie froze the lad's blood. "Ye thought the MacLeod's visit was important enough to trouble me with it?"

"Aye, my apologies." Jamie bowed his head. "Angus and Brodie told me I shouldna do it." When he felt a brisk slap on the back, he looked up.

Callum nodded at him. "Ye were right to tell me. Ye're a braw lad. That's why yer brother sent ye, and no' either one of these sorry excuses fer men."

Brodie knew enough to keep his mouth shut. Besides, his blood-rusted sword spoke well enough about his bravery in battle.

"What's that supposed to mean?" Angus bristled. "I was ready to break the bloody door doun to give ye the news."

"Then ye must be sadly disappointed that I opened it, Angus." Callum tossed him a foul grin. "Meet me ootdoors after ye break fast and ye can prove to me that ye can still lift yer sword."

"We've already finished supper, Callum," Brodie informed him without shielding his smirk. "A quick glance oot the window woulda told ye that if ye cared to look."

"Shut up, Brodie," Callum ordered.

Angus sputtered for a good five breaths after Callum strolled down the hall and disappeared inside the garderobe. Brodie whacked him on the back to induce breathing. "Best go practice, cousin." He grinned, winked, and exited the hall with Jamie, leaving Angus there alone to rifle through the folds of his plaid for his pouch of brew.

When Callum left the garderobe, he found yet another

one of his men waiting for him. Graham leaned against the opposite wall with his arms folded across his chest. The cool scent of fresh air drifting off him attested to his recent return to the castle.

"'Tis good to see ye among the living," the commander said with a casual smile.

"'Tis good to know I was missed."

"Ye weren't. Kate was."

Callum nodded and then had to smile as he headed back to his chambers. What a pack of miserably ruthless bastards he had saddled himself with. God's blood, he was fortunate, indeed.

"Jamie gave ye the news about the MacLeod?" Graham came up beside him.

"Aye. When is he comin'?"

"He'll be arriving on the morrow. But there's another matter of more urgency to discuss. A band of Campbells was seen in Glengarry."

Callum's steps halted. "How long ago?"

"Two days."

"How many?"

"Forty, mayhap fifty horsemen."

"Send William and a dozen of his best fighters to scout the coast, and I want Rob and twenty others in Glenelg by nightfall. I want to know where the Campbells are. I want to know their every move." When he reached the door to his chamber, Graham held back. "Come," Callum invited him inside. "There is one other thing I wish to discuss with you."

Graham entered the room, lowering his gaze when Kate, still lying in bed, bare as the day she was born, yanked the fur blanket up to her chin. She glared at Callum, but he only winked at her.

Shaking her head at the callous brute, Kate cursed under her breath and sank deeper under the covers. She peeked out at Graham while Callum dressed.

My, but the commander looked especially comely today, she thought, admiring him from her bed. He wore a white wide-sleeved tunic beneath his plaid, and his kid-skin boots were scrubbed clean of mud. She particularly liked the way he donned his cap backward, with the brim behind his head rather than on the side of it, his spray of burnished curls peeking out at his nape.

Graham caught her admiration of him and tossed her a smile she was sure felled many hearts.

"Are ye both done?" Callum yanked his plaid off his waist and dashed it to the ground, then reached for a fresh tunic.

Graham and Kate looked at Callum at the same time. The commander cleared his throat and picked an imaginary mote of lint off his plaid.

"Callum, Graham is comely, but surely his buttocks are not as well formed as yours." Kate blinked her long black lashes at Callum so innocently, he swore he saw a halo hovering over her head. That is, after he finished blushing a dark shade of crimson. He snatched up his plaid again and tossed it swiftly over his form.

"Kate, I dinna think 'tis proper to speak that way in front of Graham, especially if ye're to be my wife."

She popped her head out fully from under the blanket. "Your wife?"

"Aye." He turned to Graham. "Send fer Faither Lachlan. Last I heard, he was in Moray."

"Ye have my blessing." Graham was happy to hear such news and smiled at Kate again.

"We're goin' to need it," Callum mumbled. "And quit starin' at her."

"Just a moment, please," Kate said from the bed. "I don't remember being asked."

"Asked?" Callum barely looked up from securing his plaid.

"Aye, asked," Kate repeated stubbornly. It was difficult to challenge him on this issue, especially since she wanted to leap out of the bed and fling herself in his arms. But hell, the man was too arrogant for his own good. "I will not be *told* who I am to marry."

Now he set his eyes on her and scowled for all he was worth. "You were willing to be *told* to marry Lord Mortimer of Newbury."

Mortimer of Newbury! Kate almost slapped her thigh at the recollection of her imaginary betrothed's name. And what was this? Callum knew it all along? The fact that he remembered the name with such clarity warmed her heart for some odd reason.

"Well?"

"Well what?" Kate blinked at him through dreamy eyes.

Callum glanced heavenward, then back to her. His jaw clenched, and beside him, Graham tried hard to conceal his grin. "Will ye be my wife, Kate?"

Graham slipped out of the room as Kate smiled, nodding her head, and Callum near sprang for the bed.

⁓

Callum did not meet Angus outdoors that eve, and the burly warrior was quite astounded to hear his battle-hardened laird's laughter filling the great hall.

"I'd never be believin' it if I didna see it wi' me own

eyes." Angus pulled his head back from its spying position behind the thick curtain separating him from the hall.
He snatched his pouch of brew from Brodie's mouth,
spilling a godawful amount on his cousin's plaid and
cursing in the process.

Brodie stepped around Angus's bulky form and peered
around the curtain while his cousin guzzled a long swig,
covered his mouth, then belched.

Pulling back, Brodie offered him a look that said he
was the biggest dimwit ever to wield a sword and he deserved to be killed for it. "What the hell are ye coverin'
yer mouth fer? He canna hear those swine sounds ye
make over all that laughin', ye drunken fool."

Angus bristled, his broad shoulders stretching his
plaid across his chest. "I was tryin' to avoid freein' me
delicate breath in yer face."

Brodie snorted. "The only thing delicate on ye, Angus,
is yer swing."

His neck near broke from the force of Angus's enormous fist meeting his cheekbone. "Would that be what ye
were meanin' by delicate, eh, Brodie, ye son of a whore?"

His cousin merely shook the stars away from his eyes
and then threw the full weight of his body upon Angus.
They toppled over backward, taking the curtain with
them when they crashed to the ground, already swinging.

Everyone in the hall craned their necks to see what the
fuss was and then went right back to their conversations.
Only Kate gaped and rose to her feet.

"Good Lord, they are going to kill each other! Callum,
do something!" He looked at her like another head had
just sprouted from her shoulder. "Are you simply going to
sit there?" she demanded.

"Aye." He nodded. When she folded her arms across her chest and glowered at him, he chuckled. "What would ye have me do, lass? They fight all the time. Dinna they, Graham?"

"Aye, they do," his friend happily agreed.

Kate could not believe her ears. She had seen them tossing punches here and there while they rode to Skye, but this was preposterous! "Well, if you are not going to do anything about it, I will." She hefted her skirts before Callum could grab her and pounded off toward the two men hammering each other into the rushes.

"Stop it this instant!" she shouted at them. When that failed, she bent neatly and slapped Brodie, since he was on top, across the back of the head.

Behind her, a collective gasp rang out from the inhabitants of Camlochlin while Callum, Graham, and Jamie leaped over tables to get to her before she found her own face embedded to the back of her head.

"She's a damn braw lass to put her hands to Brodie!" someone whispered, astonished.

"Aye, I heard she stabbed our own laird in the leg when first they met," said another.

"I heard the laird is takin' her fer a wife."

"A fittin' choice fer a MacGregor, I'd wager."

Before Callum reached her, Kate had Brodie up on his feet, his ear painfully pinched between her thumb and index finger. "That. Is. Enough!" She emphasized each word with another harsh tug. "And you, Angus. Get up immediately so that I can get a hold of you."

The massive MacGregor lifted his head off the floor and turned it toward Callum. His laird's pitiless gaze told him to do as he was ordered.

When Kate held both men firmly by their ears, she stomped her foot. "This fighting will cease. Do you hear me?" She shook both hands while she made her demand, rattling their heads. "If you both enjoy fighting so much, mayhap a bit more training will do you some good." Immediately, Angus's worried eyes darted to Callum. "If I see you hitting each other again, you will have to come outside and wield your swords against me."

Every jaw in the great hall dropped. "Ye?" Angus looked mildly ill.

"I dinna train wi' women," Brodie drawled, then yelped when she tugged his lobe nearly off his head.

"Well, you will with me, Brodie MacGregor. Won't he, Callum?"

"Nae," Callum informed her sternly.

Kate's head snapped around with such force her hair fanned across her face. She regarded Callum with a look he had never seen on her before, and one he would not want to see her wearing while she was wielding a weapon.

"Aye?" he amended.

She nodded coolly and then turned her attention back to his newly tamed cousins.

"Did you both hear that? Your laird has commanded you to fight with me the next time you feel like tossing your fists." She released them, slapped her hands together, and turned crisply on her heel.

The crowd behind her took a unified step back, but each face wore a smile of respect. Kate's heart leapt. If she'd known that slapping a few of their most ruthless warriors around would win her their favor, she would have done the like sooner.

Chapter Thirty-Four

KATE LEANED OUT THE WINDOW to steal a glimpse of their guest before actually meeting him. It was the first time in her life she had ever received anyone of import at her home. It was the first time she had received anyone *at all*, for that matter, save for her uncle and his guard. Her heart raced and her cheeks flushed with worry. What if the MacLeod did not like her because she was a Campbell? Would he consider her a Lowlander? She had learned from almost everyone living in the castle that most Campbells were considered Lowlanders. And no Lowlander was deemed worth his weight in spit. Keddy the cook even went so far as to say Lowlanders were as bad as the English. And Rabbie the tanner called them Protestant whoresons. Kate squeaked with apprehension and patted her cheek with her palm. She looked down at the dozen or so men whose horses clopped up right to the doors.

She chewed her bottom lip while she regarded the lead rider, uncertain, by the looks of him, if he was a bear or a man. He wore a thick fur overcoat of sable brown, which matched his long hair. He was not altogether feral, though. For when he saw Graham, his smile was like a ray of light piercing the gloom. Still, Kate gulped when he dismounted and threw his tree-trunk-sized arms around Callum's commander. Whether gentle man or savage, Donald MacLeod was enormous.

Callum came up behind her and slipped his arms around her waist. "What worries ye, lass?"

"Him wanting me dead worries me." She wrung her hands together. "Did you see the size of him, Callum? Why, he's bigger than you! I'd say one—"

Callum leaned down and captured the remainder of her words with a slow, sensual kiss. Her body relaxed in his arms. "He'll no' want ye dead," he promised when he withdrew. "Donald MacLeod is one of the finest lairds I know. He took Maggie and me in when we escaped yer grandfaither's dungeon. He fed us and clothed us, and then he allowed me to build Camlochlin on his land." Callum released her and moved to the window. "D'ye know the risk he took fer me, Katie? He convinced his clan to live with MacGregors, and no' one of them has ever uttered a word that we dwell here. It's his men as well as the MacKinnons who patrol the shores of this isle, aidin' in keepin' us safe." He reached for her again and kissed her brow, speaking there. "Dinna be frightened of him. He and his sons are good men."

Kate nodded, keeping the remainder of her worries silent, and followed Callum out of the room.

She almost hightailed it back up the stairs when, reaching the bottom, the great beast of a man lifted his charcoal gaze, and then the rest of his body from where it bent to Maggie, and bellowed. "When are ye goin' to teach yer sister how to speak like a proper Highlander?"

Kate decided then and there that she could imitate their speech and the MacLeods would be none the wiser. It was clear that she would have to do the like—the man was obviously disturbed by Maggie's Lowland inflection.

The brute's eyes narrowed slightly when Callum chuckled at his query. And then Callum MacGregor, giant of a man that he was, was enveloped in a furry embrace that made him look like a boy of twelve. "Ye remember Alasdair, Rory, and Padraig." The MacLeod turned to his sons, and the three giants standing behind their father swallowed Callum up next. The rest of the men who accompanied the MacLeod were greeted with warm salutations and hefty pats to the back.

When Donald MacLeod's eyes settled on her, Kate straightened her shoulders and forced herself to smile.

"I dinna believe we've met."

"My betrothed." Callum appeared at the man's side. "Katherine Ca—"

"Kate," she cut him off before he had time to say her full name. No reason to have the visiting chieftain hate her so soon.

Her fingers were gently pried off her plaid by the MacLeod and lifted to his lips. "Well met." He kissed her hand, then angled his bent head to Callum. "I'm sorely pained that ye didna send word to me of yer betrothal."

"'Twas sudden," Callum told him and pounded him on the back. "Come, I've opened my best kegs of whiskey fer yer visit."

They moved on into the great hall, where tankards were dipped into barrels of aged brew and conversations drifted from the coming winter to which clans would be best for raiding in the spring. Some sweet meats and fresh bread were laid out on the tables, but the true feast would come later, after the MacLeods had time to refresh themselves. For now, the men were happy to warm their bellies with good whiskey and their feet by the massive hearth fire.

Kate listened to the clan chief MacLeod's hearty laughter when, after he had taken a seat beside Callum, Maggie plopped Henry the pig into his lap. Kate decided the MacLeod might not be so bad, after all, as long as she did not open her mouth. Now that she thought about it, he had not even mentioned Lowlanders when he spoke about raiding. She began to suspect that living so far from the iron fist of England's rule provided the MacLeods with little chance—or desire—to fight. Why, he seemed not to care at all about anything that went on below Fort William.

"Kate."

Jarred from her thoughtful reverie, Kate blinked her attention to the deep gray gaze fastened on her.

"Tell me," Donald MacLeod said, leaning back in his chair. "D'ye have any sisters of marriageable age? I'm lookin' fer a wife fer m' son, Padraig."

Kate's lip twitched. It was about to happen. She had hoped she could get through the morn without speaking, but she had to answer him now. Her eyes cut to Callum, but Donald's son, Alasdair, was leading him away from the table, back to the barrels of brew.

Kate reminded herself that she had faced far more terrifying men than this one, and cleared her throat before she spoke. "Nae, my laird. I have only a brother."

He arched a speculative brow at her, then sipped his drink. "I see. Where, might I ask, did Callum find ye, lass?"

Kate remembered to breathe. God help her when the man found out she was a Campbell. She inhaled a deep breath. "He saved me from a neighboring clan who were raiding my land."

"In?"

"In Glen Orchy, my laird."

"Och, what in blazes was Callum doin' in Glen Orchy? Was he warrin' wi' the Campbells again?"

Before Kate answered, Callum returned to the table. "Kate, Maggie asks that ye meet her in Netta's chambers."

"Of course." Kate rose from her chair, grateful to be leaving. "I will go right away."

Callum's gaze lingered on her as she raced up the stairs.

"Ye love her," Donald announced, unable to believe what was quite clear to see with is own eyes. When Callum turned to him and nodded, Donald raised his cup to his lips to drink. "'Tis aboot time is what I say, lad. Mayhap now ye'll find some peace and quit tryin' to kill every damned Campbell who crosses yer path."

"Mayhap," Callum allowed, taking Kate's seat opposite Donald. "Since she's a Campbell, and I dinna want to kill her."

Donald MacLeod sprayed his brew where it belonged after such an announcement—across the room. "What?" he bellowed, wiping his mouth. "Och, saints be wi' me and tell me I heard ye wrong. She's a what?"

"A Campbell."

Donald rolled his head back and shook it at the heavens. When he thought he had gathered enough wits to continue, he returned his stunned gaze to Callum. "Jesus and Mary, a Campbell. Ye fell in love wi' a Campbell."

"Aye, the Duke of Argyll's niece." That sobered the MacLeod well enough. Callum waited patiently while his friend choked out a few unintelligible sounds. When he deemed it safe to continue, he motioned for Lizabeth to bring the laird more whiskey. "I had planned to hold her fer ransom and make Argyll come to me."

"Which is exactly what he's doin'." MacLeod dropped his head in his hands and sighed.

"Aye," Callum agreed. "I expected him to come fer her. But I didna expect her to hold my heart the way she does." Callum downed his brew, then peered at Donald's bent head. "I willna let her go. I wanted this to end with Argyll, but her brother will be her guardian in accordance with English law when their uncle is dead. He may come against me, but I willna let her go."

Lifting his eyes to the lad he had come to love like a son, Donald sighed and then nodded. "Ye willna have to. I know I claimed I'd never get involved wi' yer war, but the MacLeods will stand at yer side if any army comes against ye."

"Nae, Donald. I'll take care of this myself. I promised no' to harm her brother, and if I'm right aboot him, I may no' have to. Just tell me where Argyll is. He is the one I want."

"We dinna know. He reached Glengarry and turned east."

Callum was still taking in that bit of information when Jamie burst into the great hall, his whiskerless face flush with excitement.

"There's a new MacGregor in Camlochlin!" he shouted. He cut a path to a table, snatched a tankard of brew from Alasdair MacLeod's hand, quaffed its entire contents, then swooned on his feet for a moment. He blinked and found Callum standing before him. Feeling a belch of immense proportions rising within his innards, Jamie fought to contain it, not wanting to do the like against his laird's chest. He paled considerably in the process, swooned again, then grinned up into Callum's face. "Brodie has himself a son."

"A son!" Callum turned and called out to everyone in the hall. "May the Lord bless the lad." The hall erupted into cheers of good wishes, and more kegs were opened. "And Netta?" Callum asked Graham's already inebriated brother.

"She does well. Aileen and Murron are with her. 'Tis Brodie who'll need lookin' after. I vow I saw tears in his eyes."

Callum looked around the hall and lifted his cup to Donald MacLeod. "Another MacGregor!" he called out. "And if I have my way, there will be many more to come."

The MacLeod chieftain laughed while Callum turned his attention back to Jamie. "Tell Kate to bring the babe doun so we can have a look at him."

Jamie hiccupped, then blinked to better focus on Callum. "Kate's no' with Netta."

Now Callum turned to face him fully. "Aye, she is. Maggie sent fer her."

Jamie shook his head. "Maggie's no' there, either. She wanted to go to the barn, but I told her to wait doun here fer me."

Callum dashed out of the hall and was outside the castle before anyone had time to follow him. *Please, God, let them be in the barn,* he beseeched. Hell, Maggie knew better than to leave the castle without Jamie. "Kate!" His voice exploded into a roar that echoed off the wall of black rock behind him. He did not wait for an answer but raced toward the barn.

When he reached it, he heard the sound of women's laughter. He thanked God silently before plunging inside. Kate sat with her legs curled beneath her in the hay, with Maggie lying beside her. Both women looked up, and when they saw him, Kate lifted her hand to her mouth, fearing the worst by the looks of him.

"What's wrong?" she asked. "What has happened?"

Callum leaned against the wall, certain that his legs would not hold him up if he didn't. He ran both hands down his ashen face and then, in the time it took Kate to blink, stood towering over them both.

"What the hell are ye doin' in here?" Though he shouted, his voice was laden with emotion. "Ye must tell me when ye wander off." Kate rose to her feet while he turned to his sister. "Maggie, blast ye! How many times must I tell ye to . . ." His words faded into a tight groan when Kate touched her fingertips to his jaw.

She wanted to weep. Not because he shouted, but because he was so frightened for them. For her. "Forgive me, Callum," she said, barely able to resist the urge to throw herself into his arms.

She did not have to. He hauled her against him, crushing her in his embrace until the breath left her body. Neither one of them heard Donald enter the barn, nor his gentle call to Maggie to follow him back out.

"Callum, I cannot breathe," Kate gasped into his chest.

He loosened his hold just a bit and bent his head to her until his gaze was level with hers. He had not wanted to tell her. He did not want her to fret over something neither one of them could stop. But she had to know now. She had to know how dangerous it was to be out of his sight. "Kate, yer uncle was seen near Glengarry a few days past."

Her complexion paled. "And my brother?"

"I dinna know if he accompanies yer uncle. We dinna know where he is. I feared—"

She covered his mouth with her fingers. "Ssh," she whispered. "We will save Robert, and then all will be well." She pressed her lips to his, silencing whatever else he thought to say, until words no longer mattered and the only thing that did were his passionate kisses.

Chapter Thirty-Five

⁓

DUNCAN CAMPBELL SPAT on the body at his feet. Godforsaken MacGregors did not talk even under pain of torture.
No matter, he would find the rest of them. He was close.
He had to be. He was sure he would have found them by
now if not for the skirmish with the MacKinnons a pair of
days ago. He smacked his leather riding glove against his
thigh, and a small cloud of dust rose to his nostrils.
Bloody MacKinnons had cost him over twenty of his men
before they were questioned and then disposed of.

Squinting against the high afternoon sun, he scanned
the misty glens until he found Robert appearing over a
small ridge with the rest of his men. Duncan's lips curved
into a challenging smile when his nephew scowled at the
body crumpled on the ground.

"It is only a MacGregor, nephew. Remember they have
abducted your dear sister and have most likely killed her."

Robert held up his hand to halt Duncan's words.
"Enough, please. I do not wish to think on such things
anymore."

"You *must* think on them," Duncan insisted, moving toward him. "It will take all your fortitude to kill the outlaw." He regarded Robert with a narrowed look. "Or are you going soft already?"

"Nae," Robert ground out between clenched teeth, but his gaze drifted back to the man lying dead a few feet away. In truth, he might be going soft, after all. For he was sickened by his uncle's cruelty, disheartened by the ease with which Duncan killed anyone who refused to aid him.

"I've had much time to think on this. I drank and laughed with Graham Grant many nights. I do not think he will harm Kate." Robert continued despite his uncle's laughter. "I do not believe he would serve a man who would kill a woman."

Duncan's eyes glinted with malice, piercing the mists. "Ah, you mean the clever commander who infiltrated my very own holding in order to find out where our dear Katherine lived."

"They were looking for you," Robert reminded him. "They did not kill any of the women at Kildun."

Duncan shoved his glove over his fingers and reached for his horse. "I do not care. The hunted has become the hunter." When he gained his saddle, he lifted his head and squinted west, toward the giant black mountains in the distance. "I fear we were deceived by the Cameron when he told you those we seek rode east. The only thing we've found so far are wild animals. And I do not mean Mac-Gregors." He eyed the bloody corpse on the ground. "Pity it was not the traitor Grant, aye?" He slid his gaze to Robert, daring him to disagree. "When we find them, I will leave that one for you to kill." He kicked his mount's flanks and disappeared into the thick gray mists like an apparition returning to the churning bowels of the Earth.

~

A lark soared over sheep scampering across the glen. Somewhere close by, children laughed and cattle bells rang while the music of hauntingly beautiful pipes dragged over the distant moors. Lying flat upon a carpet of purple heather, Kate turned her face to smile at Maggie, who was spread out beside her. Tiny blossoms tickled Kate's nose and filled her senses with their wild fragrance. Thoughts of the last few days brought a satisfied sigh to her lips. The MacLeods had left Camlochlin, but not before the chieftain had told her his wistful stories of faeries and romance and heroes long dead yet held forever in the heart. Faither Lachlan had not yet arrived, but Kate did not care. Callum told her that in the Highlands a man need only claim a woman for her to be considered his wife. And he had most definitely claimed her. Angus and Brodie had not thrown a fist in a se'nnight, the latter being too busy carrying his newborn bairn around and wearing an arrogant grin plastered to face to care about fighting, drinking, or anything that did not resemble the downy sprinkle of mink that covered his babe's head. Kate touched her fingers over her own belly, hoping Callum's babe grew there. It was too soon to know. She breathed a perfect sigh again, thinking of how often her beloved worked at planting his seed and the passionate mastery of his endeavors. Even knowing her uncle was close enough to give cause to worry had not stopped Callum from taking her to bed every chance afforded them. Why, he'd even stormed into Maggie's chamber the day before, a thin sheen of sweat from a long day of practice defining the sleek muscles in his arms, and carried her away to his chambers. Kate giggled remembering how angry Maggie had been at her brother for interrupting their session of careful primping. Primping that had begun after Kate had convinced Maggie that a certain young, handsome warrior truly did fancy her.

Kate suspected that Maggie already knew. It was clear to anyone with a decent pair of eyes that Jamie's heart was hopelessly lost to Maggie MacGregor. Maggie's heart was not faring any better, though she was as stubborn when it came to matters of love as was her brother. Still, it had taken only one very appreciative grin from her admirer, aimed at her unstained face and neatly combed hair, to create the meticulous little hellion lying beside Kate now.

And a hellion she was.

Kate had no idea Maggie possessed a temper that could rival Callum's! Despite the lovely day, Maggie's mood was as sour as four-day-old milk. And "'twas all Jamie's fault." According to the wee brooding MacGregor, her would-be suitor had found a new companion. A big, hairy, drunken sot by the name of Angus.

"Do not pout so," Kate said softly and patted her dear friend's hand. "I am sure Jamie would rather be with you."

Maggie angled her head and tossed Kate a sharp look. "Then why are *ye* lyin' here near me instead of him? I have done everything to win his favor, Kate. But he still has not announced his feelings to me. He would rather spend his days with a man who belches more often than he blinks!"

Kate hid her smile behind her fingers.

"I told him this morn that I would prefer it if Graham kept watch over me from this day hence. He had the bollocks to grow angry! But my decision has been made. Graham smiles often, while Jamie looks pained." Maggie paused her tirade for a moment and squinted her large blue eyes on the sky. "Mayhap he *is* pained by having to follow me all over the blasted castle."

She was most definitely in love, Kate decided while Maggie went on to list Jamie's faults. "Aye, you have it right, sweeting," Kate said glumly. "Spare yourself the suffering of his ungracious manner. Jamie is certainly not what any lass, save mayhap for Glenna, would want in a man. More than once have I seen her ogling Jamie with affection dancing in her eyes. Let her—"

"Glenna?" Maggie pushed herself up and tugged on Kate's sleeve. "But I have seen her draped over Graham's arm."

Kate shrugged and closed her eyes, basking in the warm sun. "Mayhap Glenna would be content with either brother. Or both. Now that Jamie is free to . . ." She drew her shoulders up around her ears when Maggie shrieked, and then she said a silent prayer of forgiveness and one of protection for poor Glenna when Maggie stood up and marched toward the castle.

With a satisfied sigh, Kate rose to her feet and wiped a few heather blossoms from her skirts. On her way to the castle, she waved at the women hanging their laundry to dry in the cool breeze outside their cottages. They greeted her in like manner, most coming—she hoped—to accept her as one of their own. Good Lord, but she loved Camlochlin. She loved the MacGregors, and she loved their mighty laird so much it almost made her weep. She prayed that Callum might someday come to love her in return. Dear God, she would give anything just to hear him speak the words. Misty-eyed, she passed the western wall where Callum usually practiced with his men and looked around. He was not there. She turned on her heel to go search him out inside the castle and stepped directly into his crushing embrace.

"Lookin' fer me?" His voice was as deep as an erotic drumbeat against her ear, his breath warm as it fell to her nape.

Aye, she loved him well.

"Kate?" He slipped his arms around her waist and bent to look into her eyes. "Somethin' troubles ye?"

She shook her head. "I was just pondering some things. It is naught to fret over." She blinked back a rush of unwanted tears and stood on the tips of her toes to kiss him on the mouth.

She couldn't help herself and watched the sensual way his lush forest of lashes closed over his eyes. His lips molded beneath hers, firm, yielding, while his fingers splayed over her spine and drew her closer. She wanted to live and die in his arms. She loved him, and it filled her heart to bursting.

"Now tell me what troubles ye, Katie," he coaxed in a low voice when she withdrew from their kiss.

How could she ever begin to tell him the depth of what she felt for him? He would pull away. Tell her it was too dangerous. He cared for her. It was clear, but how could he ever give his heart to the granddaughter of Liam Campbell? Still, when he looked at her . . . She reached out and swept her fingers over his brow. "Your eyes tell me things I do not understand." The words fell from her lips before she could stop them.

"Aye?" His gaze softened with some deep emotion that made her heart thud in her ears. "Is it so difficult to understand that ye mean more to me than anything I am willin' to admit?"

"You are afraid." She nodded, understanding.

"Of many things, but that never stopped me from doin' them."

"Aye, because you are brave and strong. But this is different, Callum." She looked up at him and cursed her quivering lower lip. "This has naught to do with your brawn or your pride."

"What has it to do with, then?" He played with a curl winding down her temple, her trembling lip not escaping his attention.

"Your heart."

"Ah, that."

"Aye." Kate dragged her sleeve across her nose, then broke free of his embrace and stepped back. "Forgive me. It was foolish of me to—"

"I love ye, Kate."

Her lips parted, but only a short gasp fell from them. He smiled, and finally his eyes fully revealed what was there all along.

"I'll love ye until my dyin' day, and if I have any say aboot it, long after that."

She leaped into his arms, quite certain that had he been a smaller man she would have knocked him clean off his feet.

Angus and Jamie watched from a parapet along the castle walls. With a world more experience than Jamie might ever possess, Angus waited with relative ease until Callum carried his wife inside the castle before his belch erupted from his lips.

"I think she was the only one in the whole bloody castle who didna know he loved her. Women are thick-skulled. Dinna ferget that, lad." Angus passed Jamie more brew.

"Aye, thick-skulled," Jamie brooded and almost teetered over the edge of the wall.

Angus caught him easily enough by the scruff of his plaid before the younger man toppled over. "Hell, but ye canna hold yer whiskey."

"Get off me, ye flea-ridden son of a barn rat." Jamie tugged and almost fell over the edge again. His mood was even more sour than Maggie's. But Angus had not been happier since the day he first broke Brodie's nose. He'd thought all hope was lost for any more good, clean sport when Kate demanded that he and Brodie quit brutalizing each other. Doom settled over his heart every time he watched his ruthless cousin tenderly kissing his new babe's head. But now, oh now, a new spark of hope and exhilaration gleamed in Angus's eyes.

"Did ye just insult me, Jamie Grant?" he asked carefully. He would not want to injure the lad in error.

"I did?"

Angus decided to ignore the glassy, bewildered set of big blue eyes staring back at him, so desperate was he for a hearty fight. He nodded and sent his fist into Jamie's guts with a satisfied sigh that rivaled any belch he could produce.

In response, Jamie promptly emptied the contents of his belly onto Angus's boots.

Chapter Thirty-Six

⌒

DUNCAN CAMPBELL BLEW DIRT out of his mouth. He waited in the thick brush until he was sure the MacLeod scouts had moved on before scrambling on his belly toward his men.

Cutting his uncle a contemptuous side glance, Robert realized just how much of a serpent the Earl of Argyll really was. For the past three days, they had done naught but kill until the sight of their own blood-soaked plaids churned Robert's stomach. He had met the Devil, looked into those eyes filled with raw contempt. Aye, Callum MacGregor thought naught of killing Campbells, but Duncan was no better. Feuds, for whatever truth lie behind them, were one thing. Cutting the heads from the dead was another entirely. And Duncan Campbell had done the like to a score of men already.

When his uncle reached him, he looked out first amid the thick tangle of bushes that separated him and his men from the rocky cliffs of Elgol, then at Robert.

"Now do you see why I traded the horses? They would

never make it over those crags. We will travel over the cliffs on foot," he whispered. "If we meet up with anyone, we will tell them we are MacLeods. If they try to stop us, we kill them."

Fearing his uncle had finally gone mad—or mayhap he only just now noticed it—Robert was tempted to laugh. But it would have been a joyless sound. He was sorry the poor drunkard they killed the day before had not only admitted that a clan of MacGregors lived on the isle of Skye but had directed them toward the right path. Only sixteen of them remained, and Robert knew it was not enough to take the MacGregor holding, should they truly find it.

"Uncle, hear me," he tried to explain for the hundredth time that morn. "I do not think your plan will succeed. We cannot simply slip into their midst. Think you Mac-Gregor does not know the faces of his people? I want my sister. If I must kill the laird to get her back, I will do so. But I do not intend to murder this Margaret MacGregor, be she the Devil's weakness or not. There is no honor in that."

"Honor?" Duncan sneered. "What do I care of honor? I suffered the greatest humiliation any son should have to endure because of that ill-bred bastard. Callum MacGregor is an outlaw. He defies every decree set forth by England."

"Then arrest him and see him punished in accordance with the law. Why are you so eager to kill or injure everyone but the man you seek? And why did you not seek him before he took my sister?"

"Enough questions," Duncan snapped at him. "Get

up." He rose and hauled his nephew up by the arm. The rest of his men followed.

"Do you fear him, then?" Robert demanded, seeing the evidence of it clearly now on Duncan's face. "Am I to do that which you cannot?"

Chuckling, Duncan began climbing the first of many jagged cliffs. "When the time comes for such a task, I fear your heart will fail you, nephew. But after he cuts the withered organ from your chest, I will prove my worth when I kill his sister."

Prove his worth? Robert wanted to ask him what he meant, but the path was a treacherous one. He needed his wits to make it up the cliff.

As if to confirm his decision to remain silent and concentrate was the right one, a stone came loose beneath Duncan's boot and fell, though not far, since they only just began to climb. Nonetheless, it smashed against the serrated precipice and disappeared into the raging current below. Robert made no move to steady his uncle, shamefully imagining it was Duncan's head instead of the rock that took such a beating on the way down. A short while later, and a bit higher up, Alasdair Drummond followed the rock and plunged to his death. Finally, Duncan stopped the troop and commanded Kevin Menzie to return to Sleat and procure a boat.

"We cannot return this way." He peered over the edge to the water below. "Hire a captain and return here to meet us. Once we are done, we will return to the mainland upon Loch Scavaig. Go, make haste."

Robert's fingers were raw by the time they reached a narrow ledge more than one hundred feet above the thunderous whitecaps. He decided he did not care for this desolate place, and then decided it did not care for them, either, when the skies suddenly blackened and opened up like the mouth of some great beast spitting its torrential vengeance upon them. Duncan pressed onward, losing two more men before he conceded his defeat to the elements.

"Uncle," Robert said while they sat with their backs pressed against the sheer sheet of rock and waited out the storm. "Graham told me that MacGregor and his sister were imprisoned as children. Is this true?"

"Aye."

Robert's stomach balled into a knot. He closed his eyes and leaned his head back. What else of what Graham had told him was true? "Why was this done to them?"

"There were many reasons," Duncan said. "Mainly because they were MacGregors, enemies of the realm. The MacGregors have tried for centuries to convince anyone who would listen that our clan had wronged them. They pitifully sought excuses for their savagery against our kin. The Devil's father was a known rebel who had taken up arms against the Campbells."

"But they were children," Robert said quietly, heartsick.

"It does not matter. Liam Campbell did what he wanted to do. I did not question him."

"Did my father question him?"

Duncan's expression darkened as he stared out over the landscape that was as harsh as the memory of his father's face. "He was given his own holding at Glen Orchy and chose not to hunt the outlaws. When he found out about the children he sent word of his protest. He was naught like our father. But my father forgave him." Duncan swiped the rain from his eyes. "Even when Colin

later argued the Devil's reasons for killing so many
Campbells, my father forgave him."

Chilled by the seething emotion beneath his uncle's
smooth veneer of indifference, Robert turned to look at
him while he spoke.

"I think your grandfather was glad MacGregor had
brought chaos to Kildun. For it forced his favored son to
return."

"So my father was not at Kildun when the Devil escaped," Robert said softly, as facts he had never been told
became clear to him now. "When did Callum MacGregor
put the sword to him, then? You did say it was The Devil
who killed my father, did you not? Why did he do it if,
as you say, my father did not fault him entirely for his
actions?"

Duncan slid his gaze to Robert's. A trace of unease
flittered across his features but lasted only an instant before his cool demeanor returned.

"Nephew, if you insist on knowing the shameful truth,
then here it is. Your father was a sympathizer. A fool who
received a fool's recompense."

"Nae," Robert argued. "It is not foolish to show mercy
to others. Amish and John taught me—"

Duncan's voice dipped low so the others could not
hear as he turned to stare at his nephew fully. "Pray they
have not made you heir to such weak-minded sentiments.
Pray more that your sister does not adhere to the same
folly."

"And if she does?"

"Then she will suffer the same justice as they. It is the
law of England."

For a terrifying instant Robert thought he would be the

next to fall to his death when he shot to his feet, enraged, stunned, and quite literally dumbstruck. "By whose hand will she suffer, Uncle?"

Duncan's tight shrug was his only answer to that particular query. "Let us hope she fights them even now."

"I tell you if you harm her, I will stand with the Mac-Gregors and see you dead! Christ." Robert tore his fingers through his hair as another grave truth dawned on him. "My father was a sympathizer. He never spoke unkindly of the MacGregors. He never spoke of them at all." His frenzied gaze fastened on Duncan. "Tell me truly who put the sword to him."

Robert would have preferred it if Duncan shouted at him, erupted in indignant fury at what his nephew was suggesting. Instead, all he received was an icy smirk.

"What will it gain you to know of it now, Robert?" Duncan looked up at the heavy pewter clouds overhead. "Rain's stopped." He turned to the others, just ahead of them. "Let us continue."

Robert did not move. He was certain that if he did, it would be to fling his uncle off the side of the cliff. Disbelief and disillusionment nagged at the edge of reason. Surely Amish or John would have told him if Duncan had been the one to cut their laird down. Mayhap they had not known, Robert considered. After all, the fatal wound had been inflicted from behind. Nae, nae, not his father's own brother. Robert leaned over the high crag, fighting to keep the contents of his belly where they belonged.

Besieged by fury he had never known before, Robert leaped after his uncle and caught him by the shoulder. "Why did you do it?" he demanded, spinning Duncan around to face him. Both men teetered on the pebbly ledge. Duncan gripped Robert's arms to steady himself.

"God slay you!" the earl spat angrily. "I swear I will do it myself if you unbalance me again."

Robert's voice rumbled like the distant thunder. "And I swear I will hurl you to the sea if you do not give me a reply."

Duncan looked over his shoulder and gave the command for the others to continue on. Though he was certain they could not hear, he leaned into Robert's shoulder and spoke in a quiet voice. "Very well, I will tell you." When Robert felt the sharp sting of his uncle's blade pressing against his ribs, he ground his jaw. "With a handful of his men," his uncle whispered, "your father set out to find the savage who massacred his comrades. He did not intend to bring him to justice, but rather to deliver him to safety. I followed him. It was night when I found him. He and his men were asleep." Duncan withdrew slightly and tilted his head up to look directly into Robert's eyes, his own gaze mildly remorseful. "In truth, I hated killing him, but there is no place for regret in war.

"My father believed the Devil killed his son," Duncan continued, unfazed by the murderous rage in his nephew's eyes. "I could not tell him the truth, for though he hated sympathizers, he would not have understood."

"Did Amish and John know?" Robert could barely keep his fury under control.

"Nae, but they were sympathizers, as well." Duncan sighed when Robert closed his eyes with the realization of what had become of the two men who helped raised him and his sister. "They outlived their purpose, Robert. You had already left Glen Orchy, and Katherine was to come with me. You've no idea how I have worried over you both through the years."

The sincerity in his voice was almost an extraordinary thing to hear. If Robert was not afraid of screaming until the cliffs around him crumbled, he would have opened his mouth to laugh.

"You worried we would become sympathizers," Robert pointed out tightly.

"Nae, I visited often enough to see that that never happened."

"It is true, I have hated the MacGregors all my life," Robert said, hating even more the honor he cherished as a boy, the glory that had lured him away from his true duty of protecting his sister. "Had I not gone to Kildun, my sister would still be safe in Glen Orchy."

"Soon"—Duncan placed his hand on Robert's shoulder—"she will be safe once again in Inverary. I vow it." When Robert said nothing, he turned and continued on his way along the edge.

Robert followed after him in silence, his features defined with steadfast determination to find his sister and mayhap, with the MacGregor's aid, bring the true devil to justice.

Chapter Thirty-Seven

⁓

THE NEXT DAY and three men later, the Earl of Argyll crouched at the summit of a grassy incline and craned his neck to gaze at a castle just as black and impenetrable as the mammoth mountain wall looming over it. He snapped his mouth shut.

"This cannot be the MacGregor holding," he said a moment later when his wonder switched to denial. "The old drunk must have directed us toward the wrong path and we have stumbled upon a MacLeod castle."

The fortress ahead had to belong to the MacLeods, Duncan told himself over and over while he gaped. He refused to believe a rebel outlaw had such a magnificent holding. It was smaller than Kildun, but far too grand for a MacGregor. He let his steely gray gaze drift over the dozens of thatched-roof bothys scattered throughout the vale and felt his blood boil.

"They can see in every direction that matters," Robert said, pointing to the Highlanders patrolling the battlements. He turned to his uncle. "What do you suggest we do now?"

"We wait here until nightfall, then make our way opposite the loch, along those hills where there is more shadow, and slip inside the castle."

Robert snorted, "You're mad. We will be shot down before we reach the front doors. And even if we do breach—"

"You will find the MacGregor and kill him while the rest of us search for Katherine. If you ever want to see her alive again, you will do as I say."

The meager group of men waited atop the crest for night to fall, but darkness never came. Instead, a heavy mist rolled down the mountain wall, chilling their bones.

Duncan insisted they wait until the mist covered the entire vale. It was as good as darkness. Even better.

Robert fully intended to follow his uncle into the castle. He did not, however, intend to kill Callum MacGregor. He prayed Katherine was alive and unharmed. Graham had been truthful with him, and he had been so in defense of his friend. Robert did not believe a man like Graham could be loyal to a heartless beast. He did not believe they had harmed his sister. He would find MacGregor and plead to speak with him. Nae, he decided an instant later, the laird would slay him the moment he discovered Duncan was inside the castle. Robert had to find a way to get inside without Duncan and his burly friends.

They were Menzies, who likely would not give a rat's arse about Duncan's crime against his brother. But would they feel differently if the earl was guilty of killing the earl before him?

Robert turned to him and, in a voice loud enough for the others to hear, said, "Colin was your father's favored son."

Duncan met his gaze. "What?"

"You said earlier that your father's favored son had re-turned to Kildun, aye?"

Duncan did not flinch, but his eyes sharpened on his nephew. "Aye, Liam favored him."

"You said your father would forgive him anything, even for being a MacGregor sympathizer. You hated Colin for finding favor in your father's eyes when you suffered humiliation in them." He looked over Duncan's shoulder at the Menzies and was pleased to see them lis-tening intently. "Tell me, uncle, did your father suspect you of treachery when his favored son was killed *after* MacGregor escaped? Is that why you killed him?"

Without even an off-pitch breath to betray his inten-tion, Duncan reached for a large rock and smashed it into Robert's temple. When his nephew fell limp to the ground, Duncan pushed back the hair that had fallen over his own brow from the force of his blow, drew his dagger, and turned on the men gaping at him.

Duncan Campbell stepped into the mists with a single purpose, to destroy the Devil and regain what had been taken from him.

Chapter Thirty-Eight

⁓

KATE OPENED HER EYES and then closed them again at the glaring beam of sunlight pouring into the chamber from the window. She really would have to have a word with Callum about hanging some draperies—very thick ones. At the thought of him, she smiled and turned over in the bed, intending to help him welcome the new day with a few strategically placed kisses.

She squeaked when she saw Maggie sitting in his spot instead, her legs crisscrossed beneath her and a comb clutched in her fist.

"I thought ye'd never be waking up."

"Maggie, what are you doing here so early? Where is your brother?"

"He's around somewhere," Maggie advised her hastily. There was no time to answer silly queries now. "Are ye intending to sleep all day? My hair and I are waiting for ye."

Kate could not help the smile Maggie always brought to her lips. "I'm awake." She hauled herself out of bed and tried to run her fingers through her own hair. She tugged on a few tangled curls. "My hair is waiting for me, as well."

"Hurry, Kate. He'll be up and about soon." Maggie sprang from the bed and pushed Kate toward the stool where she usually prepared Maggie for the day.

"Who?" Kate tried to conceal her knowing smile, but it pulled at the corners of her mouth.

"Who? Why, Jamie, of course. Who else? Honestly, Kate, sometimes I think ye and Callum are more suited to each other than either of ye realize."

Kate gave her a surprised look and then burst into laughter. "Goodness, poor Jamie hasn't a chance against you."

Maggie cast her an askew look, but then her lips curled into a mischievous smile. "At least not after today, I hope."

"What happens today?" Kate asked her, sobering. "What are you going to do?"

"I am going to tell him what I think of him before we are both too old to care," Maggie said, thrusting her comb into Kate's hand. "And I would prefer to look bonny doing it. So, if ye please?"

Kate nodded, taking the comb. How braw this wee woman was. Even Kate had begun to wonder when Jamie would finally begin their courtship. The poor lad was afraid of Callum, but Kate was certain Callum would be as happy as she was about their union.

"I think a lovely blue snood in your hair will bring out the beauty of your eyes," Kate said gently, offering Maggie the stool to begin.

Kate and Maggie made their way down the stairs, peeking left and right in hopes of spotting Jamie and sauntering past him. It would take him no time at all to follow. Maggie intended on leading him directly to the barn, where she would finally reveal her heart. She was so disappointed when they did not find him, she stomped her foot and muttered an expletive that would have made Brodie proud.

They were about to exit the castle when they walked straight into Callum. "I was just comin' back to bed," he said, pulling Kate into his arms. "Where are ye off to?"

"To the barn," Maggie brooded.

"Give me a moment and I'll come with ye."

"Nae!" both women exclaimed at the same time, which earned them a fierce scowl.

"Send Jamie, Callum." Kate offered him a wink that made his scowl deepen. "Please," she begged with a slight kiss to his chin. "I will come to you soon," she whispered along his jaw.

"Verra well," he conceded, wondering when he had become such a soft pup of a man. "Wait here and I'll find him." He planted a kiss squarely on Kate's mouth and whispered to her before he let her go. "Make haste back to bed."

He met Angus in his search and inquired as to Jamie's whereabouts.

"He's likely off pickin' daffodils fer yer sister. He's been avoidin' me company, and I'm beginnin' to feel slighted by it."

"Check the meadow, and if ye find him send him

here." Callum continued on his way up the stairs without turning. "And be quick aboot it, Angus."

⁓

Thin beams of sunshine broke through the loose-paneled barn walls, creating a web of dancing, dust-infused light. Henry squealed with delight when Kate and Maggie entered and plodded toward them on his stubby legs. Matilda honked but was too busy nibbling on a string of corn that had fallen from the rafters to greet them properly.

"Bertrid, stop chasing that little mouse." Maggie picked up her cat and nuzzled the feline beneath her chin. "Do ye think Jamie will come?"

"Of course he will," Kate assured her. "But I think we should have remained in the castle. Callum is going to be angry with us." When Maggie shrugged her concerns away, reminding Kate that the castle was but a stone's throw away, Kate sighed and reached for a large bag of feed and began filling each animal's bowl. Ahern pushed her arm with his nose, urging her to feed him first. "As soon as Jamie arrives, I will leave the two of you alone."

When the barn door opened again a few moments later, Henry squealed and took off running. Matilda spread her wings, her corn string forgotten, and honked wildly, waddling toward the door as if someone had sounded a duck battle call.

Casting Maggie a knowing wink, Kate turned to greet the flaxen-haired warrior. The barn door swung closed slowly, but no one stood at its entrance.

"Jamie?" Kate called out. She strained to see into the shadowy corners. Her gaze darted to Maggie clutching Bertrid tightly to her chest. "The wind, mayhap," she said

and started for the door to close it. She had taken only a
few steps past Maggie when the lass screeched her name.

Kate swung around and then staggered backward.

Her uncle stood behind Callum's sister, stretching her
spine straight as one arm looped around her throat and his
other hand clutched a dagger pointed at her belly. "Hush,
Katherine," he said softly. His gaze narrowed on her
across the filtered light. "You have settled in quite nicely
here, I see."

Terror gripped Kate's muscles, paralyzing her. She almost retched with the force of stifling a scream. Her skin
crawled just looking at him. He was filthy. Dark stains of
dried blood crusted his hands and plaid. Dear God, whose
blood was it?

"You do not look pleased to see me, niece." He moved
his blade upward toward Maggie's throat.

Gathering every ounce of control she possessed, Kate
inhaled, flaring her nostrils, and tilted her head belliger-
ently. "What took you so long in finding me, Uncle? I
was beginning to think you would never arrive."

That seemed to mollify him, but only for a moment before he snarled at her again. "You look remarkably well,
Katherine. Getting along with the savages, are you?"

"Och, come now." She sighed as if he were too daft to
understand. "What would you have me do? I stayed alive,
as you did." Her scornful smile told him she was remembering the fight in her father's yard with the McColls.
"Now, have you come to converse with me, or take me
home?"

Maggie shook her head and began to cry. Bertrid
slipped from her arms and fled into the shadows. "Do not
go away, Kate." Her plea was so stricken with sorrow,

Kate almost ran to her. She stopped herself, swallowing back her fear and guilt. The sooner she convinced her uncle to take her home, the safer everyone would be. She would worry about returning later.

Duncan yanked Maggie's neck to quiet her, and Kate took a step forward. "Uncle." She tried to pull his attention away from her dearest friend.

"Where is the MacGregor?" he suddenly demanded.

Kate shrugged her shoulders and was about to tell him she did not know or care, when the barn door swung open again.

Jamie stood at the entrance, his arms cradling a dense spray of yellow daffodils. His smile faded almost instantly when he saw the Earl of Argyll. He reached for his sword, spilling the flowers around his feet. Before he had time to unsheathe his weapon, Duncan hurled his dagger at him.

Kate cried out, but Maggie only gaped, stricken with horror as her beloved gripped the hilt protruding from his belly and then collapsed to the ground. Duncan moved instantly, kicking the door closed and retrieving his blade from where it was lodged. Without pause, he cut across the barn and gripped Maggie by the hair, yanking her head back.

Kate hurled herself at him, ready to fight him to the death. He swung and sliced open her palm. Blood shot outward, splattering across Maggie's face. Her blue eyes, already glazed with the haunting images from her past, went vacant and she opened her mouth to begin screaming.

Duncan silenced her with a blow to her head, using the hilt of his dagger. Kate went deathly still when he pointed the tip to Maggie's neck, his eyes wild with what he meant to do.

"Uncle, nae!" Kate took a step forward, reaching out to him with her bloody hand. "I beg you. I beg you, nae."

"You plead for the life of a MacGregor?" he accused, craning Maggie's head farther back.

"Aye, I do. I will do whatever you ask of me."

Duncan's eyes shot to the door, then back to her. "Very well. We are leaving. If the guards call out, you will cast your lovely smile on them and convince them you are in no danger. It is clear these people are your friends. Make them believe you, Katherine, or I will cut her throat."

"I will do it," Kate promised. "But you will release her now." When the earl laughed, she continued quickly. "If you do not let her go, I will not move from this spot. Are you prepared to die, Uncle? It is only a matter of time before Callum's men come barreling in here. You stand no chance against them, I assure you." Her muscles spasmed when he inched his blade closer to Maggie's flesh, ready to refuse her demands. "Do it," she challenged him, suppressing the need to scream, the urge to throw herself at his feet and plead for Maggie's life. "And then cut my throat, as well. But know this, you will die this day, also."

She almost staggered with relief when he tossed Maggie aside. When Kate moved to go to her, her uncle snatched her by the back of her neck and dragged her to the door.

"Betray me," he warned silkily against her ear while he covered his face with his plaid, "and I vow I will escape and return to Kildun—and to your brother."

Chapter Thirty-Nine

ROBERT GROANED and struggled to open his eyes. Searing jolts of fire shot through his head. He brought his hands up to cradle his forehead and felt warm, sticky blood drying over his eyes. He waited a few moments and lifted his lids slowly. A swath of bright noontide sky greeted him. He blinked as the memory of the night before returned to him. His uncle had struck him with something, a tree trunk if his tormented skull had anything to say about it. With a tight moan and a muttered oath, he pushed himself up on his elbows. He looked around, already knowing Duncan was not there with him. The madman was most likely dead. Robert hoped it was so. He dragged himself to his knees, too weak to stand, and began to crawl down the sloping hill toward the castle. He had to find Kate. If MacGregor found him first, so be it. He would worry over it when the time came.

He almost crawled over the dead body of one of the Menzie men. "Och, God." Robert moaned. His gaze glided a little to the left, where he found the others, as dead as the first. Sickened, Robert had no doubt about who had killed them.

He turned his attention to the fortress ahead. Where was his uncle? Was he already inside? Everything was too quiet. If the MacGregors had discovered Duncan and killed him, the entire holding would be alive with commotion. The Earl of Argyll was still alive, lurking somewhere, waiting for an opportunity to kill. Rising to his feet, Robert fought the desire to pass out from the pain exploding through his skull, and he began to run.

When he was just a few yards away from the castle, the heavy doors began to open. He skidded to a halt, his heart crashing against his ribs.

Someone stepped outside, his mop of golden curls glimmering like a halo beneath the sunlight.

Graham Grant!

The commander looked around and then stopped dead when he saw Robert. "Christ!"

Robert lifted his palms to quiet him. "Nae, Graham, wait."

"Guard!" Grant bellowed, dragging his sword from its sheath at the same time.

Robert shouted his name. "My uncle is here somewhere . . ." He looked around at the vast landscape. ". . . hiding."

"Step closer!" Graham commanded.

Robert took a step forward and then swayed. He rubbed his head to help clear it, but it only made the ground spin faster. The MacGregor was being alerted. Soon the chieftain would rush out of the castle and kill him. "Graham . . . damn you, hear me. My uncle is here and he means to kill Margaret Mac—"

Graham began running just as Robert fell flat on his face.

Without pausing at the barn door, Graham kicked it almost off its hinges and braced himself for an attack. "Maggie!" he shouted over the angry honks and squeals of her barn friends. His eyes settled on a body sprawled in the hay. "Nae," Graham choked and then rushed forward. When he reached his brother, he dropped his sword and fell to his knees. "Jamie! Callum!" he screamed toward the door for help.

Men began racing into the barn, blocking the sun from the entrance. Callum led them, his sword drawn. He slowed his pace when he saw Graham leaning over Jamie, but he did not stop. Panic engulfed him, so terrifying it made his legs feel like butter. He shoved heavy bundles of hay aside as if they were as light as leaves. Searching . . .

Brodie found her first. When Callum reached them, he crouched before the trembling form of his sister. He reached out and touched her shoulder and she reeled back, her eyes huge and haunted. But she did not scream.

Callum controlled himself from going mad as he looked at the dried droplets of blood on Maggie's face. She was too far away for it to be Jamie's blood.

"Maggie, where is Kate?"

At the sound of his voice, Maggie suddenly grabbed for him. "He . . . he killt Jamie."

"Nae," Brodie soothed her. "Jamie lives. He was hit too far to the right to cause a fatal wound," he said, more to Callum. "He has lost much blood, though. Graham and Angus have already taken him to his sisters. They will know what to do."

Callum closed his eyes in silent thanks. When he opened them again, he stood up and roared a command of orders that made his sister shrink back. He wanted men searching the castle, the stable, and every bothy in the vale. He wanted others saddled within the instant and ready to cover every inch of his land, in every direction. He wanted Kate found. Now!

As he strode toward the door to leave, Angus returned from the castle with Graham close behind him and Robert Campbell's collar clutched in his fist.

"Mayhap he can tell us where to find her," the beefy Highlander suggested.

Callum took a step forward and lifted his sword. There was no mercy in his gaze, only raw, uncontrolled rage. Robert closed his eyes and turned away. Callum whirled his massive blade over his head, preparing the most lethal blow he could deliver. Angus released his prisoner and leaped backward to avoid being cut in half along with Robert.

"Nae!" Graham leaped forward and landed with the full weight of his body on Callum. Both men tumbled to the ground. The sword flashed beneath a beam of light as it hurled end over end into the shadows. Callum sprang to feet, his fury fully unleashed. He snatched fistfuls of Graham's plaid and lifted him until their eyes were level. Then, as if his commander weighed nothing more than a thought, Callum flung him into the nearest wall.

With determination void of anything save its single purpose, Callum reached Robert and hauled him closer using only his fingers wrapped tightly around Campbell's neck.

But Graham appeared again and valiantly wedged his

body between his friend and his friend's enemy. "I beg ye, do not kill him." His hands shook when he placed them on his friend's shoulders. "Callum, look ye to yer sister, please. Do not make her witness this again, I beg ye."

Callum swallowed so suddenly a slight moan escaped him. He did not want to look at Maggie. "Brodie, get her oot of here. Guard her with yer life."

"Callum." Graham still had not let him go. "Ye cannot kill this man. He is Kate's brother. Ye vowed not to harm him. Hear me, we will find her, I vow it. He had the chance to ambush me outside, but he warned me of Argyll instead."

Slowly, Callum lifted his gaze to Graham. He waited until his sister was safely out of the barn before he spoke. "If she dies, he dies with her."

Graham nodded, finally breathing again, and gave Callum's shoulders a firm pat. "Just let me speak to him, aye?"

Turning to face their captive after Callum nodded, Graham was first struck with pity at the terror in Robert's eyes. He understood it, for he had felt it, as well, a few moments before. "Rest easy. He is a man of his word and will not kill ye."

Robert's eyes darted from Graham's to Callum's, then back again. "Where is my sister?" he asked, ignoring his throbbing skull and the fear that made his mouth dry.

"We were hoping you could tell us," Graham said. "Where is your uncle?"

"I do not know," Robert told him, tunneling his fingers though his hair and then grimacing at the huge knot on his head. "He struck me last eve. I awoke to find him gone. We came here for my sister, but he said he was going to kill—" Robert paused when he looked at the chieftain. "—MacGregor's sister."

Callum moved forward again and Robert took a step back. "When I find Argyll, and I will, his screams will be heard in England."

"I do not mean to stop you," Robert promised him. "It was he who put the blade to my father and my grandfather. We must move quickly. I am confident he is not still here. Your men are wasting time searching the castle."

In one fluid motion, Callum seized Robert's plaid in both hands and hauled him closer. "Then where should we be searchin'?"

His sister had been trapped here with this beast, Robert thought, unable to look anywhere but into the Devil's unholy gaze. "Leave Kate out of this feud," he managed with more courage in his voice than he felt.

Graham closed his eyes, praying that Callum would give him a wee bit more time. He knew Robert feared for Kate at the hands of the outlaw MacGregor. "Robert," he said hastily. "She has come to no harm here. Camlochlin is her home now—by her choice."

Robert shook his head with disbelief. He would have laughed if he was not so terrified.

"Aye, she loves him, I swear it," Graham stunned him further. "And look ye to him. Ye have seen him before— at Kildun—remember? Look at him now and believe that 'tis his love fer her that drives him mad with concern."

Robert looked, but he was not relieved at what he saw. Instead, his eyes darkened with something worse than horror. "My God, what have you done?" When the MacGregor's murderous glare impaled him, he did not flinch.

"He will kill her. Just as he killed our father for being a sympathizer."

"Nae," Callum breathed on a mangled groan, his dark intent fading into complete sorrow he could no longer control. He had done this. He had known Kate's life would be forfeit for loving him, and he allowed her to love him anyway. "Nae!" This time the word came down like a hammer. He released Robert and headed for the door but turned when he reached it. "You are the one who taught Kate about heroes. Tell me where to look fer yer uncle and help me save her, Robert Campbell, if there's any honor in ye."

Robert nodded. He had no other choice but to trust this man. "He has a boat waiting to sail him to the mainland. It is . . ."

Callum was already gone. Robert turned to look at Graham, and then they ran, as well.

Chapter Forty

KATE GRIPPED HER BELLY with one hand and the side of
the boat with the other. It felt as if she had been on the
water for hours. The waves crashed beneath her, rocking
and dipping the vessel until Kate's skin turned pale green.
She felt like she was dying a slow, sickening death, but
she used the time leaning over the edge to try to think of
what she was going to do about the man watching her.
Duncan Campbell looked quite pleased with himself,
smiling at her when she met his gaze.

"Why did Robert not come with you?" she asked him,
straightening.

"I ordered him to stay at Kildun. I knew I would lose
many men coming here, and I was correct." Duncan gave
her a somewhat rueful look. "Many died trying to save
you, Katherine."

She thought of Jamie, and immediately tears clouded
her vision. "How many MacGregors did you murder?"
she asked, sickened by the sight of this man who was her
blood kin.

Duncan's regard on her grew so dark, Kate thought he was going to haul her over the side. She waited, unafraid. She had no weapon but her feet, and she would use them to render his male organ useless for the next fortnight.

"Your concern for them is most alarming, niece," he said, remaining where he was.

"You find so many things alarming, Uncle," she retorted icily. "But I am no coward."

Duncan wanted to strike her for her cheek, but he would wait until she was in his bed. He felt too jubilant at his own cunning to do anything but grin. He'd outfoxed the Devil! He had walked straight onto MacGregor land and taken his niece from under the rebel's nose. Hell, but he was clever . . . and braw! His father would even have to admit it, were he alive . . . the bastard. Aye, he had stepped into the hornet's nest with the courage of a thousand men and walked away unscathed and taken back his pride. He almost laughed at how easy it had been. Colin would never have had the resolve to do such a thing. But then, most sympathizers were afraid of the MacGregors. It was why they aided the outlaws. Liam Campbell despised sympathizers, save one.

Duncan let his eyes graze over Kate's fine curves. He would not be so forgiving.

~

Robert Campbell was so relieved to be off his battered feet and on a horse that every so often he almost forgot he was riding with a troop of the most aggressive outlaws ever to inhabit Scotland. Remembering was simple enough, though. All he had to do was cast his glance left or right, in front or behind him. They were everywhere, and according to Graham, the MacGregors of Rannoch would meet up with them once they left Skye and entered the main Highlands. That they did so on horseback and not by boat was because there simply were none large enough at Camlochlin to bear the weight of the horses, and they would need them when they reached the mainland. Robert did not think they would lose too much time, for they flew across the landscape like a plague on the wind.

At first, the idea of being one Campbell amongst hundreds of his clan's centuries-long enemy chilled Robert's bones to the marrow. But traveling with them was quite different than when he had fought them at Kildun. They were a rowdy bunch, most certainly, and definitely hard as granite around the edges, but they possessed a wildness that appealed to Robert's most basic nature. He almost pitied his uncle and anyone else who came against them. They had suffered years of persecution. But instead of growing weaker, they possessed the power of raw brawn and unmatched belligerence. Who, indeed, could stop them?

"How do ye fare, Robert?" The sudden appearance of Graham Grant at his side almost startled him off his horse. Only his sense of pride kept Robert's exhausted body seated in his saddle. His surprise that Graham would be concerned for his well-being was another matter entirely.

"I fare well. You have my thanks for inquiring."

Then Graham did something else Robert did not expect. He smiled before he kicked his horse's flanks and raced on ahead.

They had to stop and refresh their horses by a flowing stream. The decision to halt was not Callum's, though he knew the animals would never make it through the night at the speed with which he and his men rode them if they did not rest. He also knew Argyll would reach Kildun before him, so he ordered his men to make haste.

His gaze cut to a large boulder where Robert Campbell sat alone. Graham joined Kate's brother a moment later, causing a scowl to mar Callum's brow. Graham had pleaded for the lad's life at Kildun, even going so far as to declare Robert Campbell his friend. He near got himself killed this day by protecting Robert yet again. Callum wondered if Graham harbored some fondness toward Argyll's nephew.

Curiosity got the better of Callum, and he strolled over to where the two men sat together now.

"Robert was just telling me how his small troop arrived at Camlochlin." Graham looked up briefly when Callum reached them.

"And how was that?" Callum asked and sat right beside Robert, who visibly paled at the sheer size of the MacGregor laird so close. Callum caught the apple Graham tossed him, tore his dagger from his boot, and began slicing.

"We . . ." Robert eyed the dagger. "We climbed along the cliffs from Elgol to Camlochlin."

"On foot?" Callum asked, sincerely surprised. " 'Tis a wonder ye were no' killed." He cut a wedge of apple and handed it to Robert.

"We lost men." Robert accepted the offering and took a bite.

" 'Tis a long way doun," Callum said, then, "Are ye certain 'twas he who killed yer grandfaither? I've wondered who was responsible fer that."

"Aye, he told me." Robert admitted and then grew quiet again.

"Ye were correct about yer sister," Graham said,

sensing the young Campbell's unease and hoping to ease it. "She is quite braw."

Robert smiled before he even realized he did. "Aye, I told you she fears little." He looked up as Callum rose to his feet.

"We've wasted enough time," the laird snapped. "Get back to yer horses." He walked off without another word. When he reached the others, he barked at them to move their arses, then leaped into his saddle with surprising grace for a man his size.

Graham rose to follow, but Robert's voice stopped him.

"I considered you my friend. The first I had, if the truth be known. You led me outdoors that night . . ." Kate's brother rose to his feet and set his gaze directly on Graham. "Was it an easy thing to betray me?"

What was there to say? It didn't matter if Graham liked the lad. Their names made them enemies, made them do things they might not have done under another set of circumstances. Finally, Graham shook his head before he turned for his horse. "Nae, 'twas verra difficult, indeed."

⁓

They crossed the narrows a little before dusk and then continued on without stopping again. Robert was bone weary, but he was grateful they did not tarry. And even more that the fearsome Devil MacGregor was going to help him save his sister.

Chapter Forty-One

THEY REACHED INVERARY leaving a trail of whispered rumors that an army of MacGregors was heading south, unharmed and unhindered by a Campbell knight who led them! Callum would have preferred the truth of it be known; they rode unharmed and unhindered thanks to the staggering fear that settled over anyone unfortunate enough to come upon them. They might be an outlawed clan whose heads were used to pardon the most offensive crimes, but they were bloody fierce, and people knew it.

Duncan Campbell knew it, as well, which was why he had wasted no time in gathering his allies to his side on his journey home. Callum and his men found themselves facing an army of Menzies, Drummonds, and Robertsons when they finally arrived at Kildun. True, the men looked less than confident when they saw the feral-looking Highlanders thundering toward them, each warrior taller in the saddle than the next. But Campbell's army outnumbered the MacGregors by at least two to one, and that, according to Callum's way of thinking, was what gave them the courage to draw their swords.

Callum was ready for battle—more than that, he was eager for it. He dragged his blade from its sheath and held it up, ready to plow his way through the wall of soldiers and take back the woman he loved.

Robert thundered past him and tugged his reins to a halt a moment before he, too, would have plundered through Duncan's army. "Put down your weapons!" he called out with all the authority of a king. "Hear me! I am Robert Campbell, grandson of Liam Campbell, Ninth Earl of Argyll. These men have come here at my request to save my sister from the clutches of a madman, Duncan Campbell."

"You speak treason against the earl," one of the men shot back.

"Aye," shouted another. "You ride with MacGregors and would turn your kin over to them. You betray your clan!"

"Nae!" Robert shouted. "It is my uncle who has betrayed his clan by killing his . . ."

One man broke rank and sped toward the MacGregors and Robert. His sword unsheathed for battle, Callum's mouth hooked into a snarl as the rest followed immediately behind, emboldened by their comrade's bravery.

Raising his sword, Callum dug his heels into his mount and charged into the oncoming legion.

For an instant, Robert simply sat atop his steed with a look of disbelief and horror on his face. Indeed, it seemed just an instant had passed while the MacGregor chieftain's heavy claymore fell upon his enemy's head, cutting down to between the soldier's eyes. The bloody blade came up again, and before his first victim's body fell from its horse, another rider's head was cut from his shoulders. Blood splashed across the Devil's face giving credence to his worthy title. A third man only had time to stifle a gasp while looking into the burning vengeance of his executioner's eyes before he was run through to the hilt.

Angus's giant sword found its mark, smashing bones like glass under the strength of his arm. And Brodie's merciless sword left even horses dead.

Fools! That was all the time Robert had to consider his uncle's men before ten of them were upon him. He barely had time to unsheathe his blade and deflect a blow to his chest before another swipe just missed severing his arm. Hell, he hadn't trained his whole life to die after just two battles, and certainly not during one that didn't even need to be fought! Lunging forward, he thrust his sword into the belly of another attacker, yanked it back, and struck at the next man closest to him. His swings were well practiced and almost elegant in their delivery compared to the brutal skill of the MacGregors. But just as efficient. Until one particularly huge soldier brought down his blade hard enough to bend Robert's suddenly meager weapon.

Seeing his opponent's disadvantage, the soldier looped his sword, holding the hilt with both hands, and brought it down just above Robert's skull.

But the fatal blow was blocked in midair. Sparks rained down on Robert as he watched Graham make a quick end of his would-be assassin.

Within minutes, most of the Earl of Argyll's men were cut down, with the same savage proficiency Robert had witnessed the first time he saw the MacGregors fight at Kildun. The rest took off running. No matter what his uncle had lied about, he had been correct about one thing. The MacGregors were to be feared.

With no one left to bar entrance into Kildun, Robert gathered his courage around his shoulders and brought his mount to stand before Callum's. "You may go inside with me to find my sister. Many have died today. I would ask that you spare my uncle's life." Callum shook his head. "I fully intend," Robert continued, "to bring charges against him in Edinburgh. He will be hanged for killing the earl. Reconsider, I pray you. There is no honor in revenge."

When Callum made no move to answer him, Robert started toward the castle. He paused for just a breath when he heard the conversation behind him.

"He's a braw lad. What think ye?" It was Graham's voice, answered a moment later by Callum's.

"I think he is the second Campbell I've met that I didna want to kill."

"Well done, Robert!" Another voice, this one less deadly than the one before, but no less chilling, halted Robert completely. He rounded his mount and reached for his hilt as his uncle stepped out from behind the western wall.

With his sword pointed at her throat, Duncan Campbell held Kate before him like a shield to ward off the enormous MacGregor dismounting a few feet away.

"Nephew, pardon me for not applauding you and your companions' swift execution of my countrymen, but as you can see, my hands are otherwise occupied." Duncan adjusted the sharp edge of his blade beneath Kate's chin. "I want you to know that I blame myself for what you and your sister have become. I should have known Amish and

John would teach you your father's ways, and killed them sooner."

Hearing this, Kate struggled to be free, but his hold on her was firm.

"Release her, Uncle," Robert demanded, "and there will be a chance you will not die this day. You need only look around to know it is your only option."

Callum spotted the flash of panic in Argyll's eyes as they swept the ground and the dead around him. Men did deadly things when they were afraid. "No one else here will lay a hand on ye." Callum did not move as he spoke. "Let her go and we will meet as men."

"Ah, MacGregor." Duncan glared at him and backed away, dragging Kate with him. "You mean as savages, do you not?"

Callum offered him a lethal smile. "If ye like." He spared a glance at Kate. She appeared unharmed. "Come," he spoke softly, calmly. "Ye were braw enough to take a swing at me once, long ago. Ye have no' turned coward since that day, have ye, Argyll?"

"Coward?" Duncan spat, enraged. "I will mount your head in my solar this very night. And if I don't, you will be dead by nightfall. You see, I've sent word to our Lord Protector, giving him the location of your holding. I also informed him that you kidnapped my niece, killed the men I sent to find you, and were on your way here to kill me next." Duncan's grin was a slash of victory. "If I die, he will know it was by your hand. You will bring the law down hard on your people for many more years to come." He turned his cold gray eyes on Robert. "I am not the man with no options. He is."

"Nae!" Kate screamed. She tried to claw her uncle's

arm away, but he dug his blade deeper into her skin. She didn't care. "Callum! Do not kill him!" She caught his gaze and held it. "You are not what he calls you."

Duncan yanked her back by her hair to quiet her and then turned to Callum. "You will not be pardoned but by my mercy, if I am alive to give it."

"It is no surprise"—Robert's voice dripped with revulsion at his uncle—"that your father found you so unworthy. You are worse than a coward." He squared his shoulders and turned to Callum. "I offer you another option. Whether he dies by your hand or the law's, I will be the next earl. Leave him to the law and you and your people will have my mercy."

"This is why we hang sympathizers," Duncan sneered.

Callum looked at him with the fury that had waited nine years for release blazing in his eyes. "Argyll, ye should have waited fer me to kill yer faither. Ye knew I would come back fer him. Ye took what was mine, just as he did, and inherited his crimes as I did fer my faither." He held his hilt in both hands and waved the blade at Duncan. "Stop pissin' in yer hose and come kill me, Campbell."

"Nae! Callum, please!" Kate screamed and was tossed aside as her uncle readied his sword for battle.

Robert leaped from his saddle and ran to her. They both watched Callum whirl his long blade with a simple twist of his wrist. "Come on."

Duncan obliged by springing at him and swinging. Callum avoided the blow with ease and returned with a backward strike that left Duncan's arms trembling. Duncan whirled around and jabbed, barely coming close to his target. Callum brought his arms down for a savage blow that near felled the earl to his knees. Each time Duncan attacked, Callum parried and returned with twice the power. It was clear to all who watched that the mighty laird could kill Duncan Campbell at any time. He chose to humiliate him first.

When Argyll finally did fall to his knees, Callum waited, challenging him to get up. With a final swing, he smacked Duncan's sword from his hands when the earl held it up and then shattered Duncan's nose with his fist. Argyll reeled backward, his eyes glazed above a spray of blood.

Not so long ago, Callum would have been satisfied with nothing less than death to this enemy. But another massive blow that broke Duncan's jaw was as sweet a victory as he would get this day. 'Twould be enough, Callum knew. For he was not a monster.

As Duncan lost consciousness, Callum turned to look at Kate clutched in her brother's arms. Suddenly, a hundred men and their mounts vanished into thin air and only a lass, more bonny and more beloved than all the land in Scotland, existed.

"Come here, Katie."

She did not move but stared at him, her dark eyes furious. "You frightened the hell out of me, MacGregor."

He ached to hold her. "Fergive me," he repented sincerely. "I had nae intentions of killin' him and losin' ye, but I would no' have had the satisfaction of kickin' his arse had I just walked away." He thought of his sister, his future with Kate. One now filled with hope. "It's over. It ends with me."

Kate smiled with him and then ran into his arms. He caught her up in an embrace that near crushed the life out of her. When he finished kissing her senseless, he swept his fingertips over her smile. He had escaped Liam's dungeon, but he had remained a prisoner to his own hatred and guilt. Kate's love had set his heart free to love again, to feel again.

Angus helped Robert carry the unconscious earl back to the castle. When they passed him, Callum stopped them, untied the leather cuffs at his wrists, and tucked them under Duncan's belt. He was alive, and he had Katherine Campbell to thank for it.

Epilogue

KATE STOOD ATOP the coal-black battlements of Camlochlin Castle and looked out over the landscape swathed in mist, suspended forever in time. She lifted her arms over her head and closed her eyes to the bracing tingle of winter's breath. Had it been only a few months ago that she did not know who Callum MacGregor was? Now she knew she could not live a single day without him.

Much had happened since Callum had taken her home from Kildun. A council of Oliver Cromwell's most esteemed nobles held trial over her uncle and found him guilty of murdering the Ninth Earl of Argyll in cold blood. He was not charged for killing her father or for any of his crimes against the MacGregors, but he was hanged nevertheless. After Robert became the eleventh Earl of Argyll and chief of the clan Campbell, he kept his promise and pardoned Callum for his crimes against the Campbells. He had since sent his sister a missive blessing her marriage to the MacGregor chieftain, along with an invitation to her and her husband to visit Kildun in the spring. Callum had torn the invitation in half, grumbling for a good hour that he'd be damned before he set foot in the "cesspit of the Campbells." Although she desperately wanted to see her brother, Kate had not argued, but merely nodded and left him to rant in the solar. It wasn't long after that he found her, shoved a parchment and quill in her hands, and ordered her to write to her brother and gracefully accept. Kate smiled to herself now, remembering how she had looked up from her writing to find her husband watching her, shaking his head, and mumbling something about how soft he had become.

She wondered if his notion of soft included hanging draperies on his windows and filling their chambers with wild sprigs of heather. Or mayhap when he thought of soft, it meant not smashing his sword over Brodie's head. He had been angry enough to do it after Kate had rushed headlong into the men while they practiced their swordplay and Brodie's blade nearly sliced off her head. Of course, it was not Brodie's fault. She had been chasing Matilda, who had escaped from the barn, and if Kate had not caught her, supper that night would have been roasted duck. She had saved Brodie's life and Matilda's, as well, with naught but a smile and a gentle peck to her husband's mouth—which seemed to melt him to his very core. If that was soft, then aye, mayhap he was soft indeed.

Even after he found out that she had not only accepted Robert's invitation but invited him to Camlochlin to celebrate Jamie and Maggie's marriage, her husband simply glowered at her and moved his lips around a few words Kate was sure would have been quite unpleasant had he uttered them. He finally managed a somewhat tight "Verra well" before he politely excused himself and stormed off to pound poor Angus into the ground. She knew he was angry, but she made it up to him that night and many nights after, proving to him that he was anything but soft.

Good heavens but she loved him. She loved his smoldering eyes that lit when she entered a room, and the sound of his deep, musical laughter, which had become a common occurrence in Camlochlin rather than a rarity. Callum MacGregor was happy, and she was the reason for it. She hoped to make him even happier when she told him of his bairn growing in her womb. Mayhap tomorrow, after the ceremony. He would be in a fine mood, for as she had suspected, he was pleased when Jamie finally asked him for Maggie's hand.

She dipped her hands to her belly and rubbed the soft roundness of it.

She startled, then sighed with joy when two powerfully large hands came around her waist from behind and covered her fingers.

"What are ye doin' up here, love?"

"Thinking about how wonderful you are," she muttered, tilting her cheek to his when Callum buried his face in the folds of her hair. She lifted his hands from her belly and brought them to her lips for a kiss.

"How many times must I tell ye, wife, that I'm a cold-hearted bastard?" She felt him smile against her nape and giggled in response. He wrapped his arms around her chest and looked out over the glen. "Ye're simply blind to my shortcomins."

"I have yet to see them, husband."

He turned her in his arms and pulled her close against his body. He traced the soft contours at her temple down to her jaw with gentle fingertips. "How long will I be blessed to look into yer bonny eyes and see a hero reflected there?"

"Forever," she breathed, her lips curling into a smile he longed to kiss.

"Then I want to live forever, Katie."

Perhaps this was the perfect moment she had been waiting for. She parted her lips to tell him, but he moved his mouth over hers, devouring its softness, and all her thoughts fled save one that made her burn below her belly.

His breath was ragged when he swooped down to lift her in his arms. He wanted to take her to his bed and make love to her like tomorrow might not come. He almost made it to the archway leading down the stairs when one of the tower guards called out, alerting him that a small group of riders was approaching.

He narrowed his eyes, looking toward the hills, then rolled them toward Heaven.

"Robert!" Kate near squealed and leaped from his arms. Callum forced himself to smile when she lifted her beautiful grin to him. But the moment she looked away, he mumbled an oath or two under his breath. Campbells in his castle! He had to be daft, damn him, daft indeed. He scowled in full force when his wife began talking incessantly about how wonderful it was going to be having her dear brother here at Camlochlin. "And will it not be delightful to see Graham again? I've missed him, but I am happy he and Robert have become such good friends."

"Aye, delightful," Callum brooded.

"I'm certain you will come to love my brother as much as I after a few months."

"A few months?"

"Aye." She offered him her softest smile. "I've invited him to remain for the winter."

"Nae, Kate." He scowled darker than Kate had seen in months. "I willna—"

She leaned up on the tips of her toes and whispered something in his ear.

"Yer what?" He stared at her, his face a mask of many emotions, anger not among them.

"With child," Kate repeated softly, then lifted her fingers to her husband's eyes, thinking that what she saw there could not be real. For how could a mere woman bring this strong, proud mountain of a man to tears? He blinked and then snatched her up clean off the ground in a crushing embrace. She thought about telling him she could barely breathe but decided against it. As he had once promised, he held her heart in his hands in much the same way, and it did not hurt. She had known from the moment he saved her from the McColls that it never would. For he was her outlaw knight in the most radiant armor.

Of course, Callum MacGregor would have disagreed. For 'twas she who had done the rescuing.